Collh Plr

M000205881

THE HEART

of

LIGHT

A Tale
Of
Solomon Star

CHARLIE W. STARR

Forest, Virginia

First edition, 2004
Revised, 2014

For information address:

Lantern Hollow Press
info@lanternhollowpress.com

The Heart of Light by Charlie W. Starr (1963 -)

ISBN 13: 978-0692261637

ISBN 10: 069226163X

Summary: In the far flung future, Solomon Star comes to an alien planet
where he will face beauties beyond understanding and vengeance in the
form of a mad man who has been sent to kill him by the Galactic
Empress, the only woman Solomon has ever loved.

Science Fiction

PRINTED IN THE UNITED STATES OF AMERICA

To Bryan and Alathia,
my best work

Acknowledgements

It would be a crime not to acknowledge everyone who read this book in manuscript over fifteen years and made numerous suggestions for improvement: Cara, Stanley, Frank and Rhonda, Alan B., Louise, Fawn, Lem, Becky, Wendy, John, Alan H., Brad, and many others I've almost certainly forgotten.

Also thanks to others who helped along the way including Laura, Tatyana, Harry, Brian and Kelly, and especially Jordan Hart, the man largely responsible for the formatting of this book.

A special thanks to Becky for motivating, to Cassie and Jason for inspiring this final vision of the novel, to JMK II for his eye for detail, and to Wendy West for proofreading the entire manuscript in a single day!

And finally, my thanks to Don, Kami, Brian, and everyone at Lantern Hollow for their faith in and commitment to this project.

Contents

It was the devious-cruising Rachel, that in her retracing search after her missing children, only found another orphan.

—Fragment from Pre-Imperial Age

- Prologue -

Program on.

New Project.

Begin recording.

Don't ask me how I know what I am about to tell you. To reveal some truths would...garner risk. Let's just say that what I am going to tell you is as much truth as I can discern and as much imaginative flair as I thought necessary to pass on the flavors of things—the rhythm of a moment...the weight of secret sins.

Imagine a story from his life. Solomon Star's. Of one man who died, another who died twice, of _him_ who would only die half enough, and of her: *I'm certasld on his part.*

Janis, goddess, Empress of the galaxy. My mother.
Millions more?

Here, in a time of empire, few are oppressed, and none feel the burden of too much liberty, least of all those who seem the most free. Hmm...that's a bad start. The last thing you need is a sermon.

Perhaps a backwards glance to begin things. Two thousand years ago: I see the founding of an age in a conversation: Two men sat at a white marble table, one frocked white, the other robed purple, casually conversing the future to be; one of them named Amric saying, "Power is an energy to be cultivated, not expended."

"If that is so," replied the other, "then the less power you expend, the more you will retain."

"You, my brother, have the wisdom of a gadfly."

"I can never be called your brother again. That is first."

"And so the power I expend shall be expended through you—"

"No, by me."

"And I," the purple robed went on, "shall cultivate—"

"—what I sow," finished the white coat.

Each smiled. One with his heart, the other with his head.

· "And tell me bro—my...Chief conspirator: Why do we expend so much energy to rule, and how shall we expand it?"

"We expend by making chains. We will save by teaching the ruled to make their own."

There. A little bit of mystery to whet your appetite. It began with the first Amric Emperor and his self-dispossessing brother. A dynasty which has yet to fall, an Empire which could hardly be called despotic, but neither could it be called innocent. I understand the first Emperor's mindset. I've met it in his descendants: how surface benevolence hides fallen vision, how pragmatic peace is hollowed by a subtle mistake—something not so heinous as it is just...ever so casually bent. But I'm sermonizing again. Stop it, stupid girl, and tell the story. While there's still time. *Narroks is a girl.*

- 1 -
2298

Spinning—falling...

Spinning—falling...

Falling ever toward the orb—lush and green—beacon in the eternal night of space.

The man of light peered through a porthole at the planet below: emerald daughter of a yellow sun, emerald obsession of a galaxy, frontier planet in the heart of an Empire; home of the richest forests in the galaxy, the most volatile people, and of his father. This was Kall, the jungle planet.

Windows throughout the ship darkened to protect the eyes of pilots and passengers alike. Like an invading virus they punched through the *toughness* of the living planet's ethereal skin. Eco-aliens in a bio-war, they pierced the vaporous membrane, burning them with its pain, shaking them with its spasms.

He watched the porthole glow—red then white hot. He did not blink. Then they were through!

The rebellious planet roared as they braked through the air and hover engines bent the atmosphere to their design. Silence again. The porthole cleared—blue light poured in. His tongue drank deep adding its own sighs to the artificial air around him.

Solomon Star felt as if he'd come home to a place he'd never been.

I turn myself now to another place, another world. Here it's dark. Oh, how I love the darkness. No. It isn't me, but this man I watch in a place of secrets. This is my holo room, my place for storytelling, for star gazing, for coming to grips with terrible truths. The planet's name doesn't matter. The men who will soon join Solomon's story do. Quint is the soldier. But Lazarus...*Lazarus* is the lover—

"Quint!"

"Huh?"

"Wake up! I want you on!"

His steely eyes were in Quint's face, piercing the darkness with their artificial glow. Or rather, not steely. Steel. A crazy contradiction in terms: Organic steel.

"A heart beat Quint."

Then the barrel in his chin.

"A heartbeat away from losing your brains!"

Breath hot and heavy.

"Take it easy Lazarus. I was just—"

Quint felt the explosion in his crotch as Lazarus's knee hurled him out of the hole.

The hunter in him made his rubbery legs stiffen and lift himself to a stance. In a second, a light wave of instinct, the safety on his rifle clicked, a laser dot set aim right between the post-dead man's eyes. He was good—Quint. But *him*. How could you do better than Lazarus?

Silhouetted by the setting sun, he arched like an industrial demon—servo helmet with complete visual/audio array, armored vest with sound absorbing net, padded joints spiked for hand to hand, bulking boots and a weapons belt loaded to hilt: plasma rifle and gun, radiation grenades, sonic ear poppers, poison gas pellets, even throwing spikes and hand blades.

Surprised that I know of such things? Even a gentlewoman must learn hard details if she would get to the heart of a matter.

Lazarus followed the beam into Quint's face. "Go ahead. But be sure."

'I could take him,' thought Quint. 'I can.'

"Just you remember," he bluffed, shoving the barrel under Lazarus's chin. "Just you remember. You got no one better than me. No one better to watch your six. Best in the galaxy needs someone on his back."

"I know you're the best, Quint." He smiled his cheshire evil, grabbed Quint's shoulders and squeezed just enough to let him know his affection could pulverize. "That's why you're not dead. I don't want you dying before me."

Yes. It was still there. The old man. The child artist.

"Spence, Crusher. Move."

There were four of them: Stalkers. Assassins. Imperial Crests on their pay pouches but not on their outfits.

Darkness had not fallen gradually. And they were hunting. They sank into a dark wood, a mat of twisting tangles: wild, clinging, brush, short, stumpy trees on a planet where green was as unknown as compassion in a city of men. In the distance a black haired youth was running scared and thoughtless. He was an insurgent's son, recognized in the nearby Imperial town, now the bounty for a father's partisan choice. Barely eighteen. Running.

"Running—"

"What Quint?"

"Is he running Laz?"

"Running scared and hardly a challenge."

"Satellite tracking working," said Spence, a rather matter-of-fact style of killer. "One point five klicks at eighteen degrees."

They followed, single file, behind Lazarus, tearing his way through the overgrowth with super human strength. Cat like in agility and tank like in grace, he dogged his quarry's step.

And the boy was running—here in the holo room I can recreate every detail, every breath. Panting: "Papa, Papa, Papa." That is how I fashion my stories. I am almost a character in them myself. Here I am the boy's puppeteer: pound heart, sweat skin, throb temples. Cry: "Papa, Papa."

And then the *Calmness* seized him. Fear is instinct and instinct can save, but there is a deeper place as inborn as fear, as unnatural as suffering. The *Calmness* welled up from archaic resources; instinct went away.

He turned to the bush from where the enemy approached. He could not hear them crashing through. But he sensed them. Thoughts flowed without hesitation. 'Sponge holes,' he said to himself. He was clear of the bush now, a grass covered hill sloping gently toward the twilightless sky. He began a steady jog following the length of the slope, jogging with the cool breeze that had settled upon the dusk. Then he was up and over the hill, doubling back and away. A steady jog, calm and easy.

Lazarus followed his trail. Even with the light completely gone, he followed the boy, followed him the same way you follow a flashing sign in the dark. The assassins topped a third hill; there was a bowl—a natural amphitheater. Not too big. Not too deep.

"Aaaah," Lazarus moaned and breathed.

"I'm getting all reflection here," said Spence.

"The play."

"Must be a natural dead zone—satellite's useless."

"The play's the thing."

"What's that Laz?"

He smiled at Quint. Not like before—this was the artist's smile. The one from long ago. He turned to Crusher.

"Infrared?"

"Checkn. Nawp. Na ere a saign, Lawzrus."

"Hmm." Still smiling. "Walk with me."

He began to stroll. Yes, *stroll* down the hill, his rifle dangling lazily in his hand. They fanned out and followed.

I can imagine what Quint was thinking: 'Man he freaks me out when he does stuff like this.'

"Starry night!" Lazarus proclaimed to the heavens. And he laughed. Then, "Shh!"

They hadn't said anything.

He was crouching now—the hunter hearing, tasting, feeling in quick succession. He threw himself out of Quint's natural sight in a second. The infrared visor allowed him to follow, but Lazarus disappeared. Then quickly reappeared.

"What happened?" came Spence on the com link.

"Come look," Lazarus replied.

They found their leader and saw the hole he had fallen into.

"You fell in a hole!" Quint laughed, his sense of self preservation running sometimes inconsistent.

"Look around," said Lazarus.

"What?" Quint's smile faded. There were holes everywhere, all over the bowl.

"Sponge holes uh," noted Crusher.

"Crazy terrain," Quint added.

And Spence: "How deep?"

"Fifteen meters or better."

"You jumped out?"

"He jumped out." Somehow Quint knew the truth.

"Cud be cawnected. Honeycaumbed."

"It isn't," Lazarus declared. Yes, he knew. "Perfect place to hide. But no escape. All or nothing."

"That's how to die," Quint scoffed.

"That's how to live," Lazarus answered. "I know him. Stay."

He threaded his way into the darkness. Minutes later he signaled—three tones over the link: *Approach at ease.*

He was standing over a hole, arms crossed, leaning against the air. The smile. Then he came toward them and, taking a grenade from his belt, said, "Call it a terminal choice." Passing them he pulled the pin, then tossed the grenade over his shoulder. They followed.

Inside my room I could see the youth at the bottom of the hole. He only shook his head, sedately disappointed with his failure to elude them. He wasn't afraid. He didn't scream.

I did. Sometimes a holo room, especially a secret one, can be...hmm...intense.

"Now we go after the father," Lazarus said.

"You know where he is?" asked Spence.

"I've got his scent on the end of my nose. It'll take us right to him."

They all thought he was joking.

- 2 -
Second Coming

Wetness hit him like a wave at the space port exit—not hot, but the sticky, drowsy dampness of a foggy morning. It told him the planet was alive.

'Wearing a dress uniform to this place,' he thought, 'was a mistake.' The dark blue double breasted jacket felt heavy in the humid air and weighed heavier by the cluster of pins and medals he wore over his heart. The high collar chafed his neck and irritated the tingling tension already aching in that first vertebrae below the shoulders.

A smell like pine and methane assaulted his nostrils—alive indeed. It's said that the natives, the Kalliphi, can tell a man's heart by the face he makes when he breathes, as if one's view of life rested in the nose. I have heard that the rare obtainer of enlightenment on the Kalli world gets used to the smell.

A private in a hover car pulled up beside him, hopping out to attention. "Colonel Star?"

"Yes."

"Governor's expecting you, sir."

The driver took Solomon's bag and placed it in the back seat of the open vehicle. Solomon climbed in not bothering to notice the several people who had stopped to stare at him upon hearing his name.

Might be a key part

They drove away down mud roads, past pre-fabricated composite hovels where term-miners, lumberers, and trappers lived meager existences getting rich. The only substantial buildings in this capital city, where men had dared to push back the jungle, were the space port, the military/government complex and the brothel.

Solomon awaited the Governor of Kall in his office: a spacious room with a peculiar mixture of ancient and modern: Stone walls—'this place has been here a long time'—and slow moving ceiling fans which cast revolving shadows over the latest furniture from Niem; mini-blinds, covering ultra-violet filtering windows; a computer holo display on the desk, and lizards crawling about or doing push-ups on the walls. He peered through the mini-blind slits and filtered glass beyond the unnatural settlement at the sun setting into the primal jungle. The land glowed with life. Did it? He imagined a green aura—I would say neon but that's too artificial, not sufficiently subtle. He imagined and could not be sure. Like a soldier, he took it matter-of-factly. Light was at that earth's heart, and Solomon felt an affinity for it that he could not explain. It tugged at him, sought to overwhelm him, as if to enter that jungle were to be consumed in life—a part of that from which separation—escape even—was impossible. He felt for the first time why his father had returned to Kall. But he did not understand.

"Colonel Star."

He turned to meet the planet's Governor hurrying through the hinged double doors. He was a paunchy, red haired man whose worry lines betrayed an age beyond his years. Jowls of fat and a burdened brow hid his auburn eyes from plain sight—perfect for an administrator. Sweat stains had discolored the armpits of his stiff khaki suit.

Solomon moved away from the window. "Yes. Governor Pylat I presume."

"Welcome to Kall." He extended a sweaty palm which Solomon took with all the sincerity he could muster.

"You'll excuse my tardiness—a little civil disturbance. The workers are getting restless with production brought to a halt and all."

He moved behind his desk, a dark wooden slab with intricate carvings that ear-marked Kalli culture: a forest filled with trees, dotted with animals and children playing together; far from primitive, the images imitated reality with subtle detail, though they told no specific story. Motioning Solomon to a seat Pylat sat himself and stared at the man of light for some time, mind musing over an unknown thing.

"Governor?"

"What—excuse me. I'm thinking how much you look like your father, especially with the beard. The picture in your dossier was clean shaven."

"It's old."

"Yes. Well, it's a bit like looking at a ghost." 'Or a god,' he further thought. And again he stared, something within struggling to carry him away in administrative myriads.

It irritated Solomon. He shifted in his chair, cleared his throat and asked, "What can the military do for you, Governor?"

Pylat snapped back from reality: "Huh! If only it were that simple. The pressure, you see is....If only it were...simpler." He almost drifted again but caught himself. And with a wry smile of resignation: "Well," and the assumption of a sterner countenance, "there isn't much time; what were you told?"

"My orders were to come to Kall."

"That's it?" asked not in surprise but for reassurance.

"Yes, but it's not difficult to determine that, if of all the planets in the galaxy, you're sent on a *special* mission to the one where your father lives, that mission will involve him."

A button lit up on the Governor's desk. He pressed it twice. "Quite simply then, Colonel, we're having trouble with your father that only you can fix."

"What's the problem?"

Pylat breathed deeply and assumed an almost comical air of formality.

"Kall is the richest planet in the galaxy for its minerals, wildlife, and trees—especially trees. A single day's produce could pay the salaries of ten thousand fleet Colonels—for life. We supply to every major world in the Imperium. But now, production everywhere has stopped." He paused to let Solomon respond. He did not.

"The land fights us at every turn. This world refuses to give up its treasures. Fifty years ago we raped her, stole from her, destroyed her. Now it's different. Now we coax the land, and she gives of her gold stingily. But for this we need the Kalliphi."

"The people."

"Yes. They won't let us into the jungle."

"They're rebelling?"

"No, technically our treaties are maintained."

"Then what's the problem?"

"They've stopped working."

"So?"

"We can't penetrate the jungle alone. Only they have the skills. I have five hundred foresters rusting on downed hover trucks all over the space port, ten thousand men counting mud lumps for entertainment. They're amazingly patient, but the exceptions might become the rule. Three incidents this month. Oh we could go in and tear up forests and dig up what we want. But...the Kalliphi and the land are one. There's a relationship—it's difficult to explain. They call it *eisos*. Besides it would violate the treaties."

"Going in on your own."

"Yes."

"What would happen if you broke them?"

He grimaced. "Hell. And I won't return to that. Cooperation has so much more to offer."

Solomon was surprised: more than a bureaucrat, this man seemed to be genuinely concerned for his adopted world—its people—but torn between that and his responsibility.

"I still can't see my place in this."

"It's the Philagapon—I'm sorry, that's what they call your father. It means, *the Compassionate*. Six months ago we lost contact with him in the interior. But we know he's alive. The *Call of Philagapon* drew the natives to the heart of the land four months ago. We have seen only a few Kalliphi in the cities since then. But they've all refused to work. We don't know why. But we know that the Philagapon has affected it. And we know that the Philagi—*the Compassionate's Son*—must solve this problem."

"How do you know?"

"The people told us."

Pause.

"What shall I do?"

"Find your father, get production going again, and let me get some sleep."

Solomon smiled. He felt a rare empathy with Pylat, even as he puzzled over the name he hadn't known he'd been given: Philagi.

"I think you'll be able to get some sleep, Governor."

"Perhaps. But this is no light matter." He hesitated. "There's a greater interest here—the greatest." He swallowed hard. "This one comes from the top."

He opened a drawer in his desk, the construction so good that, though made of heavy wood, it scarcely creaked with friction. He took a holo disk from the drawer and pushed it across the desk top. Solomon went white as he saw the Imperial seal.

'Straight from the top.'

Yes it was. A message, no doubt concerning this mission, from *her*. How long had it been? He had avoided news coverage, speeches, messages to the military—everything but unavoidable official portraits. He had not heard her voice or seen her animate form in years. A cold chill ran through his body.

"It's a private communique," said the Governor. "I'll arrange a room for you."

Solomon tucked the disk into his jacket, composed himself, and said, "It's a big planet. How am I going to find my father?"

"We have arranged help." He pressed a button on the desk. "Davidson Star wants to see his son; so do they. A Kalli guide has been sent to take you to him." The door of the office opened. "We'll fly you in as far as they'll let us, but you'll have to go the rest on foot. Ah. Come in Gai-ja."

Pylat stood. Solomon swiveled his chair to a rare sight: a Kalli woman. She entered with cat-like grace, deep green eyes fixed on the Philagi. He watched her read over his every feature, studying him like a warrior sizing up an opponent. He did likewise:

She was tall, almost his height, slender and young. Perhaps twenty. Her round, hint-of-cheek face and her hands were bronzed—that's all he could see of her skin for she wore a single-suit of a canvas type material—standard military issue but with no buttons or markings, and brown instead of blue. Her earthen hair was pulled tight behind her high, smooth forehead into a long braided pony tail. Her eyes: What shape and fullness were lacking in her lips, her nose, were made up in the round, almost whiteless eyes. Green upon green around dilated black—round like a circle not an oval. She bowed her head in greeting.

"She will be your guide."

They continued to stare at each other.

"You are the son of Star?"

"Yes."

"I see you. But you do not see me."

"Excuse me?"

"She's saying that something about her has you puzzled."

"Yes," slightly embarrassed, "I suppose I expected some sort of savage scantily clad in animal skins or something."

The Governor smiled.

"I would not take off my clothes for you."

"What now?" asked Solomon, surprised.

"You are not Philagapon. You are not Gaiton." She seemed indignant but maintained a stone cold, emotionless face. "I would not take off my clothes for you."

Solomon looked back at Pylat who said, "He would not ask it you." Silence. "Take him to a viewer and then to his room. Colonel Star, I'll visit you this evening."

Far away on a planet whose name doesn't matter, the assassin called Crusher received an encoded message. The encryption deciphered, he opened the file to play as Lazarus his *leader*—for lack of a better term—completed the killing blow to the insurgent father of the black haired youth they'd eliminated but a few hours before. A gesture of the hand let the others know that Crusher was about to link them to a new mission order—a new kill. In the visor display of his helmet, Crusher saw an Imperial Seal. Then he heard a woman's voice: "Lazarus." His name dripped from her tongue like honey...and blood.

The Word

about what he should be thinking about: his father,
this ...   But the girl kept distracting him. He had never been
comfortable around women, even less so now around this strange
native whom he followed through the drab green corridors of the
municipal building. Old hinge doors broke the monotonous color
every few yards. They were featureless, marked only with
numbers, no symbols or words: typical government building.

"What did he say your name was?"

"He did not."

"He called you something."

"Gai-ja. It is girl."

"So what is your name?"

"To you I am *savage*. I am Savage so."

"And I am Philagi?"

"You say. You are the son if I see. Watch here."

She had stopped at the door to a small room. Within was a holo
projector. Solomon hesitated, took a deep but controlled breath,
entered the room and closed the door behind him. It was grey
within: the walls, the holo screen, even the plastic chair—a
featureless box. Without bothering to sit down, he took the disk
from his coat and fixed it into the slot. He waited tensely to see
that face, to hear the voice. He felt sick.

Then it came: Not the face; not the voice. It had been just as
difficult for her. Words, generated against a blue field hovering in
the air before him were the whole of the message:

FIND YOUR FATHER

END THE STRIKE

RESTORE PRODUCTION

Solomon sighed relief. Anxious emotions flowed from his body;
tactical interpretations filled his mind: She would have retained
anyone else to do this job if possible. He was the last person. That
meant he was the only person. He must be important to the
Kalliphi, his father even more so. Solomon began to sense an

unrevealed immensity, and an intuition that the Governor had understated his role. He thought of their conversation and it now seemed almost cryptic. Had the man spoken in half truths? A problem of this magnitude, affecting so many of the galaxy's wealthy, should have a far less haphazard solution. Something wasn't right. He was being left too much to himself.

He punched up the computer's access to the on-planet library.

A black 3-D projection blinked drab green letters: "Accessing."

She had used the word *strike*. 'As if they worked for *her*,' he thought. 'Stalemate perhaps. Could the Sykols have that little control here?' He couldn't accept it.

"Ready."

"Topic search: Kall—culture, religion, history, *eisos*. Cross Reference: Davidson Star—biographical, Kall, Philagapon. Process to quarters of Colonel Solomon Star. Is that listed?"

"Affirmative."

Turning to leave, he thought about what he should be thinking about. Instead he thought about women and wood.

- 4 -
From 2288:
Grace?

To understand the events of 2298 means understanding other moments from other times as well. In '98 Solomon Star was a marginalized colonel in the Empress's regular army. Only a decade before, he had been the Captain of her Imperial Guard. Some of the decisions he made then might affect the entire galaxy. Others, like an *innocent* meeting recorded in 2288 A.E., were perhaps only a little less profound.

The main entrance of Imperial Palace possesses doors one hundred feet high and forty wide. Each is made from a single piece of a great black tree that grows only on the jungle planet, Kall. These trees climb hundreds of feet to the sky, and live for thousands of years. The doors, which required ten years to be cut, formed, and sculpted—and such elaborate sculpting!—rest on massive magnetic suspension fields (like those of a common hover car) which, in order to support and move the doors, require their own power source, independent of the main Palace generators.

Leading up to this grand entrance is an equally grand walkway, one hundred feet wide, which stretches two miles from the Palace to the Imperial City, capital of the Amric Dynastic See, commonly (if unimaginatively) called Imperial World, Amric's World, or even Amric. Along the pathway's length, placed every one hundred yards, one finds a spectacular array of fountains: circular pools, sitting directly in the middle of the pathway; each has a different sculptured centerpiece of marble trees, exotic animals, or famous Imperial leaders which spouts a kaleidoscope of iridescent colors using spectral waters from the planet Stanishglas.

At the fountain nearest the Palace entrance on a simple marble bench on a spring evening in 2288 sat Solomon Star. He was not alone.

Charisa was a lovely young Sykol. It was her job to be so. She was a feminine epitome, having learned well the lessons of her teachers: gentle, flowing walk, arms dancing rather than swinging, jet black hair arranged in long flowing waves across her shoulders and down the length of her spine, and the dress—an elegant creme gown of silken and sheer tatters, like chiffon only less tangible, layered one upon the other to flow like water with movement and the gentle breeze—like the one Solomon's mother Alathia wore. They had a name for the persona: *Liquid Grace.*

She stood watching the sun set through the waters of the fountain: green here and blue there—now yellow...a spray of fiery red! The waters danced. The breeze made them tingle and clash, catalyzing brighter and more diverse colors. It blew past her, trailing her hair and the many edges of her dress behind her. She watched Solomon as he sat rigidly on the bench, hands folded in his lap. She wondered what he was staring at.

As sunlight grew dim, flood light rose, softly (but coldly) illuminating the Palace and fountain areas. Solomon did not see Charisa approach from his side.

"Good evening, Captain."

He would have been startled if not for the melodic voice.

"Miss Charisa," he replied, standing as he spoke.

"You look handsome today, Solomon," said she analyzing his features. She saw fatigue. "Did you wear your fine dress uniform just for me?" (knowing that he had not).

"I wish I could say yes," forcing a smile.

"Please sit down," she said, moving first to do so.

Solomon sat. The fountain splashed a steady white noise behind them.

'Distancing himself from me?!' she thought. She saw apprehension in him. 'He's tied to the Empress.'

"Have you seen my mother today?" he asked.

"Yes I have. R.R. had a meeting today; we received new schedules."

"I trust your systems haven't been too disrupted."

'He's making idle conversation.' "No...I mean yes, but we've had time to recover..."

'R.R.,' he thought. 'Reproduction Relationships.'

"...but I'd rather not talk about work."

'You're working now.'

'Let me inside you.' She placed her hand gently on his. "You like to watch the colors in the fountain, don't you?" She turned him to the waters with a gentle pull. "The shifting colors are beautiful. It's a dance to me."

'Perfect,' he thought. 'Four years my younger, yet a perfect performance.' He was amazed at how, like his mother, she could analyze with cold, hard accuracy and yet respond with sincerest sympathy. The first aspect reminded him of his chief subordinate, Hal Teltrab; the second of himself. He examined her round face: deep brown eyes and no harsh features—genetically perfect to enhance the watery characteristics she had been taught to present, from the fulness in the cheeks to the gentle curve of the nose.

"Excuse me?"

"I asked, Captain, about your day. How has it been?"

"Long, Miss Charisa."

White silence crescendoed.

"Will you walk with me, Solomon?" Her eyes compelled him to stand; she took his arm and they slowly strolled toward the Palace doors.

"I do like the fountains," he said, attempting to be agreeable. "The colors fill me up sometimes."

"I don't understand."

"Oh...with memories I suppose."

"Do you remember the first time you saw these fountains?"

"No, but I was thinking of something else—some*one* else, actually."

"The Empress?"

"Immanuel Proshemeis."

"He's the young man who died protecting the Empress—one of your Pentaf, a Commander."

"When we were sixteen."

They walked for a moment in silence.

"He was an artist, did you know?"

"I think I did. Have I seen—"

"And very good at Hide and Seek."

"I—what?"

"A child's game."

"Yes, I know what Hide and Seek is." She betrayed the barest hint of impatience. This made him happy.

"Well he was very good at it. We played it with the Empress when we were boys...when she was a princess child. And he would always win, except when we were told not to." They stopped before the great doors of Imperial Palace, and Solomon concluded: "He was a good artist."

"Captain, I...you surprise me so."

"Good." He smiled and stood a little taller. His lungs were invigorated by the animate air, the breeze giving assistance as his chest expanded to capture it—scentlessness was welcomed. He felt suddenly feisty. He knew he would soon have to choose one of the four women to whom he had been *introduced*, but he vowed that the decision would be his own.

Inside, she smiled too.

Solomon experienced a rare feeling—pleasure. For a moment he was amiable: "These doors are magnificent. They dance like the waters."

"How so?"

"Most slowly."

- 5 -
A Game of Catch

The Savage walked Solomon the rest of the way to his home for the night: a small green box of a room with a computer station, an old spring mattress bed and toilet facilities. Nothing else. She followed him into the room, cautiously looked around, tenderly plucked a lizard from the wall, then turned to leave saying, "Go at the sun."

She pulled the door closed behind her and crouched down beside it to sleep, to keep watch. She lay like a cat on its side—relaxed but quick to the spring. The little lizard scurried down the corridor, making scratching sounds that faded with his tail. Closing her eyes, she imagined the man's face upon the darkness, followed by his father's. How alike they seemed—that face of compassion. 'If I say,' she thought, and began to give consideration to her task. In one of the many books Philagapon had given her to study, she had read that life is a journey. Then she told him, "This we see too." The Kalliphi knew they had come from space, but before the knowing was the myth of the journey from the darkness of no place to the light of the planet. Even with the knowing, though, the myth remained true. To journey was ever in the non-migratory bones of Kalli society, a rite of passage into maturity, a consummation with death. And so she sighed and thought, 'We will journey,' and softly hummed a song about playing with soft furry animals while reciting her stellar geography (which Philagapon had taught her years before), imagining in her mind the red star from which *he* had come. And she anticipated the coming pilgrimage with stoic bearing that even Kalli women thought excessive. This noble "Savage." She bore the weight of a world in a song curled up on an olive drab floor.

Inside the room, Solomon went to the tiny wooden desk and asked the holo screen to produce a menu of the information he had requested. As he began to review the history of Davidson Star's first visit to Kall, Solomon found himself needing less and less to pay attention to the words and images on the air before him. There are two kinds of memories, the kind you relive and the kind you recall. Reliving was something Solomon had only just begun. Here he was forcing one memory up into recollection: Consciously, he played his father and himself on the wall in front of him, each looking seasick for the influence of the drab green

brick. Consciously, rather than experientially, Solomon re-experienced, rather reconstructed, his first lesson about the jungle planet:

"What does 'Philagapon' mean, Father?"

They had been throwing knives at each other.

"You've been studying history?"

The Imperial Guard's version of a game of catch.

"I wanted to predict what the Sykols were planning for the training of my troops for the next three years, so I looked through your old annual logs. I knew I could learn more through them than by asking the Chief."

A six inch blade had come within one inch of his face before his hand stopped it.

"Good catch, Son."

"No, I misjudged the handle by half an inch. Look, I've cut my index finger."

"We'll stop for a moment."

"That's against the rules of the game, sir."

"Good man. Your best throw now."

Solomon remembered spinning and snapping a backhanded throw.

"Then I noticed the two years of almost no entries," he said.

The room was white and featureless—a dimension free cube designed to remove visual distractions on the one hand and spatial cues on the other. The only objects therein were a pair of towels, water bottles, med-kit, and the knives of varying lengths worn on belts about the waists of father and son.

The father: a handsome face, rugged frame, salt and pepper hair. And gentle eyes—the kind that glisten even when there's no light for them to reflect. The son: his casual reflection. In his memory Solomon could not recall his youthful face. Only the echoes of his adolescent voice—his voice and his father's—magnified by the rigid, blank, boundless whiteness around them.

Two knives—small double edged. Solomon had known he could not catch both. He had twisted his left shoulder out of the path of the first, caught the second with his right hand, under handed.

"Philagapon means *the compassionate*."

"Sir?"

He was not sure he'd heard him right. The chamber's echo obscured his hearing. His father repeated the phrase.

"I want to know about it."

In his mind he saw his father clap his hands together, the knife point jutting from between, within a centimeter of his nose. He lowered his hands: a wry smile; father's pride.

"Sit down, Solomon."

"Yes sir."

He fast forwarded his thoughts: sitting against a wall, drinking from a canister, toweling off perspiration.

"When I went to Kall in 2250 the planet was in turmoil. For two centuries the Imperial presence had mined and harvested."

"It's the largest industry of rare woods and minerals exportation in the galaxy."

"They said it was exploitation."

"*They* said?"

"The people. The Kalliphi." His eyes stared blank with memory. "They came there from space, years before the Empire, before Amric the first. There...they were reborn. At the center of it all was the richness of the planet. You can't understand what it's like to stand on top of a living world. Here on the Imperial world...it isn't the same life like that life—everything living. Sometimes I thought I even heard the rocks crying out." He smiled, a bit embarrassed. "Never mind that. The point is this: When we stole from her—Kall—the children fought back."

"Stole from it? It's the Imperial will to—"

"Stole, from their point of view. Remember what the prime will of the Emperor is. 'Always—'"

"'—and foremost—'"

And in unison: "'—maintain power.'"

"Even the Empire can't win a guerilla war. This is the point of the prime will. Authoritarianism always fails. Through all of history it has always failed. We win through craft—force with direction."

"And that's what you did." A son's pride.

"Oh no. That was the idea, but no. The theory, son, was send the best strategic leader in the galaxy. The theory was that the Captain of the Imperial Guard fit that role. Nothing had worked before. You fight them in the jungle, you destroy what you need to preserve, or else get slaughtered by warriors—beasts in their own territory. You overwhelm them with odds, they simply disappear into the jungle, and, here's the thing, they could not be tracked. Even with the most reliable sensors, they simply disappeared. From electronics the planet itself could hide, and only your feet and eyes told you, you weren't floating in space."

"What about population expurgation?"

"Determined by Sykol bio-techs to be potentially damaging to the fragile Kalli eco-system—the Empire didn't want to risk the trillions in revenue which a mass chemical bombardment might cost.

"But they couldn't drive us out. They weren't strong enough for our forces."

"Yes. I went with a hundred of my best men by the Emperor's command to take control of a regular army division for a year."

They sat sipping water, Solomon waiting for him to continue. But what his father told him next didn't make any sense and Solomon found himself unable to recall the memory. Fragments came to him, but nothing clear, only...only—and as the holo image reasserted its dominance, he connected the then with the now:

'Greenness. He told me how green it was.' And the son-now-man finally understood something of what his father had meant. He read on.

For eight months Davidson Star had disappeared. For eight months he had lived in the jungle. Details, like Solomon's memory, were sketchy. He had sent his entire division—regular army and Imperial Guards alike— back to the city after the third month with strict orders to the Imperials to halt all production until his return. Then nothing.

One day he came walking out of the jungle with a handful of Kalliphi—representatives of the people. Negotiations were made, prisoners released, and a treaty signed within a week. The Captain of the Imperial Guard requested an extension from the Emperor and was allowed to stay another sixteen months. During that time he insured that the treaty was honored by all sides. Then he disappeared again into the jungle, and did not come out until his second year was almost up. What he said of that time to anyone, he said only to his son with words that were too vague for a child's experience to make into his own metaphors.

Solomon recalled the terms of the Philagapon Pact, the *Treaty of Compassion*.

It called for the cessation of all hostilities, for production to resume at fifty percent of its former rate, and for the limitation of harvesting of the thousand year old "Great Black Trees" to one per Imperial century (there were those who protested until they realized how such scarcity would drive up the value of the ebony wood). A Kalliphi representative would accompany all jungle excursions, and would cooperate completely in locating the best animals, woods, and mineral deposits. A detailed restoration of harvested forests would be undertaken and would continue as long as the lumbering industry on Kall thrived. Finally, the Kalliphi were given the right to punish anyone who broke the treaty. Poaching was almost unknown on Kall.

Solomon considered the terms.

'It's they who have broken the treaty,' he thought. 'They've stopped cooperating. Only the Imperials are maintaining their parts. Or are they?'

It was indeed curious. He keyed in production records for the last seventy years. And there was the answer: Although production quantity dropped fifty percent after 2250, as per the treaty, production quality rose. The Kalliphi had done their job, guiding Imperial miners and foresters to the richest deposits. This, coupled with the prosperity brought about by peace on the planet, doubled profits by the late fifties. That was why the Imperials favored obeying the treaty.

Just then there was a knock at the door.

"Come in, Governor."

Pylat poked his head tentatively through the doorway. "I trust I'm not disturbing you."

Solomon swiveled his chair and crossed his arms. "No, not at all."

The Governor entered and shut the door behind him. "Yes, good. I wanted to make sure you had everything you needed and to wish you luck for tomorrow."

Solomon read the man with penetrating eyes. "Yes, I have almost everything now. I'll need appropriate clothing and supplies for the trip—"

"Yes, yes. All that will be brought in the morning."

Silence.

"Is that all, Governor?"

"You see into my heart. The importance of finding him is more than you can know—"

"That's not what I mean."

"Oh?"

"Governor Pylat, this is the sloppiest mission, military or political, I've ever seen. What kind of preparation is telling me—in all effect—to go get him? It lacks Imperial planning; it lacks Imperial control." He paused to let the truth of it sink in. "If I'm being used for bait I want to know it."

And Pylat thought, 'Don't lie, not to him.' Then said, "There is a secondary plan," said Pylat hesitantly. "But it won't work. We can't really follow you. I know. This is the only way. Any tricks will be theirs."

'Or is *she* in control?' Solomon puzzled.

"I'm being honest with you."

"Huh? Oh, yes. One other question. Why did the Kalliphi accept treaty in the first place? Why were they willing to give of their land, the woods, the animals?"

"We've wondered that for fifty years, Colonel Star. We don't know. We don't know what your father did. If there's anything else I can do?"

"No, thank you."

"Then I'll say goodnight." He turned, opening the door.

"Oh, there is one more thing, Governor."

Pylat turned back with a superficial smile.

"Is someone monitoring what I pull up on the computer?"

The smile faded. Coldly: "Yes."

"Thank you." Expressionless, Solomon turned back to his screen. Pylat left in silence.

'Why would they agree to treaty in the first place?' It didn't make sense, and Solomon found it a more intriguing question than the mysteries involving the mission and Imperial involvement in it. As he read on into the night, the question returned to his mind and made even less sense with each new thing he learned about the natives of this living planet.

By mid-morning he had finished off everything he could find on the culture and religion of Kall. And having learned much, he knew little. Lying on the bed, he detailed what he didn't know of the tribal people whose life was religion, whose religion was lived in oneness—this *eisos*, this life of worship whose object was a mystery, a metaphysic of very practical living. 'And tell me,' he wanted to ask no one in particular, 'by what do they measure this unity with the world, and what is morality to an earth people who would surrender even a single leaf to exploitation?'

Solomon pressed his head into the stiff doctor's office pillow. It sounded like crumpling paper whenever he moved. He drifted into sleep and dreamed of the jungle. It appeared to be a negative of reality, bright whiteness filling every crack and crevice. He did not blink. Then he heard the beating of his heart. It wasn't the world's; it was too mechanical, more a beeping than beating sound, a sound which had infected each of his dreams since youth, since before his memory could remember. The Savage was there as milk, flowing within the whiteness. She held out her hand to him and he cried out, "Father!" But he was not sure to whom he was calling. Then the land consumed him.

- 6 -
Sword of Light

The Savage stepped into the room to wake him before dawn. He was already up, dressed and packed. This pleased her.

"You are not like the others," Philagapon had said. She would not be afraid to test him. "The people still fear."

"It is you they fear," she had replied. "Musterion to them are you."

"Yes, an enigma."

"But I see you, and, truth, they do not fear."

"Yes, Gai-ja," *he* had said to her. "You see through and through, but not as much as you think." Those words still echoed doubt in the back of her mind. "And you will be the mystery to my son, *you* the fear."

She looked at Solomon, fearing in him nothing. She noticed his clothing: a single-suit, like hers, but blue; with military insignia, and a puzzle of his own: dull, dirty, white boots stained with red. Looking at his face she realized that here too was an enigma.

"Good morning," said Solomon smiling.

She stared at him blankly.

He did likewise for a moment, then grabbed up and handed her the backpack that had been prepared for him.

"They packed this for me. You take out what I don't need."

She was impressed, though she didn't show it. She took the pack and rummaged through it.

"I have a question."

"What?"

"How is my father?"

"He knows him."

"He's well, then?"

"He lives."

'Riddles,' thought Solomon. 'That's all I get.' Continuing the inquiry: "Have the Imperials kept the Philagapon Pact?"

She did not hesitate: "Yes."

'A straight answer?' "Then why have you broken it?"

"I don't say."

"You won't say." Frustration showed a little. Her eyes slapped his face: They said, *I don't lie.*

He nodded a slow apology.

The barest change of expression indicated her acceptance. She returned the backpack to him. He looked over the things she had removed: food concentrates, extra clothing, all recording instruments, the tracer installed secretly by the Governor's people, and the plasma pistol. She watched his face for a negative reaction to the gun's removal. Instead, he reached into the pack and removed his plasma sword.

"Do you know what this is?"

She nodded.

"It must go with me, even though it's a weapon."

She nodded. "Honored."

The plasma sword of an Imperial Guardsman is a truly remarkable device. Legend has it that the sword of light, obviously born of a technological age in which guns killed far more effectively, was conceived neither by science nor soldier but by story—an ancient fantasy tale lost long ago in the far away reaches of the galaxy. Some ideas, it seems are archetypal at the moment of their creation. This one held fast in the human imagination till human hands made it real. Earliest versions focused disastrously on laser light, at the cost of eye sight and lost limbs. Magnetically controlled plasma proved more stable, but wielding the weapon was still too dangerous, at least until the rise of military grade genetic enhancements. When peoples even before the days of Sykol engineering perfected human reflexes, the plasma sword became both a viable weapon and a symbol of elite guards—genetically enhanced super soldiers.

When the sword is activated, an antennae extends from the hilt three and a half feet. This "blade core" generates two things: an incandescent, green, high energy plasma which smells like burning rubber and a strong electro-magnetic field which holds the plasma to the core. The plasma can burn through most surfaces with ease like acid. Focused on the central core, the plasma makes an effective blade. But it is the magnetic field, specially balanced, which gives the sword its remarkable feature:

Imagine standing in a dark room across from someone holding a pen light. When the person moves the light, it gives the illusion of a streak, a tail—the faster the light is moved, the longer the streak behind it. Plasma swords operate in the same way. Only there is no illusion. The magnetic field of the sword, being affected by movement, makes it so that a quick swing of the blade will cause the field, therefore the plasma, to trail behind the core. The sword can be used to lash out like a whip, or to parry a number of blows simultaneously. A sword master can create a 360 degree shield about himself with quick, constant movement. New dimensions are added to the art of fencing: The adept can parry and strike at almost the same instant. He can also, if not careful, step into his own plasma laden field. Reception of such an elegant and deadly weapon is reserved for members of the Imperial Guard only. Men of the regular army speak of the sword with awe-filled whispers. The reverence that Solomon sensed in the Savage surprised and pleased him...and frightened him.

He clipped the sword to his belt.

- 7 -
The Sea

A hover shuttle flew them three hundred miles over the jungle. Solomon watched with captivated amazement as they skimmed over the green sea. No sooner did he see a patch so deeply green that he thought none could be greener than a still richer emerald cropping would appear. He didn't notice Savage who also watched below and yearned for the jungle as much as Pylat (who had accompanied them) longed for his precious sleep. The shuttle came to a halt, hovering above a clearing large enough to lower someone to the ground by cable.

Solomon watched the Kalli woman disappear below the trees. The harness returned empty.

'The bait taken,' he thought.

"They asked us to give you three months," said Pylat.

"And you said?"

"What choice did we have? Please make it no longer."

"What choice do I have?" replied Solomon as he slipped into the harness.

"Good luck."

He watched the trees come closer and closer and remembered his dream. Again he felt as if the land were drawing him to it, never to escape. He felt the branches sucking at him. A rush of pollen dizzied his sense of smell like a narcotic—honey-suckle mint coalesced in his sinuses and throat. Just as his head disappeared into the green sea, he screamed.

As he rode to his office from the space port, Governor Pylat stared blankly at the urban sprawl he called "his responsibility." Tin mansions sprung up in rows between muddied roads that air car exhaust splashed on walls and green suited passers by. In a field at the edge of town, the miners and trappers had put together a ball game—one like every other game: Men run around tossing or kicking a ball, strategizing to move in one direction or another though in truth spending most of their time mostly laughing, getting muddy most all over, getting carried away into anger only occasionally but patting backs and slapping behinds in the end while *ad hoc* participants stand drinking on the sidelines, talking about plays and quotas and that-tackle and money and making comments about the ineptitude of the Governor as he drives by.

'Good,' thought Pylat. 'Something to keep them busy.'

Walking down the drab green halls of "his administration building," the heavy set man felt drab weight upon his brain. Images of paper work danced in his head: of reports and fill-in-the-blanks and numerical columns; of quotas and complaints and uncivil obedience; of his family: 'Iany's birthday is next week,' he thought. 'Send a note. Some money to Celia.' The faces of the wife and son who spent only three months of each year with him preceded him in projections on the olive green walls. 'And Iany saying, "Daddy, I learned to fly a speeder today," and "I learned my ABC's," and "He took his first step today."' "Celia," he spoke to her wall bust, "I die a little every day."

His receptionist was gone to lunch, the outer foyer serenely empty. He stepped through the double doors into shadowy light. 'Who closed the blinds?' Tiny slits of light announced the presence of his company: a silhouette, seated there in his own chair, no features in the dimness save the crescent of an ivory cheshire smile.

- 8 -
God Said...

The sound of artificial engines dying away.

The cacophony of living jungle emerging.

She watched with curiosity the man crouched on the jungle floor. Solomon listened for the pattern of life, waiting for it to consume the beat of his own heart. When he realized he would not die he opened his eyes.

Encompassing a hundred shades of green in a moment's time overloads the mind. Dizzily he rose, engulfed in the wonder of creation:

No place had been left uncovered. Blankets of grass, weeds, moss, bush, covered the ground where the trees had allowed some room for them. The trees themselves reached hundreds of feet into the air, joined at the bases in ever increasing diameters. Even their mighty trunks teemed with the photosynthetic color. Solomon quickly realized that he could not be sure what was ground and what was not—the dirt of life collected upon the expanding bases and roots of wooden giants grown so tightly together as to leave no space for the original earth; they became a new earth, born of excrement, fungi, and the dead: things of the living. And a new heaven: a green sky—and yet brilliant. Somehow the leaves filtered light to the ground below so that no life would starve for the sun. It was no mere illusion. Where shade should have been, there was a warm diffusion of light, dull in its power but sharp in what it helped the eye to see.

The Savage turned, threading a row of trunks less grown over than others—more passable. Solomon's body followed. His mind turned to the sounds of life—fauna: scurries and gallops and scratches and leaps and chirps and barks and whistles and hums. Earth tone creatures scurried here and there, some like animals he'd seen before, others defying description. Larger animals roamed the hillock roots, others the vertical earth—the trees. High above in the branches he could hear the movement and cries of hundreds more. It was like a second planet up there. Shimmering insects, lighting from place to place, gave him brief concern about the problems they usually created. Watching these fireflies he wondered if the trees, like them, created their own radiant auras.

The pungent odor that had assaulted him at the space port was stronger here. Unlike other smells, it did not become less noticeable with exposure.

His attention turned to his guide who had been quietly watching with her back. The stiffness remained in her but not the tension. As he followed, he marveled at her agile movement, dancing across the uneven earth.

Liquid grace.

For her, there was no *place* called jungle. It was she.

"Where are we going?" he called after her.

She spoke an answer he could barely hear. But he doubted his ears and so wasn't sure she'd said, "To die."

- 9 -
There was Darkness

They listened over his com link—Spence, Crusher and Quint. From their ship at the space port they listened to Lazarus and the Governor, "the deskite" Quint called him.

"I don't understand why I wasn't informed about this contingency," the Governor was saying.

"Classified isn't classified if it's known."

He was being patient. Spence smiled that knowledge while sharpening a bayonet in his nonchalance. I looked into his mind for a moment—that is to say, into the series of algorithms I wrote for his character (based on his real history, psychological profile, and other factors) which allowed me to see his most likely thoughts. I call it looking into a mind, and when I did at that moment I saw Spence skinning a Dandan (an utterly harmless, utterly cute little creature—a living teddy bear) which had not yet been killed. Critics of my story might call his character two dimensional. I'd have trouble giving him credit for one. But I'm trying to tell a story, not a lie.

And in the story the Governor, Pylat, was saying, "We dropped them in the jungle an hour ago. But they found the tracer we planted—"

"Which was expected."

"Expected. Of course. It wouldn't have mattered anyway."

"Oh?"

"Electronics never work. Satellites are useless here—there's been a team of scientists working on..."

Crusher was a gadget man. This part of the conversation interested him especially. He tinkered with a computer assisted tactical visor, lighter and more accurate than the A.I.'s of standard military helmets.

Quint couldn't stop staring through the cockpit window—couldn't pay attention to the conversation for more than a few seconds.

"Everything's so green," he said.

"Green, yah?" responded Crusher without looking.

"You're talking weird, Quint," added Spence.

"Our job, Governor, is to do what you can't," came Lazarus's voice over the com.

"You'll follow him then, see to it that his father returns?" Pylat could not hide his anxiety.

"Our authorization," Lazarus replied.

"He's handing him the Imperial code," smiled Spence.

'Green, yah.' I recalled the sound of Crusher's words. I'm certain I got his voice right—the accent at least. The big man was from Gangi XII, an outer rim planet where standard dialect isn't emphasized. That voice imbued him with an air of peculiarity: a high tech, down to earth sort. Head in the clouds, feet in the mud.

"Only one thing more disturbs me, Mister, uh..."

"What?"

"Well, assuming you could find him, what can you do to help bring him back?"

"He suspects," Spence interpreted.

"Mark me," came Lazarus in a voice seeming possessed.

"No," said Quint to Spence. His tactical mind encompassed the entire context. "He's afraid we're going to start a war, to find their stronghold and pass the information on to the army."

Lazarus went on: "Think you that these are normal men."

"But we want him to succeed," continued Quint.

"These two are the product of generations of the most noble cause."

"If he succeeds, we kill him on the way out."

"More than mortal—a precious commodity, to be salvaged and savored."

"If he fails, we kill him in the jungle."

"The Imperium wants its prize, the genes of a thousand supermen."

"We expect him to fail—*then*

Pylat can worry about a war."

"It's manipulation, you see.
A great master plan with
such complexity."

"Either way, we win."

"The genius of these minds, the wonder—that has such as these in it. This Imperium. Do you know why the house of Amric has ruled this galaxy—something so vast—for two thousand years?" (Pylat took the question as rhetorical). "Because they are masters of conservation. The greatest recyclers in history."

There was a long pause—faint static over the link.

Then, nervously, Pylat's voice: "And how will you find him?"

Quint could feel his smile on the com waves.

"By the beating of his heart."

- 10 -
Images

Night fell arduous hours later for Solomon Star. He and his guide rested between two large tree roots in a niche of obvious human hewing. A fire burned in a specially cut groove. The blackened area around it betrayed the tree's long time use as a Kalli resting place. Solomon rubbed a soothing ointment over the brush cuts on his face while noting that the indestructible single-suit he wore was already filled with tiny tears—the beginning of its conversion to rags.

Night had fallen but had not engulfed the jungle. The strange luminescence that Solomon fancied he had seen the previous night asserted the certainty of its existence in the heart of the jungle. He thought perhaps some phosphorescent micro-organism might produce the glow but then decided he was wrong. The medicine on his face relaxed him. Blood pulsed in his cheeks and forehead. There was a life to the light, almost of itself. But nowhere could one point and say, "There is the source" (except the little stars, the fireflies—floating points of light). The intensity of the life that encompassed him seemed to generate the glow. It was light you couldn't quite use to see with. Nothing was clear, but images danced before the vision, and Solomon experienced memories of a garden place he'd never seen. He felt fragmented images of orchards and flower beds, bushes in rows by height and color, rivers flowing east and west and north and south, meandering with a gurgle, rushing with a roar. Animals great and small roamed freely without fear of man, without inspiring it in men; he knew their names without voice. The greenness of the center place in the vision called him back to the Kalli Jungle. There was peace in the life—harmony.

'This must be *eisos*,' he suggested to no one within. He looked at his tearless tunic: torn. Then to the Savage: unscathed. 'Oneness.' Not the absence of being, or the melting of consciousness, but the lowering of it—both awareness of self and of the surrounding microcosm; and ultimately of how they fit together—the macrocosm of things. Solomon found a strange affinity for these thoughts, as if his childhood had prepared him for them, or as if he had been born to them and made to forget. But he still felt that he lacked control and this was disturbing. He felt what might have been fear, but inexperience made it difficult to know.

"Sleep here," said the Savage interrupting his introspection. She was sitting against the mighty trunk, patting with her hand the space beside her. Solomon moved to that spot, stretched out, and placed his head where she had put her hand.

He lay on his side while she, hands and extended legs crossed, closed her eyes and settled in a sitting position against the trunk. Night brought cool air—no breeze—humid—thick in the lungs. In Solomon's ears the jungle began to slumber. In his nose life and death were quite awake.

But one more word was spoken that night:

"Sleep."

At first, he did not. Instead he gave thought to choices. What was a man to do who had spent his whole life training to do only one thing? Solomon Star was a strange blend of confidence and compulsion to duty. The life he knew was the life of a soldier. Not three months gone from Amric's world, he walked into a recruiter's office on the planet Niem on his twenty-fifth birthday, 2288 A.E. Apparently he found no emotional obstacle in serving among the millions in the Empress's regular army.

Nor were there any physical obstacles. Of course they didn't know whom they had, at first. The white boots were the giveaway. The red stained white boots he wore ever after, even trekking through the jungle on Kall. Though with some considerable disturbance at first (a long chain of requests, confirmations and apprehensive approvals), Solomon was accepted into the army, rushed through basic training, and given an officer's commission to a rank which he quickly raised to colonel in the service of the seventh fleet at the Empire's edge.

He thought of that time as his mind drifted toward sleep, and as thought led on to thought, he recalled a conversation with a superior some years later. Something in that jungle reminded him of experiences he'd never known. He met with a sense of having been there before, a sense buried deep in the consciousness—something communal, something he had seen in another once before.

- 11 -
From 2295: *kestar*
Kokkinoscardia

"I've never been to the Imperial World, Colonel."

General Scott stood at the bay window of his greeting room aboard the *Kokkinoscardia*, looking out from his battleship ready room into the huge inner dock of *Fleet Seven*, the world ship that served as fleet headquarters.

"I've always been straight military. Like my father before me, and his before him. No politics." *Family business*

The General's rough voice contrasted the graceful waltz of maintenance ships in the expanse beyond, but fit perfectly the military regalia about the room: medals in glass display cases, and weapons—even swords of steel from ancient times, and models of famous fighting ships, and large oil paintings of colorfully dressed men on horses or in hover cars poised in positions of attack, faces convulsed with grimaces of battle lust, weapons lopping off heads or blowing spines out backs and the General's own uniform: trimmed and polished. Solomon sat, rigid, studying the man.

"Magnificent. The size of a moon. Fleet Seven could destroy a star."

Grey hair, rugged brow, and a pronounced nose—he turned his face to the best of his Colonels.

"But it's nothing compared to the minds that created it, the hands that built it. People, Colonel. People are magnificence. Raw action power, resources of decades of experience, wealth of knowledge...oh yes...and intuition.

"...the Battle of Corto Mat: I was a young captain—younger than you." Something of the waking in his eyes drifted away. "We were a small unit spearheading a pincer movement against a clan army. There was no moon. Pitch black darkness...they came from everywhere, a hundred infrared blurs before my face. We dug in, fired till our guns were drained. It wasn't technology that won. Ten men against hundreds. We fought with our fists until our servos gave out and coolants became overloaded with our own sweat.

"That's how men used to fight: clashing steel, bullets tearing flesh against flesh, mind and might. And I have been there. They found us the next morning, in a sea of blood...a war shattered warehousing cache. Heh, they called it a minor frontier skirmish.

"I lived a thousand battles that night. I met them all: Alexander, Napoleon, Kirigei, Leif'K, Amric I. They showed me their wars, their methods, their honor. And I was them all along.

"Look at my eyes, Colonel."

Blue depth.

"I understand."

Awkward, comfortable silence followed. Then, ending his reverie, General Scott moved towards his desk, a wide, black varnished cube with golden trim and handles, topped (of all things) by a darkly grey marble slab complete with computer, miniature Imperial flag stand and picture of wife and son ("in his third year at the academy"). Solomon sat in wondering silence.

"I'm impressed with your training techniques, your strategies."

"Thank you, sir."

Sitting in the high backed, wide armed leather chair: "Thanks nothing man, thank you! Brilliance, Colonel, needs recognition."

He paused—stared, deep and penetrating.

"I know you. I know why you've come. And I know: *You* understand."

Solomon nodded blankly.

"I want you to tell me if I miss something, Colonel."

"I see."

"You see things, yes. Let me know if you see something that I miss." Scott pulled a three-inch square case from his pocket and handed it to Solomon. "Sykol Central has given us a little job." Solomon looked at the mission disk inside the case. "We're going to conquer a world this month."

❖◇❖

One thing in Solomon's sleeping mind associated with another and a reminiscing hero became a soldier in an electrified suit of armor—blood bathed, not shining—recalling a fight with his unit: laughing at the triumph, scoffing the pleasure of decimation, then reverent of an enemy's courage and loyalty, lastly awed and ached by the carnage.

Then everything shifted, as in dreams they will: Heads bowed—now the sky, not his dress uniform, was red (rose pink rather) and, head bowed, the red stained white boots were only white—shining new, dulled only by the heavy hearts of five boys bidding farewell to a soon empty coffin. The wind gusted and blew the young Captain of the Guard into a new uniform and an older body, and Colonel Star found himself sleeping near a woman whose stiffness had released in sleep. A forest lay about him, a green glowing jungle of pine and methane, of life and death, but mostly life. In the dream negative of the world he listened to hear the beating heart but heard instead the still mechanical sound more beeping than beating though not so un-lifelike, not as much as before.

- 12 -
Darkness was in the World

Pylat's people flew the assassins into the jungle, wondering what good they could do though suspecting why they were there, wondering how they would be able to track Solomon and fearing that they could. The orders Lazarus had handed to Governor Pylat had only mandated that he and his team be dropped off at the place where Solomon had been taken. Pylat and his people were then to leave them alone.

"Perimeter."

They acted with practiced expertise, spreading out in four directions, scanning the area with eyes and machines (and machine eyes in the case of one).

"I can't see a thing," came Spence's voice in the com system.

"Open your eyes," said Lazarus.

"No. I mean infrared—it's going crazy. We should be burning up down here—heat everywhere."

"Temperature's faine. Systems are ouwt crazy. Dampers down't work, saight and sound awgmentation ahr failed."

"Cause?"

"Down't know, Lawzrus."

Then Quint said, "What the Governor told you. It's the planet's effects. They don't know why." His voice was scratchy.

Spence: "We'd better do a weapons check."

"Not now," Lazarus decided. "We'll take two of our three remaining daylight hours to follow, then camp. Tracks?"

They looked.

"Nothing visual."

"Negative."

"Nor here."

"I can't see anything either."

But the way Lazarus said it was strange—as if he fully expected to see something, as if shocked that he could find no visible trace.

"Come."

Quint watched curiously as Lazarus pulled the device from his pocket. He switched the little box on; it began to beep.

"Some things are eternal," he smiled. "Time to hunt. Follow."

He took them in the direction he knew they should be going.

'He always knows. How?' Quint wondered. 'And how does it work when nothing else does? And how did Lazarus plant a tracker on Star?' But Quint was not one to wonder for long. His philosophy was shoot first and questions were optional.

They marched in single file for an hour, moving at a Lazarus pace while bugs flew into their faces, bark knocked them around and branches scraped their skin.

"What's the hurry Laz?"

"No hurry; this is how fast he's moving."

A second hour: The jungle fought them. Animals ran from them. Lizards darted up and down trees and scurried across their path. Birds sang and cawed and rattled the trees above, the noise seeming always loudest directly over their heads.

"Biv here," Lazarus finally ordered.

"They'll get ahead," said Quint.

Holding up the box: "Never too far." The smile. "We need tonight to check systems and learn this terrain. We'll move to within a few miles tomorrow night. Crusher, see what you can do with sensors."

The big man was relieved. He had been brooding over the failure of his precious machines since the landing zone. The jungle, this world, were too alien for him. Lazarus should have seen it in his sweat. The big man felt a vague twitching (not quite a knot yet) in his gut. The chance to gadget about was a relief.

"Check weapons Spence, Quint."

"Looks fine."

"No anomalies."

Then, looking past the infinite non-rows of trees, he smiled: "Let's be sure." He walked away from them, eyes pulling body toward an object. As always, they went after him.

"Target Practice." Bam! The shot rang out. Bam! It echoed on the leaves above. Plasma bullets fried lizards off trees. Lazarus laughed. Bam! A little mouse squealed. Spence was overjoyed, and turned loose in another direction. Bam! Animals like mice, and squirrels, and chipmunks and otters squirmed and contorted while blasting in arcs through the air. Quint joined in; shots rang endlessly one after the other like a timeless drumbeat, drowning out (finally) the clatter of the birds. 'The birds!' and Quint turned the gun skyward. He fried them in bursts; smoke trailed behind the falling creatures as if from a crashing ship. I looked inside and saw what he felt: pride, not blood lust—that was for Spence with eyes aglare and Lazarus, laughing uncontrolled: raucous hysteria, wild but precise—not blood lust but pride in his skill: the value, the artistry of dealing death. Bam! Two birds with one shot—

'Got 'em when they crossed. Watch this: Bam! Bam! Bam!'

Three targets, three shots—bird, beaver, reptile—three in one second.

Together they blew a hole out of the forest, obliterating trees and underbrush as well as animals. They cleared a space of green, replaced it with ash, a space to make Crusher (so he thought) feel more in control.

Ahead of them, Solomon had heard nothing, but Savage felt something stinging in her neck. She looked back only briefly down the trail from which they had come. She looked and then turned and then led him on, deeper into the wilderness of Kall.

The killers stood in the midst of their handiwork, satiated like lovers. Except him. Lazarus gasped the air in excitement, chest heaving. He stretched his grin to inhuman proportion—stretched it till his lower lip cracked, a single drop of blood spilling onto his chin—posed triumphant, poised like a god.

Until he turned his eyes toward Quint, and saw the expression in his face. And turned and walked away.

They set up a heating light, set up sonic screamers to keep the animals away, and the night fell. Quint loved it. Loved that night, though it wasn't dark enough for him. It comforted him nevertheless, eased the not knowing why he had been afraid earlier, why Lazarus had seen it in his eyes. His mind worked overtime. That's how he kept control when questions were no longer optional. Think it out. Enumerate the variables, plan the contingencies, fit everything into its place. Like death: moral, psychological, political, even spiritual implications. But for him set aside. Non-sequiturs to the factor with which he found himself most associated: economics. His career—dealing death. That simple. Pigeon hole all else for non-practical review. A pragmatist, that's what he was. A non-philosopher. But he thought. That's how he kept control. That's what I saw when I looked inside. It made frightful sense.

Crusher had managed to get short distance perimeter sensors to work. No one had to patrol there though one of them would be awake throughout the night. They sat around the heat light in the space that they had cleared. Green forest covered their heads high above—no visible night sky. The birds had either quieted down or been scared away. Silently, they watched Lazarus watch his little beeping box.

"They've stopped," he said. "Twelve miles ahead."

"What is thawt thing?" asked Crusher.

"This?" He looked at each of them as if about to tell some secret. "This is queen Mob."

"What?"

"The Sykol's midwife."

'Talking weird again,' Quint thought.

"You know what he is, this man we're chasing? The Imperium's finest."

"An Imperial Guard."

"That's right Spence." His voice was grave. "A priceless piece of flesh. A Gene King. Something his trainers, the Imperial Sykols, always wanted to keep track of," he added showing them the device. "At birth, the soft part of the baby's head is opened, a tiny pulsing unit placed inside the skull. They can be tracked anywhere."

Quint perceived: "And they don't even know it's there."

"They don't even know it's there."

Pause.

"But whay does it awperate? Awl else I cawn't get to wark."

Lazarus didn't know. He suggested angels smiling upon them or the like. Neither did he know why the one Davidson Star had been implanted with had stopped working years ago. Then, what had been a mutual (if silent) sentiment among three of them finally surfaced.

"Laz," Spence voiced it for them, "these Imperials. They're good, the best—well, everyone says—well, anyway, we got some sort of plan for dealing with this Star?"

What they meant to say: "Can we beat him?" It was something they had never experienced. Not fear. Doubt. They simply did not know, for the first time, if they could win.

Lazarus knew what they were really asking. He stared blankly at Spence for a moment. Then he was gone—not gone really, but moving too fast for them to see. He leapt over the light, ten feet into the air, flipped, landed, clamped his hand around Spence's throat and hauled him up, suspended above the ground, all in two blinks of the eye.

Quint jumped up: "Lazarus take it easy!"

"You don't think I can win, Spence? Is that it!"

He gurgled and gagged.

"Let me squeeze the doubt out of your mind."

"Laz." Quint didn't dare touch him.

Spence tried kicking him in the crotch, then the face.

Quint was calm: "Laz put him down." He pressed the barrel into his leader's temple. "On three, I pull the trigger:

One,

two..."

He let Spence go. He didn't say another word. He didn't challenge Quint. He turned and walked away, point made. This had been only the second time ever he had attacked one of them. 'But the last time was only days ago.' Something was wrong.

But Lazarus, he was good. Perhaps the best in the galaxy. Perhaps more than man could ever be...only...ever so casually bent.

- 13 -
Bel

The average man would've been dead.

Solomon woke to full awareness minutes before the danger reached its climax. The Savage was gone, slipped from beside him—he did not know how long ago. Before him stood a beast, a three foot high reptilian creature resembling a cobra but with fore-legs (none behind) which, along with its neck, held high its demonic head. The trunk lay behind on the ground. The tail curled up above the head to a sharp point, like a scorpion's. But these things went unnoticed. Nor did Solomon give thought or fear for the slanting eyes or flickering fork of a tongue. It was the redness.

Amidst all the green upon green of that planet stood this living stain, a red blemish on the land. But without brightness. It was a dull red, lifeless, lightless, crimson. Ironic: the color of blood lacking any ties to a beating heart.

"This Bel, is—" he heard a voice say. Without turning head or eye, he shifted his attention to his left, to a figure crouching ten yards away— "the one who does not belong. The poison of his tail paralyzes; only enough that you feel him eat to your brain through your eyes. More merciful, the fang. It quickly kills. This one separate, is."

'This one dead, is,' thought Solomon.

"Moving not," she said, as if in reply.

Instead she moved: strangely, awkwardly. It seemed a step without pattern: two quick steps, pause, one slow step, pause, one quick, one slow, three quick, pause, and all the while with eyes closed she bounced up and down, her whole body undulating, at times like an ocean wave, at times like a spring. She moved behind the creature and closer to it. Within arm's reach she stopped and began to sway, slowly.

Bel was like ice, unmoving, unshaken by her rhythm. Then it occurred to Solomon that she wasn't trying to attract the creature. What then? He hadn't the time to learn, for he blinked. The creature lunged at the movement, mouth gaping, then snapping just short of the mark, pulled up, as if by an unseen force. The neck curled under and between the feet to lash out at the foot that was no longer there, then up again in an impossible contortion to bite the hand that no longer held its tail.

She let herself fall naturally to the ground. Bel did not lash out at the movement. Instead he watched in that direction, as if waiting for the hidden enemy to reappear.

Solomon's hand inched toward the plasma sword at his waist. The creature's tail bent toward him. Bel wasn't about to let this prey go. The Savage lifted her head, then lowered it, lifted, lowered, lifted, lowered. Then she raised her torso, back arched, head dropped, and lowered, spine curved, head tucked, like a wave. The one who does not belong seemed to take no notice. Was he blind? Did he operate primarily on some other sense, or was there something more?

Solomon's tactical mind worked in a frenzy. Surely not sight. Nor hearing—it would have attacked her before. Sense then. Feeling. Movement causes vibrations, which could be felt in the feet or body. But then why didn't it attack her?

'This one is separate,' he thought. Then: 'Is there a frequency to life? No, frequencies.'

The creature was chaos in the pattern of things. Solomon sank within. Survival equals adaptation. The good soldier survives. He penetrated the pattern. It took him in. As the Savage moved again toward the creature, as the reptile turned again toward its meal, the man of light was washed with the rhythm of the planet, washed by the sound of falling rain echoed in the ears by the pulse of one who lies down to a sheltered sleep.

Bel set himself to strike.

She knew there would not be time.

The movement of his hand was as the waving of a branch in a breeze, and Bel did not perceive it.

She prepared to die.

Nor did it know what happened when the blinding light of Solomon's plasma sword pierced its brain.

- 14 -
Underworld

"I see you," had been her only response.

Following her again in what Solomon could only suppose was afternoon light, he pondered this continual silence. And he perhaps *saw* her. This was a different silence: not confident leadership; something else. Not wanting to underestimate her, he tried to suppress the recurring thought, refusing to think it. 'Awed silence?'

Just then, an insect flew into his face. He grabbed it with a warrior's reflexes and dashed it into a tree trunk with a slight stumble. He wiped a tear where it hit his eye and blinked wide to regain focus. When at last he looked up, the Savage was standing before him as if from nowhere. He felt blind to her movement.

She stared at him blankly, without derision, or condemnation, and certainly without approval, then bent down and picked up the cicada. A brown, foot long lizard had been sedately watching them while clinging to a nearby tree. The Savage held the little corpse out to the reptile which betrayed its supposed lethargy with its tongue's whip-like grasp. She stroked its head and turned down the path without a second glance toward the man of light.

By evening they reached a gorge, a deep chasm torn into the flesh of the planet. For the first time Solomon could see the true earth. The skin was cut in a cross section for the observer's dissection. A tangle of massive roots spilled over into the cut, sandwiched above by the earth of life, built up upon the bases of the trees over millennia, and below by the true earth of first creation. Below that, the hard black skeleton of Kall, shards of rock reaching deep into the darkness, untouched by the surface's teeming life. Here was darkness. Again, Solomon felt the tug of the land, the swallowed sensation, and for a moment he teetered on a precipice. But he wasn't afraid, because somehow this darkness did not oppose light. It was its own light, a place of seeing too solid for human eyes.

"What is this place?" he asked, half aware.

"'Al-Ga;' division."

"How deep?"

"We must go on."

She led him to a great tree root protruding from the ground's edge. They walked out, careful of the slippery vegetation, following the root's winding path, picking up the path of another until it dwindled to a foot's thickness halfway across and thirty feet down into the gorge. Solomon looked up from the giant's mouth at the endlessly rising trees above. He wanted to reach up for their arms. The Savage did.

Taking hold of a long vine, its anchor upon the highest reaches of the forest, she lowered herself into the abyss, into the darkness. He watched her disappear, watched the vine jiggle with life for a minute, then stop.

'A long way down.'

He followed suit, falling into the substance, the damp fabric of the blessed darkness, the black that weighs heavy with the burden of proof. Here dwelt a strange new breed of animal, many species—birds, reptiles, mammals—but all of a kind—not a physical similarity, save perhaps for a hint of grey in their plumage, fur or skin. Theirs was a similarity of being—there's no better way of saying it, except, perhaps, to say that the creatures in the gorge were children of the same Wisdom (Solomon even fancied seeing an owl nested in a stygian cleft)—and leave it at that.

The air grew cold. The scent of life became dim. His nasal passages cleared and he breathed marble air. It relieved the burden in his chest even as his heart grew heavy with the darkness. Still, he continued his descent, unable to understand a sudden fear of falling that came upon him and remained till he touched ground unexpectedly.

He was standing on a smooth, solid surface in the midst of nowhere. Surveying his surroundings in the pale, dim light, he beheld a thirty foot disc of glistening wet rock. From below, a great stone column had shot up between the ends of the earth. Solomon had descended to its flattened top.

His Kalli guide stood in the middle near the narrow circle of a pool. He approached and stared with her deep into the crystal ring. Tiny phosphorous creatures like ice crystals swam in random patterns upon the water. They danced to the rhythm of the planet without apparent meaning or purpose. But the more Solomon watched, the more he could see shapes and designs behind the randomness. The hidden order, a graceful geometric precision swimming below apparent chaos, drew him deep into its content, and into that near freezing soup, Solomon was plunged.

'No,' he thought, 'I was pushed.'

The pool was deep and dark, without direction. It stung his face and burned his eyes. He tried to surface but hit a ceiling instead. The cave expanded beneath the pool. He calmed himself, attempted to slow his heart rate and recover from the shock of the cold. Even so, his sense of direction did not return. Up and down became meaningless. Then he felt movement. The Savage grabbed his ankle and spun his relaxed body around. Taking his arms, she turned away from him and wrapped them around her neck. Then she began to swim.

'Down,' he thought. 'We're moving down.' He wasn't sure, though. His lungs began to feel uncomfortable, but he knew he could endure another minute or two. Two minutes later they were at the surface, a different surface. They had been going up after all. Maybe. Where were they? He could not tell. Savage's lungs exploded with relief. She had had to do all of the work. Solomon pulled himself out of the icy water onto dank rock, then pulled Savage up, quietly shivering, behind him. They rested.

As a soldier, Solomon's thoughts should have focused on his surroundings. But he did not notice that he was resting against the side of the great granite column, that they had emerged onto a ledge some fifty feet below its top which jutted out from the pillar almost to the canyon's far wall. Nor did he wonder how water which rose above this point to the top did not push the water here below out over the edge with a pipeline's pressure. Instead, while working the numbness out of his fingers, his thoughts turned inward where he discovered that he did not feel any different. If he had seen deeply into the pool before, if he had undergone some rite of passage, he did not experience a change, at least none that he could perceive. Perhaps he had missed something. Perhaps there was nothing to learn or perhaps it was too early to tell. What he *had* missed was the fact that he now thought of the journey as more than just a trip from one place to another.

Solomon looked to the Savage who peered back at him through dripping hair, draping her eyes. Whatever she might have been thinking remained a mystery to him. It would not be the last time. She brushed aside a single tangle of her hair to see him more clearly and wondered if he knew there had been no necessity in coming this way, wondered if he knew the image of a

52

bearded man in a blue single suit—touches of grey in his hair—running about on a giant tree with a little girl on his back, arms wrapped around clinging tightly to his neck: choking tight so that he wheezed a little but kept running anyway. In truth I do *not* know if these were her thoughts. But they make for good story, and I trust my sense about such things.

After a few minutes, the Savage took Solomon by the hand and led him across the far extending ledge to a solitary vine which led them back to the root network. They followed along the maze of twists and turns, rooting their way back up to the living land, emerging onto a wide trail, a natural separation of trees, almost perfectly straight, an easily discernable path.

"Walking, we'll be, all night," she said.

"Looks like they'll be walking all night," Quint said, smacking a bug from his bug bitten face.

"How do you know?" asked Lazarus. He was steadying the line while Crusher crossed the gorge on a servo-pulley.

"The cadence of your beeper hasn't changed—they're still moving. We're not any closer."

We pulled Crusher in and he detached from the line which held tight by the claws of a grappling hook shot from the other side. The tree was not very happy. Spence started across.

"We don't have to get closer yet. Tomorrow—" he smiled, remembering something, "and tomorrow and tomorrow." Nodding in self agreement: "We have time."

"Whar you get thawt strange talk Lawzrus?" asked Crusher. It was a question without thought—one of those "hellos" you give when passing someone in a corridor—a question meant to help hide his increasing sense of anxiety.

"Strange talk, Crusher? Have you listened to yourself?"

Spence was half way across.

"From somewhere in my memory, that's where. From things I came across, sounds I like repeated."

Quint rubbed salve over his face, though he was becoming used to the biting.

"Sounds I like repeated..."

And as Spence finished the crossing, pneumatic recordings reeled in Lazarus's brain, reeled with memories of a white room where he lay in a liquid manger, of two men in long white coats cutting him and feeding him too many bytes to swallow in a single mouthful.

Pause program.

How can I explain the thoughts and memories of a stained glass shattered man? None of them, these assassins of Imperial making, was entirely whole. I could see it inside them, even in my earliest attempts to tell this tale. Hmm. Even that needs explaining. Writers in ancient days often wrote many drafts of a story before sharing it with an audience. I write many drafts of personality programs. The earliest versions had Lazarus killing the others as they walked through the night, following Solomon's trail. But that's not how it happened. Still their thoughts were ever erratic. Something in the planet was affecting them. I know, for example, how Quint was thinking:

'I'm not well, not well. Coordination's off. I'm hallucinating. These missions. The darkness helps. I love the darkness. Counting helps—helping. Think of numbers. Numbers are solid: count forward and backward by ones and twos and tens and sixes. Solve for X and round out pi. I can think. I can think. I can think. Think of pi. Solve for...'

And Spence: 'Everything's red, infrared, red stained lenses and animal red—that's blood, blood red; making things bleed, making my heart beat red.'

And Crusher, thinking more Imperially than he spoke: 'Planets have magnetic fields. We've solved for that. Gravity does nothing to our technology. Why is this planet different? Scanners useless. There's an interference here. Interference. Why aren't there any satellites? Something in the planet. Something in the planet.' And deeper down, hiding: 'Nothing to be afraid of. Nothing to fear.'

Still Crusher feared, while Spence thought of atrocities, and Quint remained cool but on edge, edging a place of surety in his mind:

'Control. Control and be sure. Best in the galaxy needs someone on his back. Be the best. These missions.'

I knew what Quint meant. I know.

But what of Lazarus? How to explain him? I have seen the recordings of the event he was remembering, the precision records of the precise moment two long deceased Sykols raised Lazarus from the dead. I have read the reports and in more daring days have slipped from my rooms through the dark corridors of Imperial Palace down to even darker sublevels— forbidden places—where Imperial Sykols once kept and completed their experiments with scientific precision and horrid results. Men in white coats in white rooms too often coating walls in crimson. I can hear the panicked voices of the two men bending over his body:

One saying, "He's convulsing."

And the other: "Programming's off the scale."

"Do something!"

"All over the files!"

"Do something!"

"He's everywhere!"

"We'll lose him!"

"Oh God!"

"EEG is flat-lined."

"Oh God."

"What?!"

"He's tapped into files we'll never see. Gone so far back we'll never know."

How could they know what they had made? How could they know that a part of the man they'd chosen to revive had refused to die. They tried to program his mind and freed him to program himself. But that doesn't help me explain what he was thinking.

He thought of Solomon Star: 'Rip your throat, demon. Winged demon, rip it out! Take my hand and rip it out. With my hand.'

But like the broken shards of a stained-glass mirror, his thoughts of the present were just as much memories of the past, especially his memories of the white coated men in the white room:

One saying, "Can you wire a new path?"

And the other: "His brain's a sieve already."

"Hole after hole."

"For all we know what we feed him runs from his head to his buttocks."

"Then let's start over. Chop it off and try again."

'Follow the red wires,' Lazarus thought. 'Wire jambalaya: green, yellow, blue, white, coming out of my chest. Red heart—demon with an Imperial face. Shoot you dead, blow your heart out your back with a plasma bullet—one bullet, one shot. Blow out your temples with a sonic burst, make your eyes bulge in your skull.'

He remembered when they first woke him:

"What is your name?"

"I am Lazarus."

"Your name is John."

"I am Lazarus."

"No! John—"

"Lazarus."

"—Doe."

"Risen from the dead."

"No!"

And then he remembered her face:

'The goddess in my brain.'

The woman they taught him to love.

'Goddess in my brain.'

Who came to watch the progress.

'Goddess, mother, I love you.'

Whom Solomon Star abandoned.

'Demon! Kill you—rip your—'

The woman who seduced him.

'Command me goddess.'

My mother.

'My queen.'

And one more thing: Lazarus constantly saw wires, the multicolored wires pouring from his chest or pouring electricity into his brain. Red, green, violet, yellow. The colors attracted him—they attracted the man he'd once been. The Sykols had hooked him up to their computers in their attempts to make for him a completely new mind. But something of the old man in him, the child, the artist, the innocent—something of his old self would not let go. It took over his programming—*he* took it over.

And he sailed on beams of light through the totality of human knowledge stored on a galactic web of zeros and ones, bytes too large for a single mind to chew. He made himself new, a broken picture, fragmented and holed. He made a new man and drove that self insane.

I do not think I can explain it any better than that.

Resume Program.

"Target!"

With a word from Lazarus they snapped out of their private thoughts and once again became killers.

"Where."

"There." Lazarus pointed. "Seventy meters, ten degrees lateral."

They watched and listened in blind silence, tuning in fighter's senses too long dulled by reliance on machines.

Crusher asked, "Visuawl?"

"No, audio."

'How could he hear?' thought Quint. Then: "Visual."

"Made."

"Made."

Spence: "Not."

"Sixty meters, nine degrees."

"Now."

The shadow moved casually in their direction. It was big.

'Numbers are solid,' Quint thought.

The shadow was dark.

'But there's not enough dark here.' He thought of the chasm they'd crossed earlier. *'Not enough to love.'*

"It's an animal," said Spence.

"Dart," Lazarus ordered.

Spence was quick: The gun whipped from a shoulder pocket, took aim and shot silent death. The poison was too fast for pain.

Thud.

"Check it."

Spence moved quick and silent. The elk was still and stiff—somehow rigored. He drove his knife into its flank. Its mouth was fixed open. Spence noticed the white cadaverous smile, familiar smile.

In casual disgust he thought, 'Don't any of these beasts eat meat?' The teeth were white and shining and perfectly straight, edged straight. He wiped the blood across his chest making a red X on his suit.

"Just an animal," Spence reported nonchalantly returning.

And Lazarus: "Let's move."

Morning. They stopped to rest in its pale light. One watched while another drank and another sat and another saw something strange beyond believing. He said, in his peculiar accent, that it was red (which perked Spence's interest). There was a fallen tree, waist high. It sat perched on top, sat hunched on its two feet and tail. Perfectly still, like a mannequin, not even breathing. Crusher couldn't believe the red beast was real, sitting there, staring at him with slitted pupils, smiling its secret knowledge, knowing its secret and laughing to itself: 'a little closer, a little closer now.' Crusher couldn't believe it so much that he couldn't be afraid either. And he smiled, laughed that it wouldn't "boo!" away, how it even let him come right up to it. For a moment their eyes locked and Crusher thought he should be afraid but he couldn't believe. So they stared, and then he cocked his head to a side, considering how unlikely the beast was, staring at him with a cobra's devil face. Then he turned toward Spence, smiling, watching him cock his rifle for the kill. Then he turned back smiling at Bel, who then swung his tail with unliving speed, up and over and buried its tip in Crusher's skull.

- 15 -
The Mountain

On the morning of the third day Solomon and the Savage came to a river. It surprised him; no clearing was visible before the river, and no sun shone through to glisten on shadeless water. The trees extended their canopy even over this liquid space. Only the increased buzzing of insects, which he had just now noticed, gave any sign that they had been approaching water.

"Wait here," said the Savage, leaving Solomon by the bank. He did not notice her direction, only the water: gently flowing liquid light of pale green hue. Insects danced on the surface, a regalia of ripples collided in their ever increasing concentric circles, forming patterns, designs—like the creatures in the chasm pool; perhaps they were a language in liquid form—an ephemeral etching of the rhythm of Kall, written in stone, or rather ice that had forgotten not to melt. Beneath the pine and methane, the river smelled musty, mossy. Bugs buzzed in and out of his nostrils—he had to take short shallow breaths, snorting out insects with each exhale.

The Savage emerged in a simple wooden canoe twenty yards up stream.

A gentle current carried them into the night. They did not stop but rested in the cradle-on-the-water as it carried them into the heart of the morning sun. The glow of the water faded and emerald light emerged. Solomon rose from the bottom of the boat in a fever. Mosquito like insects had tasted of his flesh, left their marks and their deposits. Sweat mixed with blood in the exposed places on his face, hands, and on his body where the tears on the tearless fabric of his tunic had widened to the beginning of tatters. He looked at the Savage, steering and staring.

'No weakness,' he thought. 'Show no weakness.'

He turned away and quietly watched their journey. Hours passed with only the sounds of the living planet, especially the buzzing. His condition worsened. Casually, with a soldier's discipline, he measured his decline: head pounding, metabolism weakening with the fevered expenditure of energy, heart racing, stomach rebelling. Just as casually he leaned over the side and silently heaved.

'No weakness.'

He sat back up without hesitation. The buzzing became a cacophony.

"You are separate."

"What?"

"You are apart from the world. Not pleased with you."

"My body is not one with it."

"No. You."

"The mosquitos don't bite you."

"No."

"Why?"

"As Kall lives, we live. Earth has..."—she searched for the word in his language—"...*ways*. It says, 'Live this way.'"

"*Requirements.*"

"That sees."

"What does the world require?"

"*Eisos*. Have this and the earth is pleased."

"Sometimes you speak my language the Kalli way, sometimes more like I do."

"Sometimes."

'A game?' he wondered. Then: "The earth is pleased?"

She nodded. "And it blesses."

"And you worship the world."

"What is?"

"Praise. Honor it—as God. Kall is God."

"No." She paused, looking down river, but unable to shake Solomon's gaze. Returning attention to him: "The made must live with the made," and nodding her now familiar affirmation, "*eisos*."

Solomon recognized the finality of her statement and turned away to the buzzing, giving the Savage his back.

"I'm not dead yet."

His stamina pleased her. He was his father's son. This she knew, had really known from first sight. But loving him was not her responsibility. Had she only remembered that. Playing the detached role of guide and keeper she balanced his insight upon the scales of evaluation: 'Perceptive; yes, like you speaking I can see.'

She caught a glimpse of someone familiar and so remembered the father through the son, and thought of him with fondness. She remembered growing up and listening to the stories the elder folk would tell of him, how she would conjure up pictures of him in her head, and go to sleep with them underneath her eyelids. When he came in her tenth year from his time with their brothers and sisters, the dream tribe, he was nothing like she had imagined. Learning of him all over again was a joy to her.

She recalled a time when Philagapon was teaching the Gai-ja of her village. He had asked which was stronger, the giant tree or the tini-squirrel which eats its bark.

"The tree," one had answered. "It can crush the squirrel in its limbs."

"Then the tree would die," said another.

The Philagapon nodded his pleasure. Were there no squirrel to eat off the dead bark of the tree, which could not shed its skin on its own, the new bark could not grow and the tree would choke.

Yet another concluded, "The squirrel, then, is strongest. If it does not eat, it can kill the tree."

"Then the squirrel will die," had been her response.

Again the nod. And he went on to tell them of the Queen of the galaxy.

- 16 -
Respite, Respite...

By night his fever had reached its peak and he slept fitfully in the bottom of the canoe, his personal symphony flying about his ears. In his dreams he saw the great doors of Imperial Palace made from the giant black tree of Kall. The doors slid open and out spilled hundreds of Beli, the red serpents, squirming in mounds for solid footing. They separated, going out in all directions, all but one. One creature slithered toward Solomon who stood motionless in dream-world indecision. It spit up scarlet blood on the white boots of his Imperial Guardsman's uniform, and still he did not move. Then its hands embraced him and they were face to face, and she kissed him, and sweet saliva dripped from the menacing beast as it pulled away into the darkness of waking morn.

When Solomon woke, his fever was gone. The Savage stood by him in the water having tied the canoe to the bank. Immediately she squeezed the sap from a leaf onto his face and rubbed it in. He watched her pretend to look through, not at him. The burning stings in his skin were soothed but the medicine, rather than dulling his senses, sharpened them. She repeated the process on his hands and then turned away. Climbing the bank, she disappeared into the jungle. Solomon sat up in the boat and surveyed his surroundings. The evergreen world looked little different here than up stream. Perhaps the greens were a shade lighter. The water bugs performed a ballet to the tune of the much reduced buzzing in his ears. The caw of a bird out spoke the panoply of sound above for a moment—that was new. He pulled himself up aching onto the seat of the canoe and tried to stretch the stiffness from his muscles. He then took up his pack and checked the date on a chronometer within. Only one day had passed; he had not lost consciousness from illness, only drifted to sleep. The Savage returned shortly bearing a large leaf that had been ingeniously shaped into a basket with its stem as the handle. In it were fruit, green, with fuzzy skin, like a peach, along with cut lengths of a stalk, celery-stringy in consistency. With the ease of experience she twisted the fruit in half, revealing a pulpy orange meat with tiny black seeds at its core. She carefully handed Solomon a half, opened end upright so as not to spill it.

"Duna, is—strength. Eat it this way." She opened her mouth wide and pressed the fruit against her teeth simultaneously pushing at the center from the back with one finger. She bit down and sucked, separating the meat from its skin, then pulled the formless shell from her lips and cast it into the river. Solomon watched it as tiny fish appeared to tug upon and take their fill—nothing wasted. Cautiously he sniffed at the fruit: indescribable, but exhilarating. Then he repeated her movements with less coordination, almost choking with the sudden surge of energy that passed from heart to extremities. Eyes, fingers and toes tingled, and he felt a clearing in his head. He breathed heavy, every breath doubling his strength; he gasped for air, not out of breath but as a hungry man gobbles up a feast of bread and beans. Before the sensation passed, he relished the air. The green of the jungle deepened, though not in color. For a moment he wanted to weep with joy and did not understand his feeling—elation. The wonder of pure sensation.

'A natural stimulant,' he thought, and he attended to his heart beat for concern that the chemical would be too alien.

The Savage next handed him a stalk—"Pi-lar"—and began to eat one herself. Solomon crunched the plant, taking in its texture and taste—stringy, salty, bitter.

"People would kill for that fruit," he noted casually.

"Yes."

Then, more deliberately: "No one outside knows about it, do they?"

"No."

'And well they should not,' he thought. It was a drug. Narcotic. An army would have died for it. Of its existence Solomon ever only told one person, and even here, in this secret place, there is danger in the mere mention. Hmm...no...let it be. Let all the secrets be told.

They filled up on the stalks and shared only one more piece of the fruit which was to the pleasure of both Solomon's desire and prudence. 'People would kill.' Then they took to the river again, and traveled for two days, stopping only for food and toilet.

As they traveled, she became more conversational, teaching him with meticulous detail the names and uses of the plants and animals they saw along the river. Of Shields and Cetologies he became well versed.

She showed him wonder:

There were long tailed monkeys called Chos, colored incandescent yellow, which clung to each other's' tails in chains. They stretched themselves across the river or swung trapeezing circles. "Crack the whip!" they eeked, sending three poor brothers in an arching plunge—sploosh! Using their whip-like tails to tread water, they clamored to the shore.

Now look—those floating logs rolling over and over. They're wooly hippos—there's one lifting his shaggy head. Neumators, they're called—listen to the yawning bellow: smooth, unnatural, more instrument than animal. They eat a moss that grows on reed shafts, right up out of the water. When the Neumator sounds, his basso vibrates the hollow shaft. The reeds whistle different notes depending on their height—but somehow, the music always sounds in perfect harmony.

See that orchard? No, not orchard—not fruit. But why are the trees in rows? It goes on for miles. Here is where all Kalliphi come to plant a tree on their twelfth birthday, each in a row following from generation to generation. How the subtle eye could see the movement of age from tallest and widest, close to the river, to the shortening of years and height several hundred miles away where grows a sapling shoot (in one of the few places on Kall still open to the sky) inearthed but a few years ago by a so called Savage of true civility. The people keep their history on pages that haven't been pulped and processed.

Children are taught design here. No tree is as another, but all trees bear marks of making—marks from the first shouted foundation. Regardless of kind, all trees share this language, written in their skins—Yes, *Being* patterns—archetypes—like the patterns of the luminescent insects, seeming random until the eye—illumined—reads cryptic clarity in the bark of each living giant, and each giant's child—Yes, you learn to read them here. The likeness of the designs makes the language, the uniqueness of the individual tree allows for noting landmarks in every foot of jungle. Here the mind can dive into complexity or be released from revery:

"We had rows of trees on Imperial World. But not like this."

"How so?" She saw an opportunity.

"Not so natural—more rigid."

"Your word: *artificial*."

'Father taught her that.' "Yes. More controlled."

"Because of control, you left?"

"I left because she lied to me."

"That sees not."

He looked at her—probing green eyes. 'You want to learn me now.' "No I suppose it doesn't, not completely." 'Or do you want to teach me?' "But I know it wasn't because of control."

"How do you know this?"

"Because I'm still controlled."

She thought for a moment. "You are controlled by old ways."

"Yes. You might call it, *duty*."

"Or *slavery*?"

A piercing glance.

"Duty is what I know."

'I'll teach you more,' she thought. "For duty the army you went?"

"I left the Imperial Guard and joined the regular army. Of all the stupid choices."

"Not so."

"Why?"

"It brought you here.") ((u/ poinð

Here the river widens. Look—Dolphins! But two feet long. Silver, swimming air breathers in the hundreds! Leaping in companies, chirping in schools. And now they leap in high arcs over the boat, a tunnel weaving left to right and right to left, showering the canoe as water streaks from their shimmering forms, a fanfare welcome—Smiles, I swear smiles—Yes. And swimming up beside they offer smooth skin to stroke, or a fresh fish wriggling its life out for dinner. Flipping and spinning and dancing on their tails— self trained professionals teach wonder. There a six inch baby jumps into the canoe and lies fearlessly still. Mother peers over the edge for self assurance. Here they send the child home with a kiss. Fingers smell of sour sweet oils. The armada sends escort as far as where the river narrows from its lake-distance width.

He thought of a long lost friend. Caught up in that beauty, a solid memory, a good memory pushed its way to the surface. 'Immanuel would have loved to paint this world. We'd have never gotten him to leave.'

Watch the dandelions—giant dandelions—white marshmallow puffies shaking loose butterfly seeds in a windless air. Those are Artosi (like otters) walking among the stems, releasing the dandelion snow—it surrounds and overcomes and whirls out of touch like sunlight dust through mother's window, and sticks to wet clothing turning tattery blue to cloud billow white. The otters beat rocks on mollusks in the otherwise quiet, hammering for that soft chewy center, wary of the large reptiles scaling about the river, themselves in search of warm blood.

"Keep your hands in. They only bite the foolish."

"There's no other world like this."

"On no other world we could live."

The river narrowed. The canoe increased speed with rushing water—moving quickly but not with danger, nor over rocks. Berry trees hung their branches low under the weight of the burgeoning purple fruit. The Savage remembered the place with too intense a memory: six year olds smashing long poles into the ripe reddish clumps, bursting the balloon-tight skins, drenching each other in the sour sweet juice until so royally bedecked with purple goo as to have lost any semblance of their natural hue. Remembering, she forgot and, wryly smiling, lifted her oar among clusters. The quick moving boat shot them through showers of violet rain—oar smashing branch smashing the next in chain reaction.

"Hey!" Solomon shouted—half annoyed, half surprised, and covering his head.

Remembering, the oar and her smile dropped. Adrenalin welled embarrassment into her face but he could not see it for the purple covering. She wanted to look away—how she wanted to! Play the aloof and in control. Couldn't stand the feeling—'fool'— lost control. Openness was for later. First she had to *see* him. 'Think too much. I too much think.' He deserved better: She settled on a half-truth:

"It gives the body sweet scent."

He accepted, and to him she was nebulous as ever.

'Only a mistake,' she told herself. 'A mistake.' But her heart continued to race long into night, even as she showed him the world, giving names to many things. Names he diligently took in memorization.

At night, with never yet a breeze, the trees moved, rustling a whisper which sang to her heart and soothed that Savage breast, and began in him to dull the machine, that less beating than beeping unnatural rhythm.

- 17 -
Imperial World:
Nine Months Before Solomon's Arrival on Kall

I made a choice a very long time ago that I would speak the truth, or, in the event I could not, remain quiet. Prudence dictates an Imperial Princess, even second born and no heir to the throne, should not always speak her mind. And so I am often seen in silence. Why then would I suddenly turn from Solomon's journey to reveal a scandal in my own home? Why tell a story which, if told by any others, would have them executed? I am not the Empress's confessor, and I am guilty of none of these sins—crimes committed decades before my birth. But the compulsion to confession is strong, as if the blood were staining *my* hands and no others.

The short of it, then, is this: I am adding a subplot. It is not Solomon's story, not directly. But the two are too inextricably tied to ignore either one. Here it is then: nine months before Solomon Star went to Kall in 2298, a seed was planted on Amric's world which would give birth to war.

Hal Teltrab was the best there was at a job he'd never been meant to do. The Captain of the Imperial Guard had the most important responsibility in the galaxy. Hal had not been born to it, but that hadn't mattered in years.

He sat staring at a holo screen in a room walled with screens. The screens watched for him—a thousand eyes—and thought for him where such might be the need: a thousand programs designed to watch trends and communiques and economic forces and political voices. Some screens watched the grounds and chambers of Imperial Palace—priority one. Others watched with graphs and lines and color codes. A spacious dark closet lit by hallucinogenic pixels.

But Hal Teltrab wasn't watching any of those. He sat staring at a holo screen on a wide glass-top desk, doing what Hal did best. Doing what he *had* been born to do. Doing what he had so little time to do since becoming Captain of the Imperial Guard. Hal was digging.

Analysis.

It began with an innocent comment only a few days before. Here in this room, the *Con*, as Hal called it. A meeting of five. The Pentaf—leaders of the Empress's body guard.

"Look," said Jo Isacson, "it's an authority issue. We've got Sykol directives conflicting with Guard priorities."

"Don't be reactionary, Jo." Simon Lazar was second in command. "It's a procedural problem. We've got some gray areas to work out. It's been this way since the Emperor's death."

"Look, I'm not overreacting here. Last week—look at this report—last week specific orders from Hal—direct orders—countermanded by a Sykol sub-supervisor."

"You're right," came Hal's calm calculating voice. "But that's because of the disruption of Sykol timetables."

"Captain"—Isacson forced restraint—"that was almost ten years ago. The excuse is getting old."

"But so is the system. The Imperial machine, gentlemen, is over two thousand years old and it has never seen the kind of upheaval—"

"You mean Inmar's threats?" questioned Paul Tarsoon, Commander of the Air. "There have been threats, even wars before, I—"

"He doesn't mean Inmar," said Lazar.

"At least not entirely," added Hal.

"He means the *Incident*."

Hal smiled as he recalled the conversation—they called Solomon's dismissal the *Incident* now. "And the Emperor's passing," he concluded. "All these together have meant a restructuring of sociological predictors—the ramifications, the variables—Sykol probability computers are working overtime...as are my own."

Isacson fell back in his chair. "Why am I the only one who sees this?"

"Are you saying the Captain is missing something?" Lazar was defensive, but his point was well taken—not this Captain.

"Here's what I know." Isacson was more careful. "He's my Captain, you're his Lieutenant. I command the Infantry, Paul the Air and Fagan the Mobile. Why isn't that clear to the Sykols?"

A pause.

"Concern noted, Commander Isacson."

And that was the end of it. Except that Paul Tarsoon, who was incredibly efficient, except in committee, tossed out a thought for no particular reason, one which he claimed had been running about the back of his head for years: "Why do Sykols pass their jobs by heredity like we do? Soldiers I can understand."

"Genetic engineering."

"Increase performance by increasing human ability."

"Yes," Tarsoon continued, "but the brain pool is much larger—the Sykols can draw from a talented galactic intelligence base, but they don't."

"But they're supposed to be the most intelligent people in the galaxy—very wary of outside contamination."

"*Most intelligent* barring our illustrious Captain."

Wry smiles.

Hal smiled too but remained silent while the others talked. He had started to think. That's what he did best. What he was made for.

As the others left, Simon Lazar turned to Hal at the door: "He never should've left, Hal. Never should've left."

Hal noted the emotion.

Then set it aside.

And he thought.

And he dug.

- 18 -
Summit

On the morning of their third day on the river the Savage turned their canoe up a small tributary stream and rowed up the narrowing channel for an hour.

At a sudden moment, like the coming of a revelation, the stream widened...

        ...into paradise!

They floated in the midst of a pool below a waterfall (which was neither big enough to roar nor so small that it could not applaud), surrounded by a dome of bloom bearing vines: red and cream petals showered them, filling the place with a scent from creation's dawn. Both breathed deeply; their hearts were lightened. Methane and pine were notably absent; the scentedness was welcomed. The beauty of the place awakened memories the man of light had not known he had: images he had seen flitting before him on his first night in the jungle. They were of a place like this, one to which all people belonged. He felt a joy of discovery, an emotion of finality which he could only express by thinking, 'Of course. This is the way it's supposed to be.'

The Savage paddled the canoe through the red/cream sea, parting it with her bow, to a sandy shore near the fall where the light seemed brighter than any place they had yet been. Together, they climbed out of the boat onto the sand. Solomon's feet sank slightly into the grains. His steps away from the water left impressions—footprints for only a moment. The fine white dust sunk back making little oval craters. The Savage did not follow. She had sunk to her knees and was digging—even playing—in the sand, running it through her fingers like water. Even close to the shore it was dry enough to flow—two elements so different, here alike. Like two people: a man and a woman.

Then she stood. "Bathe here." She began to undress.

"I thought the body was a personal thing to you."

"It is."

"Then why are you—"

"It is not the same as said before. You have not two words for it. There is taking off clothes and taking off clothes. The body is the body. The mind is important." She looked *at* him, not *through*. "Where the mind is of Philagapon's son?"

Solomon looked at her a moment, and then the pond behind. An old image filled his mind—remembering him too well.

"Elsewhere." He turned to walk away.

"The son of Philagapon would not have such a mind."

"The son of Philagapon would recognize his limitations."

"The son of Philagapon would not have limitations."

He did not reply.

- 19 -
From 2279:
Gambit

A sixteen year old Captain of the Imperial Guard walked through the corridors of the vast Imperial Palace on his way to the family apartment for a rest. He had just completed a training session with Immanuel Proshemeis and certain select groups of the Air Battalion. About to enter a lift to the residential area of the Palace, he was stopped by the beeping of a device built into the belt which he wore under the red sash girding his blue Imperial singlesuit. He pressed a button through the sash and answered:

"Star."

"Private transmission," replied a voice from his waist.

Solomon reached into the sash and pulled out a device which he fit into his ear. From this he pulled a wire that reached to his mouth and fixed in place.

"Ready."

"Solomon Star is to report to Princess Janis in the Private Gardens at once. Authorization two-one-one-two. Respond."

"Understood. Identity: one-zero-two-zero-one."

Solomon turned to another lift. As the doors hissed opened he wondered why such a routine message had been for his ears only. While motionless in the moving lift, Solomon thought how pleasant it would be to see the Princess. Work with the Guard had vastly reduced his time with his charge. He missed her. He longed for the time when they were younger, when he had spent the most of each day with her. But the young men of the forty-fourth Guard, were entering their mid-teen years. Five thousand boys born in the same year (or near to it) as the Princess, Janis, heir to the Amric throne, would soon find their duties as protectors of the future Empress increasing. It was Solomon's job to make sure they were ready.

The lift door opened and Solomon stepped out to stand before the entrance to the Emperor's Private Gardens, a two-hundred yard square area that rested in a niche of the Palace. The space was roofless and surrounded by walls on all four sides except for a ten yard gap in the outer wall which connected the Private Gardens to the larger Imperial Gardens surrounding the Palace. The area was filled with rare plants and trees and, at its center, a bathing pool in which members of the Imperial family would often laze on warm summer days.

When the Princess Janis bathed in the Imperial *tub*, the Guard unit assigned to her would move to perimeter stations. One man from this unit would move to each of the four garden entrances to insure that no one wandered in accidentally.

The doorway was empty. Solomon headed toward the center of the garden. The sky was clear and pink. The sun danced about the leaves of trees and tickled Solomon's eyes while scents of a hundred different worlds darted past his awareness. An alien tree which had a bothersome habit of spraying excess water out of a spout at its top, did so. The rainbow effect was beautiful. The tree's leaves danced in delight of the refreshing mist, while Solomon's arms covered his head trying to protect him from the sappy liquid. He hurried by. Pausing under the giant leaf of a giant fern, he looked about, wondering why there were no guards in the area. Someone should have been patrolling there. He concluded that the Princess must be on the other side of the garden.

Twenty yards later he was surprised to find, as he peered through a natural curtain of vines, that the Princess and heir to the Imperial throne was at the center of the garden, and that she was bathing.

Solomon was stunned. He thought of turning away but could do nothing but stare, mouth half opened, at the porcelain skin, the gentle symmetry of the one standing knee deep in the pool while servants poured water from ancient urns over her. Delicate China. She was not the girl Solomon had grown up with. Not the sassy pony tailed girl whose sandy hair would not be the only thing that darkened with age; not the hide-and-go-seek (and make sure she always wins) player squealing about the garden in delight, the white jumpered baby soft skinned, screaming at him when he wasn't playing right though laughing at his jokes, slapping his arm in need-to-release anger when she fell down though sharing her candy with him at lunch time when no one was looking; not the baby who woke him to cry in the night by her crying nearby; not the chess player so intent on beating him (when they told her he had permission to win) that she perspired on her pieces every time, screamed (most unlady like) when she won, fumed (most ungraciously) when she lost. No, not a girl. She was a woman. Her body was slender, elegant, yet formidable. Her face was long, the cheeks high and pronounced—regal—as the nose: thin, like the lips, and pointed and turned slightly upward. Her eyes were a piercing blue with a hint of steel and a slightly more than usual tapering at the outer edges. Her shimmery blonde hair was long and silky.

"You're beautiful," he whispered. A tear ran down his cheek. He closed tight his blurring eyes and turned away. He stepped. He staggered. He grabbed at a tree trunk and let it support him to the ground. His manhood welled up into his body: mind aware, heart pounding, limbs afire; chemicals in his brain sought to betray him. He drew his legs in and hugged himself close, pushing his head against his knees as if trying to push the memory from his mind, the feeling from his heart and from his glands.

Within the silent reaches of consciousness a battle raged. The power principle, that pervading wickedness of the Imperium, was making its darkest attack on the young Captain. Following their statistics and charts, timetables and theorems, Imperial Sykols, the master manipulators—psycho-engineers, scientists who kept the Empire running—were seeking to manipulate his darker recesses, to increase that all too important dependence on his charge to include a bond of sexuality, of primal desire (can't have too independent an ego, can we?). Of this little "trick," I can, at least, say Janis was unaware.

But there was one factor the Emperor's Sykols could not fathom, let alone take into account: Solomon was a child of light. Some, it seems, are drawn to their life directions. They have almost an inbred affinity for the path they are destined to follow, good or bad. Others have more freedom, and therefore a more difficult time walking with integrity whichever road they take.

It was his compassion that won the battle within Solomon. It would prove to be at once his salvation and his downfall.

"I love you," he concluded, at last relaxing. "I love you."

And so he did. Not the dark love. But the love of charity, of compassion. Solomon became vulnerable. In later years it would make all the difference.

He left the garden in a daze. He was about to enter the lift to go home when interrupted again, this time by the Chief Sykol, a presumptuous figure of a man whom Pylat would have reminded Solomon of when he bothered to make the connection years after 2298, who himself seemed royal in bearing and might have been royalty in some deep past long renounced by labyrinthine Sykol agendas.

"Captain Star."

Startled: "Oh, hello Chief."

"Are you alright? You look pale."

Worried: "Uh...yes I'm fine." Thinking quickly: "Just a little tired."

The Chief smiled recognition.

"By the way, sir, do you know where the guard unit that is supposed to be attending the Princess is?"

"Why...with her I should think. Where is she?"

"I was told (he chose his words carefully) that she was in the Private Gardens."

The Chief looked to the garden entrance and, pointing: "Ah, and so she must be."

Solomon turned to see a member of the forty-third Guard (the Emperor's personal body guard which Solomon's father Davidson Star commanded) approaching them to take up a position at the door.

He turned again to the Chief who purposefully did not look at him.

"I...thought that one of *my* units would be training here."

The Chief looked at Solomon, smiled: "I see. Well, Captain, you had better get some rest. You have a full evening ahead of you."

"Yes, I have." Solomon turned toward the lift, and pressed the call button. He looked briefly at the Chief who stood watching him with the same plastic smile. He entered the lift.

The Chief lifted an electronic note pad and pen and made a notation. He was satisfied that Solomon's reaction to the garden scenario had been exactly what Sykol engineering had expected—the relationship they had designed between Solomon and his charge for the past sixteen years.

He could not have been more wrong.

- 20 -
The Demons

What I am sharing with you is not about me, and it is a mistake if I have led you to believe so. Therefore, I should end any mysteries which might draw you from the story at hand.

I am Janis's daughter, born fifteen years after Solomon's visit to planet Kall in 2298 A.E. Younger sister to a brother destined for the throne, I may not marry, by decree, lest my own children become a threat to a stable monarchy.

I am not interested in secret lovers. So I occupy my time with secrets, or rather with uncovering truths. My mentor taught me a passion for truth. It is a dangerous love in my world.

This "secret room" is just that. No one knows it exists, not even Captain Teltrab—or if he knows, he feigns a good ignorance. Here in my holo room I sift information, ferret out lies, and figure out truth. Here I tell the stories of my family's guilt. Solomon's story is one of many.

Bam!

"That's another one."

"Report Quint."

"Another one of those red lizards."

"That makes a dozen today," said Spence.

"To me."

They joined Lazarus at the river's edge. Insects swarmed about them. They could barely hear each other's transmissions over the buzz of tiny biters. Quint's face, and Spence's were swollen with welts. They wore gas masks as long as they could stand the heat, and then had to open themselves up to attack in fresh air. Lazarus's cold copper skin was unaffected.

"They've gone down river. We'll have to follow."

"Lazarus," said Quint.

"Quint?"

"Assessment."

"Go."

He chose his words carefully. "Most equipment has broken down." In part to appease Lazarus. "We've suffered our first fatality ever." In part to be sure that he wasn't losing his mind. "Spence and I will soon be too sick to keep up." In part because he wanted it to be dark again. Blood and sweat mixed on his face and hands. "We're fighting the planet more than this Star. You have him under tracking—we can't lose him." There were holes all over their suits. Rips and tears—Lazarus's back utterly exposed, Quint's pants missing a leg, Spence reduced to a few tattered cloths. "We can pull out and regroup. We can follow him from above." They had left or lost most of their equipment: rifles and a few conventional weapons remained as well as some rations and drugs. Quint spoke calmly. But in his mind his thoughts about Lazarus were chaos: 'You freaking ghost—you hell born invulnerable—why don't you suffer?!'

Lazarus stared his steely brow bent stare.

"How are you doing Spence?" he asked.

'Don't be an idiot,' Quint thought.

"Kill kickin' ready, Laz."

'Moron.'

Lazarus laughed. "Can't handle it Quint?"

"It's your call. Doing my job's all. You need a good back. You don't have it." He didn't say everything he'd wanted to: 'You're going to get us killed.'

Lazarus gave no reply, and he didn't bother to tell them the signal which allowed them to track Solomon Star was mysteriously growing weaker.

Pulling a cylinder from his near empty pack: "You can make it." He depressed one end; the other popped off and a rubber raft began to inflate from it.

Quint finally showed his anger: "We're not machines!"

The eyes looked up darting. Spence thought of blood and his own choking neck.

"Feeling surer Quint?"

Quint squeezed the handle of his rifle until it creaked.

"We're killers. Not robots," Lazarus continued, "oh yes. Cold, professional but," lifting his hand to grasp the air, "warm flesh and bone. A machine, Quint? Look at your reflection." The cheshire smile: "If you shoot me, do I not bleed?"

Quint didn't say what he wanted to: 'I have no idea.' Lazarus drew his eyes. 'Those teeth, too white. Perfect, straight, too white. Need dark.'

He focused all the more and saw in that terrible whiteness impure—the colorless all color—a reflection so true he could not blink away.

- 21 -
From 2279:
Sacrifices

It was a lovely day for painting: a clear sky, a gentle breeze on a warm day, birds of the air active with song, the low hum of small harvesters in the distance lifting tart citrus to the breeze. It was a lovely day for painting. Immanuel Proshemeis, age sixteen, preferred the natural light of the sun when painting in the old style of canvas and watercolors. It was more true to the color—especially in its subtlety. Immanuel was in the Imperial Gardens standing before an easel. A multi-colored palette hovered near him. Olive grass stretched out before him reaching to fat leafy trees gathered together on his left, and to the lights of Imperial City behind him. His brush hand moved lightly across the canvas. He paused a moment to examine his work: a painting of the Palace at sunset. Lit up to the appearance of daylight, only the rich red sky above gave evidence that the Imperial house was sleeping.

Immanuel looked to the real Palace a thousand yards away. He was not too far from the outer entrance to the Private Gardens. He thought of the Guard on duty within and was pleased to have a day off from his responsibilities as the forty-fourth Commander of the Air: one of the Pentaf, the Guard's five leading officers, and third in command to Solomon Star.

In the Private Gardens, Janis was bathing. A unit of sixteen forty-fourth Guardsmen and four forty-third Guard trainers patrolled the outer areas of the garden. Lieutenant Hal Teltrab, Solomon's second in command, was monitoring the unit with a forty-third Guardsman. They stood at one of the Palace entrances, wearing their private communicators, talking casually.

"Have you been to Arché, Lieutenant?" asked the trainer.

Hal chuckled. "Are you kidding? In the Guard? None of us leaves the Palace, let alone this planet, not until we're eighteen."

"I remember. I thought they might make exceptions for the Pentaf. Anyway, I went there once. Imperial visit. It was cold, and you could feel the age. They've got ruins there that pre-date the Empire; and temples, and priests or whatever they are. Not too many like you, though—pure blood."

"I want to go some day."

"It's really quiet too. Makes you think—about life and God, just like everyone says it does."

They became quiet themselves. After a moment Hal opened his mouth to speak but was interrupted by a sudden "Code R—!" over his communicator. His hand went to his ear as did the trainer's. Silence.

"Who was that?" Hal demanded.

Silence.

"Trainers count off." Stern but cool.

"One" (with Hal).

"Two."

"Three."

Silence.

"T-four respond. All outer wall guards respond."

The trainer took over: "Let's go red. Outer guards converge on charge; inner guards: T-two take two and report com loss, the rest of you on charge."

Hal and the trainer had already begun to move. With the orders completed, they took to a full run.

Immanuel was pleased with his project. He admired the painting as he walked back to the Palace, holding it before himself. He walked alongside the creek that ran through the Gardens by the outer entrance of the Private Gardens and along the Palace wall. Immanuel turned his eyes to the water. The creek bed was deep, but the water within varied in depth from a pale few inches to several feet. Immanuel followed the water's path with his eyes, looking up toward the Palace. Then he stopped. In the distance he could see several black figures in the creek moving toward him. He squinted. At first he thought them to be a group of garden workers. Then a siren seared the air.

Not the third level siren: prepare for attack.

Not the second siren: under attack.

The first—a member of the Imperial family in danger—sounded out a revolting basso. The young Air Commander's mind was shocked to unbelieving stupor. His instincts (well trained) took over his body. He ran as if possessed. As he approached the dark figures he could see twelve men dressed entirely in black including masks that covered all but their eyes. One of them was carrying a limp white burden over his shoulders: surely Janis IV.

Immanuel steered away from the creek's edge so as to keep his approach secret. And then he was upon them. The beautiful painting, still held in the young man's hand, became a flying weapon. It struck the front most kidnapper causing him to stagger. Immanuel leapt from the bank and drove his feet into his first opponent's chest. They landed with bone crushing impact even with inches of softening mud as a bed. A quick punch to the neck made the number of assailants eleven.

The painting landed nearby, its top half immersed in clear creek water.

Immanuel sprang to his feet. His enemies moved to surround him. Light flashed. A familiar hum. They had plasma swords. The scum carried the sacred weapon of the Guard! Even so, they were cautious. They were many against one, men against boy, and armed. But this was an Imperial Guard: the best in the galaxy. They had already lost five men at the hands of the three guards whom they could not avoid in the capture.

The running water was turning the picture's dusk to dawn, the sun seeming to rise as the paint faded to daylight pink.

The man carrying Janis tried to move his burden up and out of the creek, away from the fight. Immanuel directed his attack to that end of the circle. One man stood between him and Janis. The boy was a muddied blur. The blade struck downward. Immanuel stepped to the right. His blow to the head was ducked and the assassin's horizontal swing came flashing. Immanuel dropped onto his side with a splash, and in a single motion: legs lock in legs; spin opponent to ground; roll; hands pry at weapon; roll over opponent; up on one knee; strike! The enemy numbered ten, and they were breathing hard.

Immanuel spun, his enemy's weapon in hand, and swung a parrying trail shield just in time to block three enemy blades. Liquid steel shrieked and sparked with the contact. He did not feel the fourth strike at his shin; he did not have time. He fell back from the impact of the blows. Not Guardsmen, but they were good—almost certainly genetically enhanced, like the Guard.

'But not that good,' Immanuel thought.

He rolled and blocked and struck and rolled, but he could not gain a stance. Water sizzled as it struck flying plasma—a wafting smell of burning meat in the cauterized numbness at his shin. A slashing whip of plasma, and he cut the legs of another kidnapper off at the knees. But he still couldn't get to his feet. A strike near his head splashed boiling water into his ear. He was running out of space. He took a gamble and kicked himself up—right into a slashing trail of light that kills. Immanuel fell limp into the water, blood pouring from his chest.

He laid on his side, clutching his wound, eyes closed, breathing shallow. Humming died away with footfalls. He could feel the warm flowing past his fingers. He was at once angry and sad: he had failed. He thought of crying, but did not have the strength. He opened his eyes.

Immanuel could see the painting a few feet away. The sun was setting again. Blood flowed, a trickle in the stream. It passed under the canvas and collected there. The pink sky darkened to scarlet red. Dusk over the Palace. The boy's heart smiled. And then darkness fell.

Two silent ships glided silently through space. Seventy-five hundred men sat silently within. Solomon Star sat in darkened quarters. He too was silent, except within. He could not believe what had just happened. The foundation of his existence was rocking on a precipice. He could not believe that Janis had been kidnaped. He thought it impossible that anyone could have penetrated planet security, Palace security, and charge security. How could anyone hide a ship in the Imperial Gardens? But they had. Janis was gone and Immanuel Proshemeis was dead. 'How lucky,' he thought, 'that Immanuel managed to get a tracer on the escape ship.' They could follow the kidnappers wherever they went.

The Guard had been scrambled in secret. The Emperor had no intention of letting the peoples of his precious Empire know that the heir to the throne had been abducted. Nor would he wait for ransom demands to be sent. The entire forty-fourth Guard and half of His Majesty's own forty-third had been sent after Janis. She had been traced to a planet in a binary system that had no name, only a number. They would rescue her. They had to rescue her—and crush the enemies of the Empire! Solomon knew the price of failure.

He stood to leave the room with the thought of that price looming in his mind: If the Princess were to die there would be no need for a forty-fourth Guard. Immanuel would not be long without friends. In two eons of inheritance, never had there been such a failure. In a lineage of fathers stretching farther back than he could remember, never had a Captain of the Guard failed so completely. The cabin door hissed open. The light of the ship's corridor streamed passed him. He did not blink.

Military File: 1001001

Ship Recording: 3142279.1201

Air Commander Retton: 43 Guard:

"Gentlemen, we're in orbit about the planet, directly above the Princess's signal, exercising detection shielding machinery. Reconnaissance ships have located the enemy position as you see here on the viewing screen.

"Closeups show that this fortress is not well guarded, but formidable, nevertheless, given the context of a hostage situation. Light and medium assault weapons, no air cover to speak of. Heat sensors approximate seven thousand bodies."

Mobile Commander Simon Lazar: 44 Guard:

"Have you located the Princess?"

Retton:

"No. But we know she's in there. Commander Adrian—forty-third—is in transit with reconnaissance information. His stealth squad could take none of the enemy alive. But we will use what information he did obtain to manufacture uniforms and infiltrate the fortress. Captain Star."

Captain Star: 44 Guard:

"We'll send a group of men in, disguised, who have digested what records we have of this culture. Fortunately our language specialist found specimens of their communications in his archives. He'll be leading this group. Then we begin a frontal assault. Air barrage."

Lieutenant Commander Hammill: 43 Guard:

"Thank you. We'll blanket the fortress in low yield grenades—cut power and raise smoke without endangering the Princess. We have it easy this go. We've coordinated with mobile for phase two."

Star:

"Mobile assault."

Lazar:

"Our troop carriers will land out of range and be on spot fifteen seconds after the air assault. My armored groups are curious as to why they're being held back?"

Star:

"We have to think of the—"

Lieutenant Commander Andrews: 44 Guard:

"Sir, why are we only attacking from one side? Why not take up two offensive positions or surround the fortress to prevent escape?"

Infantry Commander Joseph Isacson: 44 Guard:

"In the back door."

Andrews:

"What?"

Star:

"Go ahead Jo."

Isacson:

"While the assault presses, a small group will infiltrate what we have found to be a stealth access point—"

Retton:

"Yes, here."

Isacson:

"Yes. We'll free this opening in the wall where we will link up with our group inside who should have located and secured our objective, unnoticed, we hope, by the general confusion of the main assault."

Field Lieutenant Spitz: 43 Guard:

"Hopefully."

Isacson:

"We will."

Star:

"Because of the importance of this group, Jo and I will personally accompany Commander Rann's rescue force."

Infantry Commander Rann: 43 Guard:

"Fifty of us will assault under my command. Thirty forty-third and twenty from the forty-fourth. She is *your* charge. We all feel the weight."

Star:

"Thank you sir. Lieutenant Teltrab will lead the entire frontal assault. It is vital that you all remember the risk involved in this strategy. The enemy will not harm our Lady if they think they can defeat our little charade or use her life for leverage. There is strong evidence from cultural studies that suggests these people are completely ignorant as to whom they are up against. The point being this: You must do so well that you appear to be losing the battle. That will give us the time we need."

Lazar:

"How will we be able to do that—to...look bad?"

Star:

"That remains for the troop session. Hal, uh, Lieutenant Teltrab will lead that session."

Retton:

"The point of emphasis in that area will be commitment and withdrawal. Emphasize this to your small unit commands. Mistakes make you expendable.

"Gentlemen. You have heard the speeches, you know what the implications are. Your hearts weigh heavy. Especially that of your Captain. But talk is over now. So is thinking. Now is doing."

Sergeant Urya moved a quiet hand about his body, checking the links and systems of his body armor. Imperial Guardsmen wore a light armor system, not like the heavier cybernetics of the regular army. They didn't need that bulk. They were Imperial Guards. The synthetic rubber like suit held thin maneuverable body and limb shields—plastic looking pieces that conformed to the body—and an electrical system for life support and servo connections. The bionic features of the suit were limited—no increased strength or speed. This was the trim uniform of the Guard. Only oversized white jet boots (for extended leaps—fifty yards) and A. I. helmet showed resemblance to regular army technology. Nothing else was needed. Urya breathed artificial oxygen—cool and crisp, it reddened the blood.

The helmet, like the uniform, was blue. It completely enclosed the head: a tinted face shield from brow to chin, and an Imperial crest marked the forehead. The helmet was linked to an Artificial Intelligence computer that worked in direct conjunction with the brain. It processed communication and sensory information, monitored life support systems, and, upon mental command, fired the boot jets. It was a Guardsman's partner. Urya stared through artificial eyes—dull auburn images framed by lines and numbers augmenting his vision's perception toward the execution of death.

Urya reached down to the red belt that had replaced his sash and unclipped his plasma sword: perfect. He picked up his rifle as the transport ship began to slow. He had checked it before. The weapon shot green *bullets* of plasma. A magnetic field was generated around tiny particles in the gun. These attracted plasma from another compartment as the gun fired. The shot would strike its target before the field collapsed. The rifle's output was almost limitless. Urya heard orders and updates and the roaring of engines—voices tinny in communicators, ringing his ears.

Touchdown. Sergeant Urya looked at his men: a squad of six. Edur, Kane, Tur, Mason, Eruaf, and himself, indistinguishable behind their artificial faces, private in their fears: Coolant systems worked at an accelerated rate. He looked, then, at the exit hatch. The silence was deafening. It opened wide. They leapt into a blue skied planet of golden flora.

"This is Friberg. Two company focus on my mark. We move now! Thirty degrees of landing plane. Sergeants report in."

'Enemy scan, Uey.'

'Clear,' came the computer's inaudible response.

"Squad seven, mark."

"Mark affirmed."

"Let's move. Squad seven marked."

They were off in swift orderly units, moving in jumps like a plague of grasshoppers from some mechanized apocalypse. The land was strange to the young Urya—his first trip to another world. He did not have time to wonder. In swift mental communication he monitored group positions and the enemy objective.

"Hold back, Kane."

"Sarge?"

"You're too far forward."

They were the spearhead for the first assault wave.

"This is Friberg. Command says go. Move in your tactical units."

'It's just us now,' thought Urya.

Golden trees streaked by, and grey fortress walls loomed higher as the Guard approached their objective. A hole had been blasted in the wall by the air assault. Smoke billowed in the air. Dozens of black uniforms poured from it like ants from a mound. As the enemy came in sight a bloodlust filled the hearts of the Imperial Guard.

"To me," commanded Urya, and his five fighters gathered around him just inside the cover of the trees.

"What are we waiting for?" asked Tur.

Urya: "I want inside that wall."

Guardsmen sprang from the trees, and guns began to blaze. A thousand men clashed with gun and sword before the fortress walls.

A larger group waited a half mile behind for the final assault— the illusion underway.

"There," pointed Mason.

Urya magnified his viewer. A clearing of men between them and the wall was evident.

"I make twenty targets only," said Kane.

"Guns."

A unit of six aimed six weapons. Six computers targeted 20 enemy combatants. Locked six. Clear.

"Fire!"

360 rounds fired in a second.

"Move!"

Six young men leapt into battle. They were at the wall in three jumps.

"Eruaf, Mason—flank."

The two took positions on either side of the break in the wall. Urya and the others jetted over the rubble just inside. An explosion blew Edur and Kane back out.

'Uey!'

'Scanning heavy gun thirty meters linear, five meters vertical.'

The target lit up in Urya's face mask—a window in the fortress.

Mason: "They're dead, Sarge."

Urya's gun fired. Smoke obscured his vision.

"Infrared."

They had been the first to breach the wall. Confusion did not protect them for long.

"They're on us," said Tur.

They began a blanketing fire—a planned pattern. Fifty assassins charged from the fortress. Another alerted group moved toward them along the top of the twenty foot wall.

Voices filled Urya's head. He recognized Field Lieutenant Friberg: "Battalion override. Groups focus on sector two. Support Sambok and Green. Set up perimeters. Do not assault."

"Who's that at the wall?"

"What?"

"There's someone at the wall."

Urya blocked the communication with exhilaration. Exploding light crashed around him, but he did not waiver.

Eruaf: "We're getting cut off!"

'Danger: vertical target.'

Tur responded to his A. I.'s warning, turning to fire at assassins on the wall. His shot struck the stonework and caused a number of them to fall. Another five flew down on top of Urya and Tur.

Mason: "The wall!"

"I got 'em!" replied Eruaf.

A hundred yards away, someone called out, "We need a spear head!"

And a commanding voice replied, "Hold your perimeter!"

"Who's in there Lieutenant?"

"Cut the chatter!" Field Lieutenant Friberg cursed himself. 'Our orders stand.'

Urya thrust a jet firing boot into an attacker's face. He sprang up, sword blazing, and sliced the head off of his nearest opponent. He turned to behold the barrel of a gun and ducked as it fired. He rolled and literally sliced the gunman in half with a swing of his sword. But this assassin was good. The shot that had missed Urya struck Tur in the back.

"Tur!" He hesitated a deadly moment. But an assassin's strike was blasted short by Mason and Eruaf who had come inside the wall. They cleared the area for the moment, pinning the enemy in the distance with short, targeted bursts of plasma fire. Urya picked up his gun.

"We're cut off Sarge," said Mason afraid.

"We'll make it."

"They're going to call the retreat!"

"We'll make it."

Urya stared at the lifeless form of Tur. Reality slapped him in the face. The fervor was gone, and now he came to the awareness that he too was afraid. He looked out beyond the wall and saw a line of black troops firing at his comrades beyond. He turned and joined his teammates in firing at more immediate targets.

"We'll make a run for it. Jets at full thrust. One after the other. We'll cover for each other. Yar, you first, then Mason. I'll follow. We made it in three jumps before. Alright. Go!"

Eruaf was off.

"Go!"

Mason followed. Urya sprayed the perimeter with fire and then turned.

"This is Friberg. Retreat sound. Odd groups pull back."

"No!" Urya jumped.

He couldn't see Eruaf, but Mason was just ending his first arch.

"Friberg wait!"

Plasma filled the air. Urya twisted, tumbled and fired. Mason landed in the midst of the enemy and did not emerge.

"Mason!"

A grenade exploded: Mason gave his sergeant a chance. Urya felt beyond fear, beyond anger, beyond his charge. There was only getting back to the line.

"Friberg, I'm coming in!"

His second landing threw him off balance. As his jets kicked in, he flew parallel to the ground a short distance. He hit hard and rolled.

"All remaining groups begin orderly retreat."

Urya sprang to his feet.

"Wait!"

He ran.

"Lieutenant, wait!"

He set to jump, but the jets did not fire.

"Aah!"

He felt an explosion in his back. The force knocked him over. On his feet again, he staggered forward, thirty yards from the line. But there was no line. He did not scream when the next bullet struck his shoulder.

There was a brief silence. The sky was blue. Urya took it in for the first time. Then he could hear a quiet roar.

'Amplify.'

The assassins shouted their supposed victory. They ran forth triumphant. Urya saw several pass right by him.

"This is Sambok. They're following."

"Do not engage. No go."

'No go,' thought Urya. 'The Princess. They gotta get her out.'

Urya swallowed blood.

'Captain Star...get her sir...please.'

Tears filled his eyes.

"This is..."

'please sir...'

"...We have..."

'please...'

"...out..."

'What was that?'

"...Janis...begin assault!"

'They did it?'

"Now we fight like Imperial Guards!"

'They did it.'

"Second wave is right behind."

'Thank you sir.'

Sergeant Urya smiled.

'My life, my charge.'

Sergeant Urya died.

Minutes before:

"This is Rann. Scout report."

"Isacson reporting. We're at the edge of the wood. Fifty meters between us and the cliff and two hundred vertical to the wall. There's a hole in the wall, about one meter, covered by a metal grate—I scan easily cut. Plenty of ledging to make jumps. Two guards on the wall. Looks like our little distraction is paying off."

"No one else?"

"No sir."

"We're moving in."

Fifty men (and boys) of the forty-third and forty-fourth Guards crept forward and assumed positions along the line of the woods and the open space between them and the fortress wall. Solomon crawled next to Commander Rann at a position just below the grate.

"This is peculiar. It's like they're inviting us in."

"I know. Too many things going well on this one. We have no choice." 'Chronometer.'

Rann's computer flashed a number on the visor before his eyes.

"Alright, the retreat is on; we've got two minutes." 'Group com.' "Groups four and five, hold your position; be prepared for assault and retreat backup. Groups two and three will line up along the cliff. On my signal G-2 will go over the wall and G-3 will jump up to the wall to provide cover. G-1: with me at the grate. Isacson, move in on those targets and make it quiet."

They watched in silence, faceless figures in the bush. Someone was moving on the wall—Jo Isacson—moving quickly, sword in hand. Heads rolled. The corpses tumbled to the cliff's base. Jo dropped to the narrow ledge outside the wall and moved to the grate.

"One minute. Let's move."

They approached the wall.

Ten men jetted in six leaps up the cliff and huddled near the opening in the wall. Jo finished cutting quietly through the iron with his sword. It fell forward with a clank. Rann peered through to see a courtyard. The stone fortress stood fifty yards away. There was a single entrance, large and bordered by pillars carved in the shapes of surrealistic men: massive shoulders and calves, tiny heads, and tapered waists and hips. They looked like hour glasses. There was no one in the area.

'Heat scan.'

'Scan shows no one in visible area.'

"Hmm. You sure you weren't seen, Isacson?"

"The courtyard was empty when I hit the wall."

"Too peculiar."

Solomon looked in past Rann. "How much time?"

"Thirty seconds. Isacson, get back up on the wall. They should come through that entrance."

"I don't like this," said Solomon. "Where—"

"Stand ready."

Silence roared.

"Five seconds."

The clock ticked down. Nothing happened.

"Something's wrong. Prepare to move in."

Suddenly they exploded from within the fortress. There was one man in black at the front of the group. He wore no mask and his clothes were torn and stained with blood. It was Commander Adrian. He carried Janis in his arms. They were followed by a hundred screaming, sword wielding assassins, bent on making Janis's new found freedom short lived.

"Move! Move! Get in there!"

Jets kicked in and soldiers charged. Solomon, having caught sight of the white form of the Princess, ran straight toward her. He did not strategize; he did not think. He gave no consideration to the deadly crowd with which he was on a collision course.

Adrian wasn't twenty yards into the courtyard before enemy plasma cut him down. He screamed and fell. Janis rolled a few feet away.

The back slashing assassin moved to grab the Princess. He made an excellent landing pad for Jo Isacson whose boots blasted through the assassin's back to cushion his landing. His gun flashed, and he smiled beneath his mask. He was one lone boy standing against a hundred trained killers. They didn't have a chance.

"Hold your fire on the wall! Get the Princess out."

Solomon reached Janis first. He threw down his gun, scooped her up into his arms, turned, and ran. Nothing else mattered. He didn't even notice the assassin that would have decapitated him had Rann not shot the man. He was outside the wall in an instant, jetting precariously down the cliff.

"Alright, butcher the scum!"

Solomon did not slow. He ran right past the reserve group who had emerged from hiding with shouts and triumphantly raised fists.

"G-4 with me," he commanded.

They stood for a moment bewildered, and then went running after him.

"Begin the withdrawal. Let's have some cover!" 'Command com.' "This is Rann. Objective achieved. Send the transport. Call the strike."

Solomon finally slowed his run. Awareness returned to him. He noticed his heavy breathing, his racing heart. He tried to calm himself. He noticed too that the princess was crying. Not the quiet tears that you might expect from royalty, but full fledged wailing that bordered on hysteria.

"Let me go! Please take me home! Please!"

Solomon sat her down as group four caught up and formed a perimeter around them. A transport descended slowly from the sky.

"My Lady. It's alright. We'll take you home now," Solomon said.

She cried even more as her eyes focused on the faceless voice.

"Please," Solomon pleaded. He thought for a moment, then removed his helmet.

"My Lady, please."

She focused through her tears. For a brief moment of recognition her crying stopped.

"Oh Solomon!"

She threw her arms around him and began to cry again, not in hysteria, but anguish at the ordeal's end. Solomon melted, crying with her, feeling her pain. He held her tight, yet delicately, like the most precious of china cups, unrelenquishable by the owner who prizes it above all things. He wanted desperately to feel her warmth through his armor, and the softness of her skin. Her reddened face, the tear stained cheeks and her disheveled hair were the beauty of legends, deeper than appearance, more lovely than the sunrise on a hundred planets. She was everything in the universe in a moment: the incarnation of that blessed beauty that lies at the heart of all created things. In that brief bright moment she was more his than her world could ever allow.

The transport came to rest in a clearing a few yards away. A gust of retro-fire pulled Solomon from his reverie.

"We'll take you home now."

He picked her up, carried her to the ship, and placed her on a hydro-cot. He followed as Janis was moved into the ship by Sykol medics, until one of them barred his way holding up a hand. Solomon looked at him angrily, then looked to the cot disappearing into the transport. He turned away slowly, head bowed, then looked up to see the faceless faces of soldiers staring at his. He wiped his tears away, though not in shame. One of his officers approached and handed him his helmet. He smiled and said, "Let's go home."

- 22 -
Imperial World:
Eight Months Before Solomon's Arrival on Kall

Imperial Stadium: the largest above ground structure on Imperial World. Visible from space. Once a year the Guard gave up its duty as a whole, turned planet security entirely over to the billion man army of Fleet One, the world ship that orbited the planet—perfect protection and a nice addition to the tide cycle. Once a year—for the spectacle.

A million enthusiasts filled the stands. The dome lit up with giant perspectives, multiple angles, projections of the playing field, the Imperial Boxes. The purpose: to show the genetic prowess, the tactical intelligence, the heroic grandeur of the greatest fighting force in the galaxy: the elite soldiers, Her Majesty's Imperial Guard. Over the game, which would be broadcast to the worlds, sat the Empress, Janis IV, clad in shimmering silver upon a glittering gold throne, more ornate than her official seat at Imperial Palace. She was as much the show surrounded by her attendant women and various royal houses as was the Guard.

"Tri-Ball" was *the* game of the Empire. A variation of a more ancient sport, it could be played by as few as a hundred men or as many as there was space available to move them around. The game was played on a triangular field—length (in larger contests): one mile from point to point—with 30 foot wide goals at each point, and three round plexi-leather balls. In games of five hundred players or more, another feature was added. At the exact center of these larger fields were three holes (a little larger than the playing balls) set fifty feet apart in a triangle. These holes led to underground tunnels which would move a ball quickly to an opening several hundred yards from the goal to which the "drop hole" corresponded (thus placing the ball dangerously close to a scoring position in a matter of seconds). The ball would then be shot into the air at which point it belonged to whichever team could get it under control first. The three balls were played simultaneously and could be manipulated with any part of the body except the hands and arms. For professional league and Guard games, there was an added factor. In the case of the Guard, the Infantry had five hundred more men than either the Air or Mobile battalions. These extras became the fourth and fifth teams of the game, adding an extra tactical dimension.

Tri-Ball was more than a game for the Guard. It was a ritual, a galactically broadcast gala, showcasing the teamwork and strategy of the galaxy's finest fighters. The size of the field onto which the Guard assembled combined with the simultaneous use of three playing balls required teamwork. Fifteen hundred players per single team became a link of one defense and two offenses, moving the ball up and down their ranks.

Strategy was a key aspect of the game as well. Strategy of attack: Would a team try to keep control of one ball or more? Would they form a coalition with another team to defeat one? Would they move down the sideline or to the center to risk attacking the heavily defended "drop holes"? Fifty players on each team would serve as nothing more than communicators— seldom touching the ball—to focus on player positions and coordinate with team groups over the length of the field. And defensive strategy: How many men would be risked for offense? Which way would the ball be fed? And then there were the five hundred, the extra teams of two hundred-fifty each.

Five teams marched out to the field: 1500 green clad Infantry, 1500 yellow clad Air, 1500 red Mobile, and the extra five hundred infantry dressed in black or white. These two teams were Simon Lazar's and Hal Teltrab's while the others were each controlled by their battalion commanders, the other members of the Pentaf. In this game, not only did the three teams in colored jerseys play against each other, but the black and white teams simultaneously competed in a separate contest using the first three teams.

The rules were complex but simply stated: the black and white teams could join any of the other teams at any moment in the game, provided that no ball was within a hundred yards of a goal. The first decision to join a team would be given by the Lieutenant of the Guard. The Captain's team would then immediately join the offenses and defenses of the other two teams. This play would continue for ten minutes, and then the white and black teams would return to their neutral status. The next choice in this six hour game would go to the Guard's Captain. Simon Lazar and Hal Teltrab would hover above the field in an oval observation craft and would call down their single commands via loud speaker. They could not tell their players where to move during the game. The black and white teams would move around by prearranged strategies trying to out guess each other. Meanwhile, the battalion commanders and their teams would try to guess the moves of the black and white to gain advantage or guard against it. The black and white teams would score by "decisively" (as ruled by the referees) helping two teams score on one. One point would go against the battalion team scored upon, and one for the black or white team. The battalion team with the least points won their portion of the game, the black/white team with the most points won their portion.

The teams were assembled and sent to their respective sides. Then three balls were simultaneously shot out of the center drop holes, and the game was on. The players moved in troops like the soldiers they were. Body checking was a must in this game (so long as hands weren't used). Twenty men or more would throw their bodies at each other, while others built human walls anticipating the emergence of a ball from the crowd or looking to cover for a break away.

The balls shot fifty yards in three different directions and the fiercest part of the game began. The quick offensive strategy was to move the balls back to the drop holes while defenses sought to push the balls into their own territories for protection or to the area of another team for attack. A thousand players converged into a hundred yard square.

In a minute, a ball shot from the crowd into yellow territory—the Air battalion's. A defensive link sent the ball well away from the drop hole. Red players, the Mobile, moved away immediately to support the offensive. Green did not. Instead, all of the Infantry team joined the yellow offense against the diminished red team and literally began to push a second ball toward the red chute.

Lazar saw his move: "Black join green team!"

Hal was at once surprised and then proud. "All or nothing in the first few minutes of a six hour game," he mused in satisfaction.

On the ground, black and white teams hurried to new positions. The ball dropped through the hole. The third ball had somehow moved its way into the yellow team's area, but it still floated about the center of the field. Half a mile away, the Guard was at war near the red goal.

"They're going after it hard," Hal noted. "Have we an injury count yet?"

"I'm watching their performance," Lazar answered. "You worry about how you're going to catch up to me."

Hal smiled, and then, "Not for long." Lazar focused on the game. The ball had moved into the forty yard area in which only ten players from each team were allowed. Sandor Fagan, the Mobile commander (and one of the two red goal keepers), was shouting frantically. Suddenly, the move that Hal had seen coming, came. A red player cleared the ball forty yards down the sideline where a line of red and white jerseys had formed a barrier two men thick and several hundred yards long. Communicators went to work and the line extended. The ball was moving in quick passes down the sideline and no one could break through the red line to stop it, not till it had encroached dangerously into yellow territory and the ten minute time period ended with black and white teams' return to neutral status.

Simon frowned. "My elite team would have done it."

"But we're not playing hundred-man ball."

"Don't be so right, Hal. You're too good at it."

"It has its draw backs."

"Ha! Name one."

Hal hesitated for a moment, thinking, 'Do I really want to do this?' Then he did it: "Simon, there's a problem."

"What's that, Captain?"

"A potential security risk."

Lazar looked away from the game and at his Captain. "Really?"

"Yes."

"And you wanted to talk about it here?"

Hal pressed a button on a console to his left.

"It's one of the few places I thought we could speak safely."

"What's that system? That's been added."

"A universal jammer."

Simon's recognition was quick: "It's an internal problem, then."

"Yes."

"Is Janis in danger?"

"Probably not."

"*Probably*, Captain?"

"As I said, it's a problem. Janis is probably safe. But..."

"Someone's going to die, aren't they?"

"Maybe."

"Someone close."

"Maybe."

"Hal."

"Yes, Lieutenant."

"I don't want to be Captain of the Guard."

"I know."

"We've had enough changes."

Silence.

"Simon, did you know there's a homing chip in your head?"

"A what?"

"A tracking device. Sykol engineering—just inside the cranium, here"—touching the top of his forehead.

Silence.

"Let's have it, Hal. What's going on?"

"We'll need Jo and two or three people I know."

"What about Paul and Sandor?"

"I don't want to trust them on this."

"Tarsoon and Fagan? They're the other Pentaf."

"But not original. Not from the first five of us."

And Lazar thinking: 'He never should have left.'

"You, Jo and I," Hal continued. "My Con at twenty-six hundred. Tonight, before the official return to duty."

Silence.

"We'll be there."

The hours passed. The game ended. The troops returned to the palace for an evening of celebration and ceremony. The green team had one goal scored against it, and the black and white teams tied at zero.

Gaheris was master of all he surveyed: three square meters of cubicle space on the fourteenth sublevel of the Imperial Palace— Sykol levels all below ten. The good doctor sat at his workstation working over a holo model, one he'd spent years designing: the perfect man. Behind him, scattered on the floor, lay cast away parts—artificial limbs, robotic servos and joints; boxes full of sensors and circuitry; rows of holo disks or piles more, pre-programmed protocols—all gathering dust in heaps and corners in this dust free environment. He'd given it up years ago. Now in his virtual laboratory, he pursued his passion relentlessly. Bio-mechanics was the future: machines that mimicked bio-chemicals, chemical molecules made out of machines. Nature had done all the work for us. All that was needed was to see the applications, the alterations. He smiled at himself. The projection before him was a DNA sequence—twenty-five percent complete. It didn't exist. It would in ten more years, after he'd completed writing it and his colleagues in chemical applications figured out how to build it one molecule at a time.

On the wall to his left hung a family tree, official Imperial seal, certifying his lineage as a descendant of the Imperial Guard. His father was a forty-third Guardsman (retired). He himself had been rejected for genetic incompatibility from the forty-fourth Guard (at age six months). With his intelligence, they said, he belonged in Sykol Medical. He'd spent his life trying to overcome his father's disappointment. His younger brother *was* a forty-fourth Guard, Gaheris's best friend in life—a brother who preferred his brother's love to his father's favoritism. Of course they never got to see each other—their lives seldom allowed "personal time." For Gaheris, less than most. No picture of wife and kids to feel guilty over while he put fifteen, eighteen, twenty hours of every twenty-seven hour day into his cubicle and his model.

It was quite a shock for him to hear, "Hey, big brother, how goes the protein sequencing?"

"Wayne? Hey little brother!"

He jumped out of his chair, yanking his long white coat from where it had caught on the arm, and gave his brother a hearty embrace.

"It's great to see you!" And then a quick change in demeanor: "Say, how'd you get down here, this is Sykols only? Are you in trouble? Sub-chief sees you, you're going to be." Looking around. "Get in here."

"Wait," said Wayne, grabbing his brother by the sleeve. "No, I'm not in trouble; I'm here to do the regular Guard sweep of the lower levels, and I can't stay, I—"

"Hey, there's no Guard sweep down here—this is Sykols only, what's going on?"

Lowered voice: "It's hard to explain, brother. Better...let me show you. Come here a minute."

"What...are you—"

"Just come on."

And then the surprise increased:

"Good Evening, Dr. Gaheris. Working late?"

"Commander Isacson—"

Jo Isacson grabbed Gaheris by the collar and walked him briskly down the corridor. Simon Lazar took his opposite arm while Gaheris's brother followed, checking behind them every few steps. Around a turn, an elevator door shooshed open and Gaheris's surprise reached almost its peak—almost.

"Ca—Captain Teltrab!"

"Dr. Gaheris. I need your help."

And the door shooshed shut.

- 23 -
The Desert

That night at the water fall, Solomon and the Savage slept in the hollow of a tree, as they had done that first night in the jungle. The sound of the falls made for peaceful dreams; an ever growing blanket of petals kept them warm.

In the morning they made for the river, and continued down stream without speaking, until he thought out loud:

"If I'd had control of this mission it wouldn't have happened this way."

"What is *mission*?"

He remembered her presence, felt a flush of embarrassment, thinking, 'That sounded insulting.' He thought to pass the question off. Then he thought better:

"The job—the work I've been sent to do. Like your mission is to guide me to my father."

"It's not that."

"What?"

"*Mission*. Not mission."

"It's not?"

"No." She was thinking, straining to remember. "The word he gave me."

"My father."

"Philagapon. Not a mission." She closed her eyes; the brows drew together in concentration.

"It's alright," he said. "It's not important." She remained focused. "It's the circumstances, our situation here. It isn't normal for them. They're hiding something."

She opened her eyes. "The offworlders?"

"The Imperials," he nodded. "If they had put it to me to plan for someone else, it would've never happened this way."

In his mind Solomon spun images of white frocked master manipulators working behind the scenes, behind screens of statistics and behavior models: 'Sykols. Could there be a place in the galaxy where they have so little control?' He couldn't accept it. The images of conspiracy became more complex. 'Or is this whole world artificial?' He looked at her. He could not see deception, nor could he discover clarity.

"Something does not see," she read the consternation in his face.

"No it doesn't."

She waited.

"This place is too important to my people. And they are too powerful to just allow the Kalliphi to determine the direction of this missio—to say if I succeed. They like being in control."

"On Kall they cannot."

He shook his head. "There's something else—they're planning something else."

"No."

"Why?"

"Philagapon has said."

"That's not enough."

Her look was shock, her voice controlled anger: "I see them."

His reply was almost fear: "I *know* them."

She *saw*...something. Then: "I remember the word."

"Tell me."

"*Pilgrimming.*"

"*Pilgrimage?*"

"Yes."

And Solomon had something more to think about than Imperial plans.

As the day wore on a chill entered the air, not a breeze or temperate drop, not the kind of chill that raises goose bumps on the arm, but a lack-luster feeling, like the chill of an autumn funeral. And the light dimmed. The river became sluggish, stalling, procrastinating, wanting to put off as long as possible an inevitable, miserable task. Mud clouded and leaves crowded the banks, and a breeze did arise, the first Solomon had felt since coming to Kall. The ever present odor of life and death lost its precarious balance: Death asserted itself on the breeze, causing the eyes to burn and redden.

He turned to his guide and saw apprehension in her eyes: not anxiety from uncertainty, but fear of the known. Suddenly, the light was gone and they emerged into naked sky. Startled, Solomon turned to behold a great grey sea of death. Ashen corpses, wooden mummies stretched out over a lifeless terrain, jutting their crumbling centers only a fourth of their original height into the sky. The sky: Grey clouds shrouded the sun's direct rays now, not green trees; mists mimicking life, but not life—not the luminescent light of the living. Wind blew dust across the open plain, chilled the pilgrims to the bone, and filled their eyes with irritating particles. But it was not for this that Solomon shed a single river swelling tear into the widening waters below him.

They had come to a wasteland, an abomination of desolation left behind by the reapers—that is the rapers from the days before the coming of Philagapon. The land, with all its bountiful life, could not reclaim its own. For though pains can be ended and sins atoned for, there will always be some lessening of things, some entropic reduction in energy, in beauty.

He was shaken from dazed imagining by the bump of the bow against the river's edge. Looking again to his guide, he was unnerved at her apparent desire that they leave their floating womb. Yet step out they did onto the sooty ground, that open tomb. Solomon led, walking to a high point sixty yards from the canoe. He turned and surveyed the grand cataclysm and wished to weep further. It was what made him unique: Imperial Guards, the super soldiers like Solomon Star ("Gene Kings" they're called in the regular army) aren't meant for compassion. But that's the very thing that made the man of light what he was. Mouth half opened, he watched his footprints effaced in the dust by the chilling wind—from dust, to dust. And he and the Savage were, for a moment, cut off there by an island of death, separated from the tie—the memory of action—that linked them to the river, and escape.

He stood silently and ached. Savage ached too, though she had been there before. Fish out of water.

Finally, he spoke, knowing the answer: "What happened here?"

"The offworlders did," she said, with the first expression of passion he had encountered in her. "Stripped the wood and burned and wanted only rock and stripped and burned to get rock and wasted." Fading off: "And they killed Kalliphi."

He grabbed her with his eyes: "I *am* sorry."

She almost smiled thank you. Then: "We are all."

The wind grew harsh; grey ash whipped and tugged at their stone expressions. In the midst of death, thoughts of death took hold....

- 24 -
From 2279:
Punishment and Crime

The sky was grey, the land, gloomy dark. Dress capes billowed and whipped in a harsh wind, tugging at the stiff shoulders of Guardsmen standing at attention. The uniforms were navy blue: slacks and double breasted jackets with gold buttons and rank insignia on the shoulder. A large medallion, the Imperial crest, hung on the left breast. About their waists girded a red sash tied right of center, a traditional mark of all Royal Guards. And the boots—purest white with almost sacred significance. None in the galaxy but they who pledged their lives to the protection of the ruler of the Galactic Empire (or his heir) could wear them.

Leaves rustled and flew into faces. The service had ended. The troops had been dismissed. Only the Pentaf remained, staring in silence at the steel grey coffin.

Paul Tarsoon thought less of his dead commander and more of the discomfort he felt with his new position in life. These had been his leaders, his idols. Now he was one of them. He felt like he was intruding. So did they. It would not be the last time.

What had the chaplain said? "Immanuel Proshemeis is no longer with us...." Solomon wondered why that phrase stuck in his mind. He looked at the new Commander of the Air, then at the casket. Things would never be the same. Decorum gave way to compassion. He began to cry. It would not be the last time. His tears were rain on the painting of the *Palace* in his hands.

A clear pink sky. A beautiful day. The red sun shone brightly. It beat down upon the field of orange dirt, down upon the ranks. Beating. Beating. Yes. It was the time of beatings. They gathered on a great dusty training field to the west of Imperial Palace: the remaining 4923 members of the forty-fourth Guard. They filed into their ranks before a long wooden platform and stood at attention for two hours. The weather had been carefully engineered for this day. No breeze blew—no relief. Silent heat rang in their ears. The platform was ten feet high. Five sets of stairs led up to it, and a metallic handrail ran the length of its center. The Pentaf stood on the platform, one member across from each staircase, near the rail. They waited two hours to be beaten. They wore no shoes or shirts, only tight chocolate trunks, looking like men, not boys: lean, muscular soldiers, broad and tall, geneticized to be men before ever realizing they weren't boys anymore. Sweat poured from their sunburned bodies, drenching their hair, tickling their faces, running into eyes that could not be wiped by sweaty hands held at attention. Red dust turned to mud beneath their itching feet. The punishment would not be severe: ten lashes with plasma whips. But they had failed in their life mission. They had failed to protect their charge. Though they had saved her, the Guard had allowed her life to be put in jeopardy. The day had come for them to pay the price.

After the two hours passed a hovercraft arrived and settled itself to the right of the platform. The dust it kicked up burned the backs of their throats. Five men emerged from the ship bearing plasma whips and wearing black masks—hoods of the executioner. A panel hummed open on the hovercraft's second level. It opened upward and out to provide shade. On the other side of a window, in a luxurious air conditioned compartment, sat Janis IV. Solomon looked at her. It was the first time he had seen her since the rescue. She was radiant: dressed in a long white gown, hair gathered to a bun with a flowing tail that draped over her shoulder. She reclined against a plush hover chair—blue like the rest of the compartment, and cool: a deliberate, icy blue. Attendant maids stood about her prepared to carry out her every whim. She did not return Solomon's gaze. He turned to the business at hand.

"Troops stand forward!"

The first row stepped forward, turned and marched in five separate lines up the ramp. The five whipmasters had taken their places by the rail, a short distance from a corresponding member of the Pentaf. For the leaders there was an added punishment: They would have to stand and watch.

Five lines came to a halt. Without further words the first boys stepped forward to the rail. A post with shackles was not necessary. They would not run. Their only fear was that they would cry out, or fall. The rail, hot from the sun, was provided that they might steady themselves.

The first guard to grasp the burning bar near Solomon was a stocky dark haired field lieutenant named Friberg. He held the bar tightly, his fingers blazing, his knuckles white. Sweat dripped from the end of his nose. His breathing was heavy; his eyes, determined. He looked at his Captain. Solomon wanted to smile, to reassure him. He managed to purse his lips and give a curt nod of support. The whips hummed on, green and glowing. Friberg turned and looked at nothing.

Crack!!

He exhaled hard through clenched teeth. Solomon flinched. A shudder went through the Guard like a wave. The whip tore flesh from backs; searing plasma burned much of the wound closed: blood loss, little; blistering, much. Ten such lashes would be a long reminder. None lasted beyond four slashes before screaming. Neither did any collapse.

The process continued. Row after row of Guardsmen filed forward, filed back to their place in the ranks, waited at attention. Every half-hour, a new group of whip-masters would emerge from the hover craft to relieve the old. The Princess continued to watch. She was not there to enjoy the sight with a twisted sadism but for ceremony and psychology. For the most part, she played her role well.

The Guard watched too. Those in the rear ranks were given the dubious privilege of viewing, in full, the tattered backs of their comrades in the fore ranks: pink-white and crisping black and liquid red and runny clear and crusty brown: flesh tones and earth tones—dust to dust.

The Pentaf watched. For three hours they watched. As Hal Teltrab watched his friends beaten, his emotional state shifted from a typically analytical Teltrab to a passionately involved Hal. As each blow struck, he felt more and more. Solomon's reaction was exactly the opposite. With each one of his guards who stepped up to the rail, and with each blow that landed, the intense burning compassion in him cooled and darkened. He grew numb and entered almost into a trance. He did not notice the coming of his turn at the rail until it was upon him.

Solomon shook his head to perception and looked about. The last line of troops was filing into place, and the other members of the Pentaf had already taken their places at the rail. Solomon turned his face to stone. No one would see his bewilderment. No one would see his pain. With disciplined steps he moved to the rail. Up to this point, though his feelings had been in turmoil, his mind had been ever set with the conviction that this punishment was just. His Guard had failed, almost completely, in its lifelong mission. Solomon felt ashamed that his charge had to watch this spectacle of Guard failure. He was ashamed that he himself had failed her. Many would be doubtful of the maturity, the stamina of these sixteen year olds, forgetting that they were bred of

Imperial stock: made in mind and body to excel, forty-four gene generations of perfection. In a far flung past they might have been mistaken for gods.

The punishment began.

One!

The whip ripped down Solomon's right shoulder blade; he clenched his teeth and the rail in front of him.

'Forgive me, Lady,' he thought.

Two!

Flesh seared closed on his spine; his breath quickened and deepened.

Three!

The whip struck horizontally across the small of his back; he arched and gasped, then stepped back and shifted his weight against his arms and bowed his head.

Four!

His lungs heaved, despite his best efforts to control his pain by controlling his breathing. He sucked in air through his mouth as if having run too far or fast.

Five!

The whip cracked across his right shoulder; he cried out for the first time, jerking his head upward. In that moment he saw the Princess and his entire demeanor changed. His mouth, opened wide with pain, shut tight. His brow, furrowed with anguish, smoothed over. Eyes squinting with the exertion to maintain control opened wide as he looked and disbelieved.

Six.

He didn't feel the blow. He only thought about what he was certain he had just seen but could not have possibly seen: the princess, his Janis, smiling. He looked again. Yes smiling; though she was several yards away, he could see every detail.

Seven.

She was eating something: a rare Kinji fruit—a glistening, bright red ball—she bit into it, red juice dripping down her hand. He lived every feature: dripping chin, and eyes filled with a heretofore unseen lust.

Eight.

There, see it! She smiled again amidst the biting and chewing; she didn't try to hide it. Why would she act that way? Pain gave way to anger; anger gave way to numbness.

Nine.

Numbness gave way to guilt: the thought of allowing her to be put through a torment that would cause her to react this way. But guilt soon gave way to confusion as Solomon's confidence asserted itself: Was this Janis—the young woman he'd held on an alien planet only a week before?

Ten.

He kept a steadfast gaze. While the whip-masters left the platform and entered the hover craft, and while Hal and the others moved to positions at the head of the platform, Solomon neither moved nor turned from the Princess. He waited; the window panel closed and the craft pulled away. Only then did he turn to dismiss his men.

Of all the members of the Guard, Solomon was the only one to withstand burning in almost six hours of exposure to the sun. This made getting into his dress uniform a great deal easier. He had only his back with which to be careful. He slipped his jacket on slowly and buttoned it. He tied his sash in front of the mirror, while checking to be sure that his appearance was immaculate. He saw his door open in the mirror and turned to see his mother step into his room. He held his hands out from his side for her to review him.

"You look handsome." Her voice was soothing.

"Is everything alright?" He was nervous. It was as if he were being called before Janis for the first time.

She approached and took his hand. "You look perfect. I'm very proud of you, son." She kissed his cheek. "Go on now."

She watched him leave, loving him dearly, feeling it deeply. At the same time, Alathia Star, mother and Sykol, made a mental note regarding Solomon's emotional state which she would deliver to the Chief at a later time. The life of the Guard was harsh. She would have had Solomon spared it if duty had not stood first in her mind.

Solomon moved with a brisk reluctance through Palace corridors. It was the first time he would appear personally before the Princess since the kidnapping. He feared her chastisement. At the same time he questioned her behavior of the day before. What a contrast it was to the image of the rescue which played through his mind. Of one thing he had become certain: Right or wrong, he did not like the image that had been revealed to him at the platform. His desire to be accepted by his charge strove against his confidence. He felt something empty growing inside him: a queer feeling he could not identify. Apathy was new to him.

Janis did not understand the *whys* behind everything that Imperial Sykols had told her (though she was learning quickly), but she understood what she was to do.

'Silly games,' she thought as she walked slowly through the white halls of the Palace. "Sometimes I wonder if Father controls the Empire or if the Chief does."

"My Lady?" questioned a servant who followed behind.

"Nothing."

Ruling the galaxy required work. She was only just beginning to understand this. But understand it she would. She wanted to, wanted heavily, like a toddler wants candy, a lover, sex. Lust hungry, she was Amric, and would spread herself for the goal of power, would break an old tie and re-knot it to their liking if not to hers. She felt the loss. She would have to enter a new relationship with the Captain of her Guard. But she chose: She would do as had been *suggested*.

Janis entered her receiving room, reserved for what little official business the Princess performed. The room was long and narrow and laden with red carpet and tapestries. These tapestries hung from high ceiling to floor, covering white walls almost completely. Each was ornately detailed with scenes from ancient Amric conquests and styled after even older hangings in Imperial World museums whose origins were unknown, having come from chaotic ages before the Empire. Some historians believe the most ancient of the hangings are Terran in origin—from old Earth, a world lost to us in the age of Amric.

In this hall, however, hangings less mysterious, though old and priceless themselves, offered stories of Imperial greatness: disproportionate Cyber-knights riding hover-steeds, jousting with lances of green plasma against backgrounds of which they seem no part, lacking dimension, relative size, and vanishing point perspective. Other heroes fight sword battles in which their pointed feet never touch the ground while holding standards no Imperial ever carried into battle with ornate images of eagles and lions or more fanciful creatures like griffons and unicorns which few could ever recognize. A lost art, all but lost in the translation, the hangings in the royal heir's receiving room were machine woven by digital artists, the finest of their day.

The only piece of furniture in the room was a great throne-like chair of gold, ornate in design, padded with scarlet plush. The chair sat on an elevated platform—a solitary slab of white marble. There were two single steps at each side of the platform and one before the chair. Janis seated herself, and two servant girls spread the train of her white gown in a fan below her feet. Other servants and Sykols stood in lines near the walls, while a Guard unit watched from key positions throughout. She nodded and the door at the end of the room was opened. Solomon Star entered and walked slowly down the room's length. He stopped short of the platform and bowed.

"My Lady," he said rising to attention.

"Captain Star. I trust you are well."

"Yes, Princess. Very well, thank you."

"Well. Much has happened since last we talked like this. I wish to commend you on your performance and leadership in rescuing the Imperial heir."

"I am honored, Lady," he said stiffly.

"You have done my family a great service. My father sends his personal thanks."

He bowed again, less deeply than before.

"Captain..." She wanted to call him by name. Something inside her fought against this formal air. Solomon would always do that to people. They could not understand his instinct for compassion. "...are you pleased with your Guard's performance?"

"Pleased, Lady?"

"Was the rescue performance adequate?"

Solomon hesitated. What did she require of him? Unsure: "Adequate, Lady? I haven't studied everything—there are holos to review... but...many died."

"Did they die well?"

'What a question!' "Yes."

"And Commander Proshemeis? Is it difficult without him?"

"He is...no longer with us, my Lady. It is difficult."

Her voice softened: "Thank you, Captain. If you will excuse me, I wish to rest now."

He bowed and began to turn.

"Oh, and Captain..."

He turned back.

"Thank you." Her voice was tender. She allowed a bit of affection to show through. It didn't help.

She watched him turn and walk stiffly to the room's end. Somehow the distance seemed great, watching him pause at the door to speak with the guards there, watching the door close after him.

Solomon walked slowly down empty Palace corridors. He stared at nothing as he went his way. He felt, again, the emptiness within him. It had grown. He did not understand why. Without knowing it, he had gone to Janis hoping to attain more than her forgiveness. He got that. But he had also gone to remake the previous day's image—the image of her at the whipping field— into a more familiar picture of the Princess: one of tender (if selfish) warmth, the image of a weeping girl moistening his chest (but the source of that image was too far away and traveling farther on a secret ship to a secret planet to live a promised "happily ever after" life). That was the image he wanted to remake. When he left her, remaking had not occurred. What held to his imagination was an enlarging picture of a sadistic red stained smile, the smacking of vengeful lips. It would haunt him for decades.

- 25 -
Pilgrim

On the third day after the wasteland, having given up the river and turned again to the forest, Solomon presumed to question:

"Why have we been going in circles?"

Her stride mis-stepped only slightly and without turning she said, "I don't see you."

Solomon stopped. "You see. I see too. And I don't have to see the sun in the sky to know where we are and where we've been."

At last she too stopped and turned. He patted his hand against the bark of a nearby tree. She paused in a moment of indecision, between two roads, two possibilities. And then she knew. It was as Philagapon had said. The moment of indecision would come, brought about by the assertion of the heart of the son.

'You learn a good lesson,' she nodded. "Come."

They changed directions.

- 26 -
From 2277:
Brothers

If Imperial Guards, even 14 year old boys whose genetic fate already had them looking like men—if the Princess's Guard could ever have a day in which their attitudes might be described as relaxed, even cheerful, it was on the day of the annual Guard "Tri-ball" spectacle. To be sure, Solomon's forty-fourth Guard had been given some ceremonial duty, but since the regular army was in the city, the Palace, and the stadium in full force, most of the young Guard were able to watch their fathers and uncles in the forty-third play the great game.

It was with this cheery attitude that Solomon and his friends (and fellow leaders) entered the Palace having watched a nail-biting ending. Hal Teltrab, a usually stoic young man, even at that age, could not hide a grin of pleasure. His father, with his 250 member black team, had emerged with a one point victory over Solomon's father's white. Jo Isacson was equally pleased over the forty-third Infantry's clear victory over the other two groups.

"That was awesome!" Jo declared.

"It truly was," Solomon agreed. "Even if my team lost."

"It was close." Hal tried not to be smug.

"Yes, but your dad was brilliant," Solomon countered.

Hal hesitated for a moment before allowing himself the pleasure of a son's pride: "He really was," he laughed.

"Yeah he was!" Jo added. "And did you see that in-air-360-volley in the hundred and fifty-eighth minute? That was perfection!"

"That was Sambok," Solomon noted.

"That's right!" said Jo, "His son's in *my* Infantry."

"But his father's a pilot," said Hal.

"That should make Immanuel happy," said Solomon. "Speaking of which..."

"He didn't go to the game," said Hal.

"What?" Jo acted surprised, but everyone knew. They had a joking ritual for it, where Solomon would ask, "Painting again?" and the others would reply in unison: "Painting again."

Then Solomon would assume a very commanding air and address his subordinate: "Lieutenant, what sort of research do you have on obsessive-compulsive disorder among Imperial Guards?"

Hal's appropriate response was always, "Are you serious this time?"

To which Solomon always replied, "No."

They chuckled, and then Jo added, "Yeah, but I am. Immanuel needs to relax."

"Painting is *how* he relaxes, Jo."

"I know Solomon, but—"

"It makes him happy," added Hal.

"I know but—"

"You wouldn't deny your own friend, one of the forty-fourth's own Pentaf the chance for a little R. & R. would you?" Solomon insisted.

"No, but—"

"Come on, Commander"—Hal's voice was falsely stern—"where's your loyalty to your fellow Guardsman?"

And Solomon joined the cadence: "Your compatriot!"

"Your friend!"

And then Jo quit before his frustration made him want to hit someone. He was outnumbered, and he knew that no one could beat his two superiors when they joined forces to win a stupid argument.

The boys made their way toward Guard family quarters, expecting to run into Immanuel Proshemeis in a corridor or courtyard along the way. They were not disappointed. Simon Lazar, the fifth member of the Pentaf, had run ahead of the others to find their absent friend and drag him to an impromptu celebration which they had yet to plan. As the friends approached each other in a corridor near Immanuel's apartment, Jo laid into his friend at once:

"So it's AWOL, is it, Immanuel?"

His friend's deflection maneuver was brilliant: "What's that? We're having our after-game party at the Isacson's place? Sounds great!"

"Hey wait—"

"Give it up, Jo," said Simon, "you can't win."

"Captain Star, sir," Immanuel said, assuming a mock formality accompanied with a salute. "I have been brilliant today."

Solomon followed suit, "Commander Proshemeis, yes we *will* be going to Jo's place for the highlights show with appropriate libations, and what masterpiece have you completed this week?"

"Completed is right," Immanuel grinned. "I've been working on this one for six months."

He turned to Simon who was admiring a three-by-two canvas which the others had yet to see.

"It really is good, Immanuel." Simon was not joking.

He turned the painting for the others to see.

"The portrait of your mother," Hal remarked. "You hoped to be done for her birthday."

"Two days early," Immanuel beamed.

"Let me see," said Solomon. Simon stepped closer to Solomon.

Jo was ever the soldier: "I can't believe you guys."

"Commander, shouldn't you be calling your parents and letting them know we're coming over?"

"You can't be serious."

"Commander!"

"Yes, Captain."

And Solomon was free to admire the painting. So he thought.

Loud voices—raucous, not angry—disturbed the attempt at a peaceful moment. Around a nearby corner came three men in Tri-ball uniforms. Guardsmen from the Emperor's generation enjoying their day's victory, they did not notice the boys till one of them bumped into Hal Teltrab.

Dismissively, and with a laugh, the man said, "Whoa! little guard, be careful, you might get stepped on."

His friends chuckled. They were about to pass on when Solomon spoke up:

"A little decorum, Infantryman. You might do well to look at uniform insignia."

The man paused but kept his smile: "Rank is mostly honorary for you cadets when it comes to us in the forty-third, boy, now don't ruin my mood."

"Ahem," one of his friends cleared his throat, and in the Imperial battle language pointed out that they were addressing their Captain's son.

But Solomon gave no time for the man to process the fact, saying, "Cadet, or not, soldier, you're speaking out of turn."

And then Hal: "They've been drinking. A little victory celebration on their breath."

"I'm sure it's within regulations," Solomon added. "Nothing we'd need to report."

"Now hold on!" came the aggressor, pointing a finger in Solomon's face. "There's a way things get done. And cadets don't make spot inspections, trainers like us do. Listen to the kid, Seamus—thinks he counts for something. Thinks he's a real Guardsman. Sorry son, that eagle's not official for another two years, and I got regs on my side."

"Wow, I think he really *is* drunk," said Simon. All five of the young leaders were shocked.

The forty-third Guardsman didn't miss the opportunity. He snatched Immanuel's painting from Simon's hand.

"Hey!"

"What do we have here?"

"Give that back!" Jo Isacson had shown uncharacteristic restraint up to this point. But his demand was not a boy's whine; it was a command backed up by threat.

"Or what?" their adversary replied. "You gonna report me? I'm looking at contraband here." He handed the painting off to the man on his right. The three of them then made to spread out and surround the Pentaf, but the boys countered setting themselves in eye line of each other, two of them—Simon and Immanuel—in flanking positions.

A moment of tense silence was followed by laughter from the forty-third Guardsmen.

"I can't believe it," the leader cried, holding his stomach, "the runts are challenging us."

Solomon looked at Hal. Hal assessed the situation in a split second—it's what he did best. Within two years the boys would be full grown and almost to a level of strength and speed they would have for a century to come or more. But now these genetically enhanced super soldier children were facing adult versions of themselves—more experienced, stronger, faster. Five versus three were unacceptable odds, even if the men were drunk. Hal shook his head.

"We can take them," said Jo.

And the men stopped laughing.

Solomon sighed a little. "No, we can't."

"You bet you can't. Now you're learning your place."

"Infantryman, that painting is not contraband." Solomon spoke evenly. "Please give it back."

"We'll hold onto it, little guard. For a lesson."

And then he and his partners backed away, leaving the boys in silence.

Jo naturally spoke up first: "We can't let them get away with that."

"We won't," Solomon assured him. "Remember your lessons, Jo. Smarter is better than stronger. And we are *very* smart."

Solomon sat in his best uniform. Across the desk in the office where he kept his back at stiff attention, Solomon's father collapsed a holo screen which then began to project in three dimensions, coalescing images in the space about six inches above its surface. The image was of a garden with soldiers—five boys and a man—fighting, and that furiously. It was no training exercise.

Davidson Star, Captain of the forty-third Guard, spoke evenly, with a seriousness proper to the moment, and yet always with a kindness which his handlers at Sykol Central could never explain the origin of:

"Solomon, it's quite unusual that the forty-fourth Pentaf would all be assigned to a training exercise which amounted to nothing more than a routine guard assignment within the Palace."

"Yes sir. We wondered if it was a mistake ourselves."

"But you checked the orders?"

"Yes, Father. They were confirmed. I can show the documentation to you if you'd like."

"I'm sure you can. I'm sure the orders would show no irregularities if backtracked through channels, either."

"That's more than I know sir, but I'm sure you're right...after all they're just routine orders sent down by Sykol Central. I can't imagine why they'd do something inappropriate."

The boys in the holo had subdued the man within two minutes of their engaging him. He was beaten and bloodied and the direction of one leg suggested the need for a complete knee replacement.

"It's also strange that the audio feed on this camera in the Private Gardens wasn't working."

"I thought that myself, sir. The Private Gardens are too important a place for breakdowns like that. Hal, Lieutenant Teltrab, checked the maintenance records after the first inquest and found that camera had not been looked at for six months. I can show you the documenta—"

"I'm sure you can, son. So the five of you witnessed one of my men, Private Starecraft, trying to...uhm...look at Princess Janis while she bathed."

"Well, Father, that's what she usually does in the Private Gardens, and the soldier was there without any authorization in a position very close to the Gardens' center. You know, sir, that one of the first things a Guardsman is taught when his charge is female is to protect her modesty from himself. There was no reason for him to be there, and, when we confronted him with the most obvious interpretation of his presence there, the guilt on his face communicated everything we have since accused him of."

"And it is a very serious accusation, Solomon. At the very least, this man will be cast out of the forty-third Guard. But if you press forward with your charges against him, it might cost him his life."

"I wouldn't want that, sir."

"Why not? A man plays pervert with your charge, and you would suggest leniency?"

"He was stopped sir. And there's always a chance that—"

"A chance of what?"

"Oh, that...we were wrong."

"Do you think you were wrong?"

"No sir."

Father and son stared at each other for a silent moment.

"Alright, Solomon. I wonder if you might look at this by the way?" Davidson pressed a button on his desk and the holo image shifted to a different scene. This is Private Starecraft's quarters. And the men entering there in the middle of the night without authorization are known associates of his. Now two minutes later—see here—they come out of his rooms with a rectangular object—we can't quite make out what it is."

"That's rather strange, Father. I agree. It almost looks like they're trying to hide the object from the monitoring camera, too. Have you questioned them about it?"

"No, not yet. If they knew Starecraft's entry code, they must be friends, perhaps running an errand for the private."

"But I thought you said they entered without permission?"

"Perhaps. I should have clarified. The strange thing, Solomon, is that this recording is from the very night after the morning on which you and yours captured Starecraft. He was incarcerated immediately after that. Incarcerated and hospitalized—in that order."

"I'm very sorry about that, Father. We violated protocols by not holding him at bay with our weapons, but he too was armed, I didn't want to shoot the man, and I feared that if we hadn't moved swiftly to subdue him, we wouldn't have been able to. A forty-third Guardsman is not an opponent to be trifled with."

"You certainly didn't trifle, Solomon: a fractured skull, a broken wrist, an eye popped from the socket and every ligament in his knee torn and frayed."

Solomon did not respond.

"So you don't know why these two men would've gone into Starecraft's quarters to retrieve this object on the night you caught him?"

"No sir."

"Very well." Davison sat back and considered the young Captain of the Guard before him. "Do you remember, Solomon, when I taught you that it was important to fight your own battles?"

"Yes sir, I do. Very well."

"Just be careful how you fight them."

"Yes, Father. It occurs to me, sir, that I would prefer charges against the private not be filed."

"Really? That reluctance again?"

"Sir it's just that…I'm certain we were right, but there's always a chance we were wrong. I'm sure he's been protesting his innocence."

"Oh, quite. He claims he received orders to be in the Private Gardens at that time and to head straight to the center. But of course there is no such record of any orders, not even on his personal comm. It would take an impossible talent to fake such orders, send them, and then remove all traces of them."

"I can't imagine anyone being capable of doing that, sir. No one with systems access below a Sykol could pull that off. It certainly goes against Starecraft's claim."

"It certainly does. No one else but the Sykols or Guard commanders—ourselves and our lieutenants—could have that kind of access. But why no furthering of the charges if that's the case?"

"I guess that banishment from the Guard seems a fair compromise, just in case there was some sort of monumental computer glitch."

"Hmm. Well it might be best to put all this behind us as quickly as possible. The Guard will likely appreciate a gesture of leniency as well."

"Or, I fear, sir, that some of them might not appreciate such a crime coming from one of their own. Some even might try to take matters into their own hands if an investigation were to drag out."

"Well that's my worry, not yours. Such men had certainly better be careful—I won't have my inferiors fighting their own battles, or rather, if they do so, they'd better—"

"Better do it carefully, sir?"

"Yes. They'd better do it carefully."

Solomon and Immanuel sat in the latter's bedroom, admiring a reacquired work of original art.

"It really is a good likeness, Immanuel. You've got talent."

"Thanks."

"And it was a good mission too."

"They'll keep quiet?"

"They'll keep quiet. And they'll be thankful they didn't end up like Starecraft. They'll owe us, and we'll end their resentment by leaving them alone."

"Solomon, why all this risk for a painting, even if it is mine?"

"Nothing matters more than Princess Janis, Immanuel."

And Immanuel Proshemeis repeated the Guard's single mantra: "Our lives, our charge."

"But one thing matters almost as much."

"The Guard? Our forty-fourth?"

"Especially the Pentaf, the five of us. Especially our friends."

The look on Immanuel's face was thanksgiving. Solomon would never forget it.

- 27 -
The Possessed

What follows is...speculation.

Several days had passed. Several. The river had given the hunters some rest. They erected a bug screen around the raft and pumped their bodies with antibiotics. They were alive, but Quint, at least, was certain they were dying. Except for Lazarus. He pulled ashore six times that last day—to take up the chase again, they thought. Something was wrong, but he wouldn't tell them. When at last they took to the jungle again, it was at a desperate's pace. The foliage reopened scabbed lacerations and added as many more. Spence popped carbs and stimulants every thirty minutes. The sweat pouring from his body left a visible trail behind him. He didn't care. Neither did Lazarus. He kept pushing, relentlessly, unaffected by the alien environment—by its attack—running obsessively, muttering something about demons. Quint was on stimulants himself. He wasn't thinking clearly, not at all—kept hearing a voice inside his head, a cold calculating voice speaking with fiery fear: *I can last three more days—three more. I'll be dead then.*

"Kill you demon, kill your face, kill your mother in me," Lazarus rambled.

The others thought he meant the red lizards.

"Sweet white mother in my head."

They had seen more of them. One almost killed Quint—dropped from the trees. Spence was a drug enhanced blur—shot the dragon out of the air, shot it to the ground squirming, shot its red coherence to bloody chaotic bits and then stomped on the pulp (staining his ragged boots red) and cussed the beast in song.

"Demon beast, demon beast," Lazarus went on. He should have looked to the man behind him, not thought of the one before. *There* was a demon. Spence was gone. Something else was there. It rustled when he moved.

"This way." Lazarus changed their direction. Then he stopped. He looked around—Quint never saw him look so puzzled. The three of them stood unmoving—two panting, Lazarus staring at his little beeping (barely) box.

"What's wrong, Laz?" asked Quint.

He held up a hand for silence. Then he smiled again. It was different. Forced.

"That way," he pointed.

Then one of the beasts, the red lizards, dropped from the trees and clamped its fangs into Lazarus's forearm. He just stared at it in surprise. Then the tail swung around, aiming for his head. Lazarus was faster. He caught the tail in one hand, pulled and stretched the beast until the neck rested carefully in the other; then he began to dance. And he danced and squeezed a life crushing waltz. One-two-three, one-two-three—he should've been dead, but danced and cheshire grinned. He should've been dead. He did not even bleed.

Watching that moment alongside Quint, we turned in stunned silence to look at Spence who was flaying the skin from his chest with a knife.

- 28 -
Imperial World:
Five Months Before Solomon's Arrival on Kall

The War Room: Imperial Palace, sublevel eight. A hundred yards square. Darkly lit—most light coming, in fact, from the large tactical holo displays lining the walls, the single holo galaxy floating in three dimensions at the room's center, every planet of the Empire lit and labeled according to a color code: green for Democratic Worlds, red for Monarchies—Dukedoms, Lordships, Baronies and Kingdoms—blue for Imperial Colonies—agro-planets, natural resource planets, engineering worlds and the like—and twelve yellow points of light for those planets tucked relatively close together in the fifth galactic arm of the Milky Way which answered directly to the Imperial political machine, among them Arché and the brightest point of all, Imperial World, called Amric. Six hundred known inhabitable worlds in the galaxy—perhaps another thousand yet undiscovered. And of these lights, fifty-seven were blinking. Some in fringe areas of the Empire—new acquisitions requiring special attention, resources, or subjugation. But in the third and fourth galactic arms there blinked in harmony a dissonant chorus of forty red and green worlds where Janis focused her attention from her position in the Gallery.

Along one wall of the War Room ran two floors of rooms for meetings, communications, food consumption, breaks, maintenance, technology, and management offices. At the center of the second floor was the Gallery, a long narrow room, artworks hanging on three sides, glassed in on the fourth, where Janis could look down on the rows of workstations where Sykol, Guard, and Regular Army specialists gathered intelligence from throughout the Empire.

She stood with a smile of satisfaction on her face while thoughts about programs and intrigues and control and a vague desire for vengeance passed before her mind in catalog fashion. She turned to face the table that ran the length of the Gallery's center, unfolded her crossed arms and placed them on her hips. She paused to survey the faces of the ten people who, with her, would decide the fate of the galaxy in the next year, to look them over even as they surveyed her present persona: sand-gold, silky hair splashing about her shoulders rather than pulled behind as usual, a sleek black tunic, high collared, double breasted, gold buttoned, form fitted at the waist and tapering in below the hips.

The leggings and boots matched: black on black, and on her chest the pin of the Imperial crest: a sharp taloned eagle, wings spread, claws clutching—one a lightning bolt, the other an olive branch. And she surveyed them:

Lord Ymar Magnus, of planet Logres, descendant (by cousinship) of the Amric line and presiding lord of the House of Royals. He would be first in line to the throne except that law prohibited the ascension of any royalty other than immediate house Amric to Imperial crown. He was the most loyal man of some power at Janis's disposal because he knew that his status as second in the Empire depended on the strength of Amric house. Janis took her seat at the table's head (raised slightly above the others—but not so much to flaunt her position as to remind of it— the pretense of democratic Cabinet sessions was important, however well those around the table understood that it was *pretense*). Lord Magnus sat to Janis's immediate left: quite the elder statesman now—long, silver hair crowning a high forehead in thick waves, a large, rounded nose and protruding chin.

To her immediate right sat the Chief Sykol who had not been known by any other name for forty years when he took over the roll at his father's death. His own son, Rejik—seventeen years old now—would by Imperial decree succeed his father at his death. Beside the Chief sat the other two Sykols in this Imperial Cabinet: Spaulding Ang, the Sykol Polit-Bureau chief and Dr. Spin Verkruyse, Imperial Communications Agency. Next to the Sykols sat the Military Chiefs of Staff: General Alexander Constantine of the Army and Admiral Miguel de Nelson commanding the Space Fleet. In terms of real power in the Imperium, this side of the table was the most significant, though the side which Magnus fronted was not pure puppetry.

Next to the Lord of Logres sat Gergrick Brodnik, the Secretary General of the Union of Democratic Worlds which made up not quite half of the Empire. Self governing and loyal to the Imperium, they represented the finest example of the Imperial *Power Principle*: maintain power without expending it. What the ancients had attempted with bread and circuses, the Sykols had achieved through measurement, tabulation, and the willingness to allow people the illusion of their own autonomy: the utopian impulse brought to the strength of its ugliest fruition.

Next to Brodnik sat the Chairman of the Imperial Reserve, Netsirk Watov and beside her Jason Bocc, the Chief Economic Advisor of the Free Market Monitoring Board.

And at the table's foot sat Hal Teltrab whose job as Captain of the Imperial Body Guard extended his authority beyond the Palace to galactic scale: He was the official Marshal of the Regular Army and the Space Fleet so that his protection of the Imperial charge might reach out from Amric's world toward all potential threats. No major military decisions were made without the Captain's approval. But Hal's case was even more particular. He was a figure head, a badly needed one since the dismissal of Solomon Star. And there were other reasons....

Janis placed her arms on the black marble before her, folding her hands together. Here she was at her best. She smiled confidently.

"Gentlemen. And lady. What shall we talk about?"

The informality perfectly calculated.

"My Lady," began the Chief, "I'm sorry to report a security breach in classified Sykol files."

Shocked silence around the room. Even Janis was surprised. This was supposed to be a war council.

"The information in the files was sensitive but not critical or damaging. The alarm to me is that it could happen at all. My people are running traces but preliminary evidence suggests the source of these invasions to be a powerful network system in quadrant three."

'Rikas IV...Inmar's world,' thought Janis. 'A nice segue into graver issues.'

"We'll know for sure inside a week—"

"I don't see how you could have come to those conclusions, Chief."

Hal's voice was as commanding as his presence. Janis smiled her pleasure:

"So, Captain. The Sykol Bureau reported the security breach to you and you have already solved the mystery."

"No, my Lady."

"No?" Her brows perked up.

The Chief's eyes narrowed.

"No. Sykol Central never reported the problem to me. That's not unusual since it didn't directly affect Palace security. Though perhaps a bit imprudent."

He hesitated.

Janis prodded: "Continue Captain."

"The Chief will not find his culprit in Quadrant Three because I am the culprit."

"Ah ha!" she laughed to hide a growing confusion. And thought: 'How is the Chief leading this toward Inmar?'

"There was a rumor of a potential security risk: a Sykol sub-group engaged in genetic experimentation in a non-bio-secure zone. Not so much a violation of rule as of protocol."

"Who are these people? I'd like names, Captain."

"No need, Chief. False alarm. It turns out that a research Sykol was running an exponential search through databases with insufficient parameter controls—it caused red flags on a hundred of my own security protocols. He simply didn't narrow his word search. At any rate, I had to break into Sykol personnel files, check his background and connections, look at research programs currently in progress, and so on, and so on...."

"Captain, that action was completely inappropriate." A calm, controlled tone. "You should have consulted me immediately. Empress—" But lacking in veneer. Janis realized the Chief had not consulted Hal Teltrab in planning his introduction to this meeting.

"No problem, Chief." Hal's own tone was matter-of-fact. "Security remained internal. The only information that *leaked*, went to nowhere but my Con. And certainly, Chief, you have nothing to fear from me?"

He smiled. And the Chief—only the slightest hesitation—smiled:

"Well, Captain. You make an important point about internal cooperation and...policing. Fine. Fine."

'Awkward,' thought Janis. 'And not a good show—at all.' She checked her displeasure with a smile and a deep breath and a mental note to be furious afterwards. As she exhaled, she leaned back in her chair and assumed a regal air: hands on armrests, back straight and stiff. She focused her attention on Spaulding Ang.

"Mr. Ang."

He looked up from a staring-at-no-particular-thing-on-the-table-before-him revery. A middle aged man, greying at the temples and not unpleasant in feature—cleft chin, rugged cheekbone, but a small beakish nose; dark eyes, dark complexion—he looked at Janis, then quickly to the other end of the table and back. And in a sonorous voice he spoke:

"My Lady?"

"Talk about Inmar," she commanded.

The Polit-Chief's answer was calculated and well-rehearsed as was each moment that followed: a slight nod of the head, increasing in vigor and speed to the climactic moment of speech:

"I think we're looking at a war here."

The responses were simultaneous:

Watov, annoyed: "Now I don't think we need to jump to those kinds of conclusions—"

Constantine, releasing: "That's exactly what I've been saying for months!"

Nelson: "Let it come."

Across from him, Bocc: "I couldn't agree more."

The Chief: thinking, 'That's more like it'; saying, "Some decorum, please. Decorum."

And Janis raising her hand and her voice: "Quiet!" She did not hide her displeasure. Silence was immediate.

And the Chief: thinking, 'Perfect.'

And Janis: "Continue Ang."

He stood and continued the orchestration:

"Here's what we have: an alliance of forty planets having made official grievances against the Empire." He began to move about the room. First to the right. "Lord Magnus and his Honor Brodnik would argue that no such alliance exists, but the mere fact that these worlds jointly submitted the grievance proclamation, however legally, is proof enough that Inmar's rhetoric is not pure bluster. Dr. Verkruyse will be glad to confirm the Polit-Bureau analysis. The Overlord has been jockeying for position in the House of Royals for twenty years. His coalition includes a confirmed twenty-seven houses, twenty-five of which are down there blinking on the Intel map in Quadrants three and four. Ten legislative writs in the last year alone have been carried through the House by this faction, all with the intention of decreasing the power of the Empress."

"That's an over simplification," protested Magnus. "Those bills—"

"Were each, with respect my Lord, rejected by the Empress. And for what reason? They were bent on Inmar's independence."

"That's right," agreed an enthusiastic Bocc.

"Thank you. Well there have always been separatists among the democratic worlds. We've sufficiently responded to their needs and assuaged their angers to keep their loyalty for years. However, the separatists support Inmar philosophically and many have signed with him in the *Grievances Proclamation*. Gentlemen, that's not a coalition, not a political party, not a power block. It's an alliance of planets. It exists in every way but overt declaration and that's coming next, I say."

"You don't know that," prodded the Chief (knowing full well...).

"Yes, we do." Charts and graphs began flashing on the holo display, changing in perfect synchronization with the content of his speech. "We know that these worlds have turned major portions of their economies to military industrial complexes. All perfectly legal but also perfectly unnecessary in a part of the galaxy that has known peace for a thousand years."

"That's not what they say," interrupted Watov. Her feminine features—a gentle, round face, piercing blue eyes—stood in marked contrast to the coarse voice. "Instances of piracy have quadrupled in the shipping lanes there in the last five—"

"That," demanded Nelson, "is part of Inmar's lie—we have cruisers patrolling those shipping lanes."

"It's a pretty expensive lie if so, Admiral. The economic losses in that quadrant are real."

"What better excuse—to charge the military with incompetence, the Empire with apathy. They're blaming us for invisible pirates, energy station disasters on three worlds, sabotage of the eco-system on Uridia, global bankruptcy on Xanthrus where last year we dumped six trillion credits to bail out an inept leadership, and there are half a dozen conspiracy theories floating around the press, not just locally mind you, but galactically, all claiming for one reason or another that the Empire is out to ruin every planet in two quadrants and everyone of these *lies* begins with blame set squarely on the shoulders of Janis IV! I don't know about the rest of you, but I'm tired of disloyal voices attempting to take political advantage of the Emperor's untimely death."

"Mr. Ang, I admire your passion."

A slight bow. "Empress." And he took his seat.

"But prudence is ever the Imperial mode. What if we were to take a wait-and-see attitude, work on solidifying our public perception, tone down political rhetoric, let Inmar make a fool of himself, or end his foolishness—"

"I can tell you why not, your Highness," broke in Admiral Nelson. "Oh...forgive my interrupting you—"

"You're not here for your manners, Admiral. You were about to say?"

"Fleet Intel has one primary purpose: to know how many and what kind of ships of mass destruction are floating about the galaxy at any one time. We have reason to believe that Inmar is working on developing mobile space fold technology."

"That's impossible," said Brodnik, himself a retired Fleet officer. "The power required would take a world ship."

"Yes. It would," replied Hal. He let the truth of it sink in.

"Madame Watov, could the resources of forty planets be sufficient for producing a world ship?" asked Janis.

Shaking her head: "I find it hard to believe, my Lady. Perhaps if they tasked those resources to the limit. But it's a farfetched notion from my perspective."

"But possible."

Reluctantly: "I suppose so."

"And it would put quite a drain on their economies." Janis let this point sink in.

"The question," Admiral Nelson concluded, "is whether or not we're willing to risk the possibility that a thousand destroyers might suddenly come pouring out of a new moon orbiting Imperial Planet, their plasma cannons trained on every major city here."

"May I point out before we allow rumor to dictate our course of action that, barring minor planetary skirmishes, policing actions, and acquisitions, there has been peace in the galaxy for six hundred years." Lord Magnus was grave and regal. "Is that something we want to throw away?"

"Here, here," echoed Brodnik, and Watov agreed with an affirmed nod.

"No. But only if it's something we can afford to keep," Janis declared. "If Inmar thinks my youth equals lack of resolve, he'll find differently in the coming months." She set her chin and narrowed her eyes. "Make preparations. Watch Inmar. I want confirmation on the world ship. Captain Teltrab, see to it personally."

"Of course my Lady, but allow me to offer that I am reluctant to abandon the possibilities of peace. I believe your wait-and-see posture is kind and appropriately cautious but should also be augmented by active pursuit of peace. We should pursue every avenue before a war, even one we know we'll win. It *has been* six hundred years."

"I conclude otherwise," the Chief retorted. "Pursuing peace will show weakness." He intended the statement to be final.

"No," said Janis. "The Captain's motivation is noble, and, if ours is less so, it is nevertheless a possibility for advantage." She was suddenly inspired. "How if the Palace were to personally take up the grievances mandate? We agree with the decisions among the Royal Houses and the Democratic Union that the grievances are unsubstantiated, but, because of...oh...because of our deep concern about the quadrant, we wish to open lines of communication directly to the forty systems. We'll send an envoy."

"Dangerous, my Empress," said the Chief. And then quickly: "But intriguing. If we sent the right people."

Janis: "Yes."

Verkruyse: "Someone from this cabinet."

Ang: "No, two cabinet members."

Watov: "I'll go. I want peace. I still favor peace, my Lady." Almost pleading.

"And perhaps I should go," offered Lord Magnus. "I'm visible and would make an impression."

"With apologies, my Lord," Hal responded, "Inmar is most interested in reaching the ear of the Empress and he knows that no one bends that ear more (even than you, sir) than Sykol Central. A visit from the Bureau, by a section chief, either Ang or the doctor will impress him as to our earnestness."

Janis decided: "It will be Mr. Ang. But plans for war go into development immediately. We will not begin a conflict. Nor run from it. Captain. I need to know if that world ship is being built. I need to know now."

"That went well."

The Chief, the Captain and the Empress in a long featureless corridor walked away from the war room up a gradual incline.

"It went terribly." Annoyed but not angry. "You throw out an unconfirmed report of espionage which turns out to be a failure on both your parts at simple communication, and then *you*, Captain Teltrab, are fool enough to blurt the problem out in front of the whole cabinet instead of waiting till afterward."

"I can't agree with you more. Captain I want a complet—"

"Be quiet, Chief." Mostly annoyed, a little angry. "That's the kind of defensiveness that made things look even worse. You should have seen the look in Magnus's eyes, the smug old wind bag. He was sure you two were going to have it out which, of course, gave the best impression of the worst lie: (now more angry than annoyed) that you actually *are* at odds with each other and we have an internal struggle in the Palace. It was so stupid!"

"If I may, my Lady?"

Stopping and turning: "What Hal? What perfect piece of analysis are you going to toss out that will explain things with such insight that you will once again be vindicated, and perfectly?"

"You did a fine job of glossing over our foolishness."

Anger eased passed annoyance, her frown to smiling self satisfaction: "I did run things rather well in there, didn't I?"

"Oh yes," grinned the Chief. "Pardon an old man's patronizing his pupil, but I am so very proud of what you've become."

She couldn't help but feel pleasure all the while knowing: "Oh yes, you are patronizing me. But," light heartedly, "it won't put you back in my good graces right away."

"No, and neither will our next order of business."

The end of the corridor. The royal lifts.

"Here's where I take my leave," said Hal.

"Where to, Captain?"

"My Con, Empress. I've got a doomsday device to ferret out in Quadrant Three." He bowed, and, walking away down another corridor hands held behind his back, thought, '...and Palace security to run, and battle plans to draw up, a Guard to monitor,

Sykols to out-sykol and perhaps...' —he hesitated to even think it—'...a traitor to expose. A traitor.'

Stepping onto the elevator, a single Guardsman to escort them:

"Well then say it."

"You're due in the medical suites."

"Oh God."

"You're ovulating, my Empress."

"And just how many people in the Palace are on familiar terms with my menstrual cycle?"

"We need to fertilize one more egg before your hysterectomy, for precaution's sake.

"Hysterectomy, right. I'm not sure."

"About what?"

"Who's the male donor?"

"Genetic material selected at random from the collected banks of the Royal Houses. It doesn't matter, really. The material will be re-sequenced to suit Imperial standards."

"I see."

"You're going to have a son, by the way."

"That's fine. I was hoping for two children."

"Hmm. Difficult. But not unprecedented. We have to be careful—worries about ascension and sibling ambitions crop up, but if the second child is many years younger and kept from reproducing...well we've dealt with that before."

"With your precious charts and tables of formulae." Silence. "Two children, then."

"Very well."

"A boy and a girl."

"As you wish. But the hysterectomy next month."

"I don't want it."

"My Lady?"

"I'm just not sure about this hysterectomy...this neutering."

"Oh no Janis, not—"

"It's how I feel Chief."

"And you can't govern your Empire by feelings, child."

She reeled on him: "But you can rule it by statistics, is that it?!"

"No, I only—"

"Who's in charge since my father's death, old man? Am I the Imperium or are you?"

Reflexively, she took a step toward the guard behind her whose body stood at perfect attention, perfect readiness though his mind raced with uncertainty. Guard training had prepared him for Palace politics, had taught him to close his ears to the private conversations of higher echelons, even the Empress herself. But this conversation was bringing a sweat to his brow.

The Chief's tone became warm like a father's love:

"My Lady Janis, I've seen you grow from a child to a goddess, far surpassing all my expectations. These Sykol rules as you think of them are of your ancestors' making. Ten generations ago the matriarch Dido decided for herself that her best advantage, the advantage of every female ruler of Amric house, was not to be ruled by the biochemical processes of her body but—"

"So for a woman to rule this Empire she must make herself into a man, is that it?"

His pause was pregnant, but seemed just short of deliberate— his countenance warmed even more:

"No." Shaking his head. "If you would change it, change it. You are my finest pupil. But you are my Empress. Say what you want and we will make your rule into our...vision" (now nodding).

The elevator doors opened and they stepped out, silently, the Chief keeping his gaze fixed on her, the Empress staring blankly at no particular distant thing.

"Alright, then, old father man. The hysterectomy next month."

"You'll find it freeing, believe it or not. The hormone therapy balanced perfectly and part of your diet. You won't be bothered by any such things."

"No. Not anymore. That will be...good."

"Feigning pregnancy will be easier than carrying the child to term."

"Yes. Yes it will. Who's the surrogate?"

"Alathia Star has agreed to carry the baby."

Her face, which had been resignation, was now shock, then...something...the grin was wide, lips unparted. The eyes narrowed to slits. Half way between whisper and speech she voiced some darkened approval, turned and walked away, her guard trailing.

The Chief watched them leave, lifted his note pad and wrote of how that encounter had gone exactly as he'd planned.

Alathia Star...she was my surrogate mother as well. Something about having a perfect womb, even in later years, as well as a perfect psyché for childbearing. She is the reason I went searching for Solomon in the first place. She and my foster father, a mildly tortured soul named Hal Teltrab.

- 29 -
Heaven

Their path was straight and true. Ten days and Solomon had learned to read the unwritten language. Only ten days. Surely the Philagi. The Savage led him at a robust pace, invigorated by the proximity of a goal. She led him into the densest, tallest part of the jungle, where the light of the planet outweighed that of the hidden sun, where animate life tugged at the indestructible fabric of his clothing, tears now tatters—still not quite one in grace. Three days to the river. Four days to the wasteland. Three days of wondering. Here the final leg—two days after he had asserted heart's confidence, asking, "Why are we going in circles?" (twelve days in all), they stopped to sleep again at a Kalli hovel. As with that first day, she lit a fire and drew him close to her protection: womb of woman and wood.

"You were as your father?" she asked.

"Yes."

"You protected the Queen of the galaxy."

"Yes."

"But you left."

Scratching his cheek: "I left."

"Why?"

He thought for a moment. "When I was two they taught me a song." He cleared his throat and began to sing, his voice rough and unpracticed:

"'The Captain of the Guard

He went to see the Queen

She scolded him for being late

and said, 'Where have you been?'

"They hit me until I was six whenever she cried. Never hard, but always in the face. We sang her, we ate her, we slept her, we died...."

Silence.

"They tried to make me in their own image—the image in their books and drills and four hours sleep a night. But I could not *be*....They say they made me feel her pain. When we were twelve, she turned her ankle and I cried. But not for their reason."

"Philagapos."

"Yes. I loved her."

Silence.

"She told me not to look at the sun. Outside, I would stare at the sun and she told me to stop. She said I'd go blind."

"You said they might plan."

"What?"

"The outside ones—your Queen."

"A plan?"

"A *more* plan."

"I said they were planning something else, but you said—"

"Philagapon says no."

"Yes."

"About Kall—I meant Kall. I was not thinking more than us. You are the Korun-ga, the...prize-thorn. You...." She was trying to say more than she could, more than language from another world, any other, could.

Solomon understood enough: "It's about me."

"The plan."

"They wanted—*she* wanted me to die here."

"That sees."

"No." He suddenly understood it all. "Not dead. Killed."

Silence.

"Here we are safe," she concluded. "We will be warned if trouble is."

And he believed it, with more faith than a soldier normally would.

But one more word was spoken: "Sleep."

As he drifted away, Solomon imagined this place of rest was like that one on the first night, and he toyed with the idea that they had, indeed, completed a circle. What he saw the next morning dispelled such doubt. (But first a note: That night his dreams were pleasant. No, perfect. He didn't remember a thing about them. Only that when he heard the sound of his heart beat, it wasn't the world's. But it was alive, a beating sound without any artificial overtones.)

It was the first of the great black trees that he had seen there. This young one, only fifty feet around, extended its massive roots in all directions and collected about itself a plethora of moss and vine. Tiny feral creatures scurried up and down its ebony trunk, foraging a rich dried sap from its dead bark, an energy food, like honey. It smelled like ripe oranges and sugar—concentrated, potent. Around the tree wove a giant vine, certainly as old, ascending spirally into the second earth. Its width made walking possible, and notches for stairs had been cut to make the steep ascent almost easy.

Up that spiral stair they climbed, with each full circle coming nearer to their maturity, like the history of heaven. Up they went, lightly touching the trunk's surface for balance. Had he time, Solomon would have stopped and stared and been consumed by the depth of the blackness of the wood. No wonder it was so desired. It held in its darkness the imaginations of the powerful. Up they went toward what appeared to be a heavy cluster of overgrowth—the second earth, or the first heaven for those headed in that direction.

They climbed hundreds of feet into the firmament above and emerged into palpable light.

The sun shone clearly, brightly, through now present gaps among the half height trees. A rich blue blanketed the sky, dotted with white billows lazily drifting, without care, wherever they cared to drift. Here, massive limbs stretched, winding and intertwining, climbing and dipping to create the frame for a new landscape—a maze of hills, valleys and holes in the earth, framed by trees, but laid over with vine, moss, creeping plants, and the remains of living things long dead. You could walk in any of these spaces, unconcerned about its strength, feet relieved by their spongy feel. Flowers blossomed in the light and gave off their own radiance, melding light upon light, making the place effervescent. The scent here was a bit more pine than methane; it wafted on a now present breeze. Never before seen animals—more mammals than reptiles—scurried about or slowly grazed or leapt and swung on vines. Squirrel creatures, tails fluttering, approached Savage and danced at her feet. An albino climbed up her clothing to her shoulder and kissed the perspiration on her face. She smiled: "Charisu bo"—her tone warm and friendly.

Solomon, too, felt relaxed; the wonder of the place, not so dynamic as the waterfall but quiet and naturally pleasing, gave over to musing. There was evidence of design here, of shaping, weaving. Had the Kalliphi created this new world with their own hands? Why else would there be only this one level of strata and not many above and below?

Birds sang a song—was it? Yes! Harmony! And antiphonal melody: they sang to each other. The song was simple and soulful, the variations complex, never the same. The dance of the fairies ended, and the white queen hurried her children off to their serious play. Savage led Solomon to the east, her step seeming lighter than before in his eyes. Was it her or this place? She led him on till midday at which point they came upon a path: a rounded black surface, almost free of overgrowth. It was hard underfoot, unlike the spongy feel of the artificial terra about it. And its blackness—deeper than tar from the world's bosom. It was the limb of a great black tree; its source could not be seen! For thirty minutes they followed it, always ascending. Then, finally looming in the bright distance, appeared the greatest, most ancient of the ebony giants, reaching into the sky beyond sight and so thick as to keep the eye from seeing its width at any near distance. It was a giant among giants—Leviathan—the heart of the planet, the home of its people, the height of their journey.

- 30 -
From 2288:
Fall

The first time I met Solomon Star, years after the events on Kall, I was struck with a sense of the man's unmoving greatness. Not for anything he had done or accumulated, but for what he had surrendered. There was a moment in his life when he could have seized it. That's what struck me. He hadn't had to. He was the perfect example of the best kind of achievement: one who sees his glory and knows...and turns his back on it and walks away.

The death of the Emperor had been a shock to the galaxy. Nature is fickle; it obeys no manuals and few predictions, and it is quick to remind even the most powerful of the annoying fact of mortality. Soldiers can guard and Sykols can calculate and bureaucracies can administrate, but no matter what controls or orders or mathematical principles humanity may impose on her, nature refuses to give up her randomness, as if scoffing at those whose heads are screwed too tightly into their skulls. The autopsy discovered a weak vessel in the brain, a genetic flaw inborn to shorten the life clock. As with all great but tragic leaders, the Emperor was betrayed from among his own ranks.

Of course plans existed, in the face of such contingencies, for the smooth maintenance of the Empire, but the transition period was far from ideal.

For Janis it meant immediate ascendency to the throne. She was not quite the youngest ruler in Amric history, but close. Nor was she not quite ready for the task—not according to Sykol manuals of development. Still Janis was forced into a shrewd political world which taxed her abilities and energy. The Chief and other Imperial advisors were overworked as well, as Janis sought to consolidate her power and complete another twelve years of training in two.

The Sykol bureau was in an uproar, tabulating statistics, predictions, new developmental schedules, and methodologies; it is no wonder that the *flaws* in Solomon's personality were overlooked.

It also meant drastic change for the Guard. The forty-third Guard was retired with honors—Davidson Star removed himself to his wonder-world, Kall. His wife, with whom he had never developed more than a casual relationship, remained behind to share in the Sykol hysteria. The forty-fourth Guard, under Captain Solomon Star abruptly ended training and entered the work of protecting the new Empress of the galaxy.

For Solomon, it meant long and frantic hours. The coronation had been a near security disaster. Oh, there was no real trouble, save for the myriad demonstrations made by small groups of activists for whatever cause was in vogue that year. But the screening of thousands of dignitaries plus millions of spectators, coupled with the organization of the more than fifty non-cooperative Nobles' Guards (each concerned with its own charge), seven divisions of the regular army (brought in as a general police force), and a planetary air space filled to three times capacity was almost more than Solomon could handle.

There was also the emptiness within him. The void inside became a gulf when he saw the crown placed upon her head. He was lucky that his schedule made him too busy to dwell on his feelings. And unlucky to long for her still, for Janis became even more distant from him than before. She became, to him, without feeling, without humanity. And so: a ruling machine who approached her new status with vigor and success.

It was three years before life in the Palace finally began to become what might be considered routine. Even so, Solomon remained drained. Apathy sucks motivation like a leech. Only his sense of duty kept him going.

The Empress played Solomon subtly (when she had time for him), holding to Sykol *suggestions* of decorum in their relationship. There was one instance in particular—nothing my mother had planned and nothing Solomon understood:

The two of them were walking together in the Imperial Gardens one clear pink day, enjoying the rare opportunity of being able to converse almost alone. Janis cherished such moments, despite her willingness to sacrifice intimacy for power.

"Carry me, Solomon," she asked.

"Empress?"

"I am tired. Please carry me to the car."

Reluctantly, he took her up in his arms. Much as he had done many years before—yes, that day. But now he remained rigid—muscles tense. He walked at attention. She placed a supple hand lightly against his chest and cuddled her head, eyes closed, into his shoulder. Solomon's mind flashed back to that time—her tears. Almost imperceptibly he allowed his physique to soften, drawing her closer. A brief moment, but intense: almost the melting. A spark of compassion nearly ignited—

"Put me down!"

"What?! I mean—"

"That will be sufficient, Captain. I feel I can walk the rest of the way to the transport."

"Your will, my Lady."

Bewildered, he had lowered her gently to the ground. Bewildered, he had followed her back to the hover car in silence.

It wasn't easy to see it in his actions. For twenty-five years he had been trained for one purpose: to be the Captain of the Imperial Guard. And there was none better. Duty drove him, and confidence managed the apathy. But the difference was there in an ever so slightly absent enthusiasm. Difference and distance.

Storms raged the day the Captain of the Guard was called to an audience with the Empress in her private dining chambers. Solomon, dressed in a Guard singlesuit, entered the round room that sat atop *Hupsothesa*, the highest tower of the Palace. The entire sphere was windowed, allowing a magnificent view in all directions of billowing dark clouds, dancing electricity, and wind whipped rain. Weather satellites were being taxed to their limits to control this tempest. The lights of Imperial City flickered dimly in the distance. Janis stood watching the display, a spectacle of Amric's World, given in her honor. To Solomon she gave her back. A red cape trailing to the floor hid her features like a cocoon. Metamorphosis indeed:

"It's lovely, isn't it?"

"Quite so, Lady."

"My grandfather thought well to build this room." She turned. "It's wonderful to come here and relax...think. I wish you to have tea with me, Captain."

His face responded confusion. And before he could decline:

"Consider it an order." An uncharacteristically wry smile.

A servant set a tray of tea and sweets upon a small floating table.

"Thank you, Stephanie, that will be all. I don't make the command lightly, Captain. I want you to sit and drink and eat with me."

"Your pleasure, my Lady." He crossed the room, a note pad in his hand, and joined the Empress, sitting on a hover chair opposite her.

"Please pour. We have Pistin tea from Ouranos."

"My favorite, Empress. I enjoy the sweet taste. And the pastries—they too are my favorites." He spoke matter-of-factly.

Janis smiled, pleased that the information she had received was correct.

"What do you have on your key-screen?"

"It's blank, Empress. I assumed the agenda for our meeting to be yours."

"Yes. Efficient as ever, Captain." Janis lifted her cup, paused, looking at him. He followed her lead, drinking in the richness of the Ouranian tea, breathing deeply the hot/sweet aroma.

"You'll receive a holo on this, but a dinner has just been arranged with the President and Governors of our Imperial World. For three years we've been running about, dealing with everyone, everywhere; we've neglected our own planet. I want to do something special—beyond the typical presents. Send a group of our own Guard to all of the invited dignitaries to escort them personally to the dinner. That should impress them, hmm?"

'And scare them a bit,' thought Solomon as he wrote.

"Will this cause any strain on the preparation for Inmar?"

"Plans for the Overlord's arrival have been designed to the last detail, Lady. The time table is in perfect schedule. We're actually to the point of having to wait until the few days before his arrival before anything else can be done."

"Excellent efficiency again, Captain." Then her tone changed. "This one is dangerous."

"I...have heard, my Lady, that he celebrated on the day of the Emperor's death."

Janis turned her face.

"Yes." And with controlled anger: "I want him to see our power!"

Something came upon her, something which had begun on the day of whippings: some monomaniacal obsession glazing over her eyes. The man before her became a hazy shadow in the single-minded reality that now swept her into a familiar world which remained yet anathema to the soul. There she had been molding a place for herself with fist and sweat and tooth and blood, almost perfect in fit. And there all doubts and questions dispelled and she was sovereign, master with infinite perfection, and absolute rule—even a substance of absoluteness, a concrete form of black and white which all but the most cunning would perceive for Truth.

Outside, lightning cracked open the sky. Solomon felt a chill: "So it shall be."

She returned.

"How are you doing with your lady friends?"

The sudden change in subject stunned him to stupor. She had become quite good at this; like the winds raging without, direction was a matter of whim. She was Amric, mistress of the universe (some in the Palace privately thought her none other than the great founder himself, reincarnate, perhaps a genetically engineered DNA structure too close to her founding roots), and she possessed a mastery of the skills required for it. She could be all things to all people. Almost.

"I've heard that they're rather frustrated with you."

"I find little time with them."

"I like that girl Charisa. She seems sharp, and rather pretty, don't you think?"

"I hadn't noticed."

Janis stood. Solomon began to, but she motioned him to stay. She moved toward the window. Then, turning: "Captain, our duties take many forms and I want...you and I have grown up together, worked hard to maintain the Empire.... If you feel uncomfortable—don't let me stand in the way of your duty, and your feelings toward the woman you m— will choose.

'You must be kidding,' he thought.

"I trust that you will—"

'You couldn't be more wrong.'

Somewhere within, she hoped she was. But he tuned the rest out. A sickly sweet expression of intimacy there—a facade of care; her self deceit bi-leveled. Solomon felt annoyed—a tiny anger at the pit of his stomach, which he did not show. He had experienced the feeling toward Janis only once before. He thought of the heat:

'So different from the storm outside.'

"Now, Captain, about this incident with my escort to the city."

Thinking: 'How did you find out about that?'

"Your reaction was most unprecedented."

'No one knew my response. Those men were sworn to secrecy.'

"Well?"

"I received...conflicting reports, Empress."

"Why did you bother to accept any report other than the one that I commanded your subordinates to give?"

"Commander Tarsoon was there himself; I can't ignore my fifth in command's log entry. His visual recorder confirms the analysis."

This time *she* was shocked to silence by the presumption of his defense. He saw the look and tried quickly to recover:

"My Lady, you were in an open mall, on foot when someone broke from the crowd lines shouting. My—"

"Yes, a distraught father looking for his lost daughter."

'Who we helped him find,' he didn't say aloud. 'Not that you care about such things.'

"Your men threw me to the ground, leapt on top of me, turned their guns on the crowd and assaulted the man."

'With an excellent 2.7 second reaction time,' he recalled with satisfaction.

Suddenly she was in his face. "Do you know what that will look like?!" He strained to keep still, to keep from blinking her spit out of his eye. Quietly: "'The Empress is paranoid,' they'll say. 'The Guard bullies innocent bystanders.'" Then more loudly: "'Who's the Empress afraid of?'" And shouting: "'Inmar has Her Highness hopping'!"

"My Lady Janis." He spoke in a tone she hadn't heard in ten years, his anger momentarily subsumed with disbelief. Was this his Janis IV? His heart spoke with the conviction of confidence and with feeling: "Everything those men did, they did according to every rule of training, every Guard procedure, every Sykol manual, every instinct in their—"

That she hit him wasn't the surprise. The surprise came when he realized she was pulling back to do so. He was so shocked that he almost allowed the instinct to defend himself to take control. As the hand swung toward his face, he had to genuinely fight the impulse to block it.

It struck.

"Who rules this Empire, the Sykols or me?!" Then a backhand on the other cheek. "Who do you serve, the Imperium or me?! I *am* the Imperium I—"

Suddenly she drew back. She'd seen for a moment the feeling he normally blanked from his face. "Oh, Solomon." And for a moment her eyes cleared, and she sounded like the child Princess of his longing. But too late: the compassion which had manifested for her in that moment was gone, tuned out of his reddened, stone still face, turned only toward his men whom he would try to protect. The anger which he had set aside began to foment in his gut. He placed his pad on the table beside him, placed both hands on his lap.

"Forgive me, Lady."

But she knew he had spoken it with all the sincerity of...of a Sykol. And the haze returned to her eyes, the command to her voice—cold and hard: the fury of ice.

"Explain yourself. You are to carry out a Second Order reprimand on yourself, and the Third Order discipline I ordered against those guards who served me in the city yesterday."

His anger grew.

"But first I want you to explain yourself." She turned to hide the unsteadiness of her panting, to hold the still stinging hand, redder than his face, to her mouth. "I'm waiting, Captain."

His voice, his face, his demeanor were blank formality. His words...perhaps not the best he could have chosen. Perhaps, unconsciously, that's how he wanted it:

"In seeking to fulfill my duty to you, Empress, I must think about my men, that—"

Reeling: "You must think about your charge, and every thought of every Imperial Guard must be to his charge! 'His life, his charge!' Beyond feelings, beyond self, duty first to the Imperium!"

"They are only men, my Lady."

"They must be more than men! Our power will not be jeopardized, especially not on Imperial World. Why am I even arguing with you—no, why do you argue with me!? You know the duty and will respect it!"

"Yes, my Empress." Solomon stood and bowed.

"Each and every one, dedicated to the Imper—no, dedicated to *me*, and the obedience of my will." The glaze in her eyes thickened. "We deal with masses, not individuals. Even I am not alone. Complete obedience. We must know that each and every one shall be willing to obey, even unto death, as was tested in the kidnaping."

One word.

But one word.

And one word: "Tested?"

She froze.

His anger flared.

Then she continued—cooly, cautiously: "You were to be informed in a year. Under pain of death, no other guard must know—not even your lieutenant, not for another ten years. To test Guard abilities and loyalties, House Amric developed an ordeal generations ago: a crisis situation. The kidnaping was planned."

Lin, Master of Turez Temple, surveyed his keep from the stone terrace of its highest stone tower. Ancient grey walls blended with distant mountains. To his left, a mirror lake, fed by melting snows. Younger students fished there. Lin could see women carrying water from the lake to the temple walls. Young masters, who had left as students, would be returning from winter ordeals soon.

In the courtyard below, Lin saw priests, reading and discussing the Cathudah. To the right, young men clad in black practiced battle designs with Disnis fire weapons: guns and swords. Lin smiled. This was a strong group. Soon they would be called to take the holy war once again to the Pepsin. He had known that the brothers at Temple Su Tico would fail. The Pepsin came with their machine men and fire birds. They destroyed Su Tico.

But the holy child was rising anew. The word had come from the Disnis: soon they would send the black bird that would carry the finest warriors of Temple Turez across the heavens. Lin did not know why the gods had brought them to Nama, nor how—such times were forgotten—nor did he understand the countless defeats down the millennia suffered under the hands of the Pepsin. His people's piety seemed ever insufficient to the Cathudah. But of one thing he was sure: This time the child would be taken and kept. The cursed Amri—the Pepsin—would whither, and the child would lead the people of Nama to paradise.

"Dear God," was all I could say. When I discovered the Nama Program in the deepest archives of Sykol R. & D. When I realized the implications—an entire culture invented for Imperial play. When I read the Cathudah....It was brilliant. Written seventeen hundred years ago by a Sykol anthropologist who named it after his daughter Cathi. Dear God.

There's more:

From: **The Sykol Manual of Guard Crisis Theory and Statistics: "Introduction to Volume One: 'A Brief Summary.'"**

Section Twelve: Justification of Risks

12.1 The founders of *Crisis* testing knew that no amount of risk to the resources of the Imperial House would be readily accepted—especially such a seemingly great risk. With volumes fifteen and sixteen, the *Crisis* committee made a special and systematic effort to develop (and explain to His Majesty) a fail-safe program for successful implementation.

12.2 Included in this section are chapters on the following:

> **12.3.1-127** Historical accounts of program development and trials.
>
> **12.4.1-56** Details on insuring transportation and mechanical safety.

12.5.1-482 Details and techniques of engineering the primitives' religious, cultural, and psychological systems toward charge protection.

> Cf. *Creating the Religion*, vol. five and *Neuro—subconscious Implantations of Kill Inhibitors and Hesitation Words*, vol. six.

12.6.1-66 Procedures for training the advanced Guard in rescue methods while maintaining the secrecy and integrity of *Crisis* testing.

12.7.1-138 Procedures for surrogate program including creation, training, secrecy maintenance and post-crisis care.

"It couldn't have been. They would never have allowed the risk," Solomon was saying.

"Do you doubt me!"

Then what he truly meant: "But men died!"

She forgave this breach of etiquette: "And well, as I recall."

"For a test?!"

"FOR THEIR CHARGE!!"

The power possessed her fully. Sickly, sweet honey smothered her senses, hell-fires burned her molten heart, and all the gods in heaven and earth shuddered as she drained their life's essence from the dark place. Power: For a moment she was the incarnation of all that made meekness a thing to be desired.

He didn't notice.

"You knew all the time. When I carried you out. And at the whipping field."

How perplexing light can be. In the ensuing moment of silence he had time to think: 'They would never have allowed the risk.' And then he realized the awful truth, the base deceit and pure manipulation of the thing.

"Oh, no." He stumbled to his feet and simultaneously backwards—"No, no"—his legs shaking with the last of his faith.

"That will be all, Captain."

"No you c—" He tried to steady himself, almost fell over.

"That will be all, Captain!"

Reality cracked.

His head would not stop shaking; his voice trembled: "Yeh—Yes it will."

"I understand your shock, Captain, but do not risk—"

"It wasn't even you...*you*...used...a genetic print!"

"Do NOT—"

"SHE WAS A CLONE!"

"—RISK A FIRST ORDER REPRIMAND WITH ME!"

Suddenly fury waned and compassion welled with its purer anger.

"That will not be necessary, Empress."

Anger at something ever so casually bent.

He reached to the rear of his sash and took hold of a centuries old piece of cloth tucked away there: a ceremonial white glove with only one purpose. He threw it at her feet.

"I resign."

- 31 -
Poacher

Lazarus lost the signal.

It was hours before he admitted it to them though they'd heard it stop themselves. What remained of Quint asked him why. He said he didn't need it. Quint half believed him.

"Why don't you die Lazarus?" said Quint. "I'm dying. Spence is dead."

Spence was casually stripping a band of skin from his thigh, peeling the cut piece off with his fingers. He had tied the X-shaped piece from his chest around his head, like a scarf.

"Why don't you die?"

"I died once, Quint. They brought me back to life."

"What?"

"Mother wouldn't let me sleep." Was that tenderness in his voice? "You can't die Quint. I need you on my back."

"Back!" barked Spence, elated; he started awkwardly slicing at his spine.

"Stay here for a moment."

Quint heard concern in the man's voice and couldn't believe it.

"I'm going to scout ahead."

Lazarus walked away casually. Something was different in him—for that moment.

Quint sat on a fallen tree and watched Spence cut himself again and again. I sat next to him in my secret room, watched the blood drip—red here, clear there—watched in fascination, living the pain as vicariously as I could. He didn't cry or laugh or scream. Just stared with a brightness in his eyes. He looked up once.

"Want some, Quint?"

"No."

Even now, I don't know how he could've gone mad so quickly. Lazarus—he was already crazy. But Spence was only a sadistic maniac when they came. I suppose the light was too blinding.

One of the serpents, Bel, came and sat next to him watching. When it was time to eat, Spence took the beast's tail in his mouth and crunched down on the stinger, shoving it deeper into his throat; the lizard, meanwhile, began chewing on his feet and they squirmed in a naked circle on the turf.

After a minute Quint shot them, the monster and the lizard. And he went on shooting them for ten minutes, until all that remained was a hole in the ground, a very large hole: round and black and asymmetrical and six feet deep.

He walked away to find Lazarus. Suddenly he wanted to kill someone. Lazarus. Or Solomon Star. Someone.

There, at the largest of the great black trees on the planet, was the largest Kalli encampment. Solomon had journeyed for thirteen days. You might have imagined grass huts or some such primitive dwellings. Not so here. The people of the jungle planet were master woodsmen. Beautifully shaped and intricately sculpted buildings stretched here and there on great limbs at all levels, every one finished like the best of indoor furniture. The tree itself had been cut into to create a network of passages and rooms. Yet the giant hardly noticed. The place seemed natural, an extension of the tree itself. *Eisos.*

Solomon was oblivious to all of this. He was captivated by the sight before him. The people, hundreds of them, stood in silent rows along the village perimeter. They stood watching—men, women, children—close together, still. Brown single-suits, hair drawn tight behind. They waited with incredible intent, watched as if for the coming of some messiah. Their eyes, all of them green, penetrated the man of light with the being of the forest, seeing him. Silence fell upon the place like a shroud, or, better, a veil. Even the animals, the birds were quiet. The breeze stilled that the leaves might not rustle but join in the solemn moment. By the presence of her leading, the Savage pulled him forward. As they drew near, the sea parted; the people moved aside giving them entrance. And still they watched. Entering the encampment, Solomon was engulfed by aromas of fresh food and scented homes: nothing sweet, nothing bitter, rather tastes of meat and vegetables and kindling—savory and subtle, like the smells of one's home. He was so quietly captivated that he did not notice the approaching figure.

"Hello."

He noticed.

"Hello, there."

A man came near, an offworlder, dressed in the grey garb of a miner. His hair was sandy; an unkempt beard had been growing for perhaps three months. He was tall and thin, almost emaciated, and a beaming smile stretched across his face.

"Hello. You must be the son." He grasped Solomon's hand and shook it vigorously. "My you *do* look a lot like him!"

"Who are you?"

"Grace's the name, Charlie Grace. I'm a poacher. Heh. They caught me a month ago I think—or maybe it was more. Heh. I don't know. I was hunting Amberleeke'—that's an animal you know—for their pelts, and they caught me. Snuck right up on me, they did. Didn't hear a sound. Had me in a minute. I thought I was dead. You know regulations and poaching. They could've killed me then."

He moved about excitedly, but he was not nervous; more like an enthusiastic child having to wait on his parents' permission to open his birthday presents.

"They brought me straight here, straight to him—tied me up and hung me by my feet while I waited for him. He's not doing very well you know—your father. I think he's sick. I've been with him though. Haven't left, though I'm from off-world originally."

Solomon patiently endured the incoherence, though with a gentle prod: "What happened after they brought you here?"

"Why *him*! The Philagapon of course. They took me to him when he returned to the tree. Did I say he'd been out? Heh. Yes. He came walking by me, right by, talking to someone. Hardly noticed me."

Grace paused, then smiled, deep in awe, eyes aglow.

"Then he turned to me, for just a moment...

he said he loved me.

And he *meant* it."

- 32 -
Imperial World:
Two Months Before Solomon's Arrival on Kall

The fire was warm. The couches luxuriant. Even Hal Teltrab had surrendered his traditional stiffness to lean back into the cushions. Janis stretched out opposite him staring up at a holo map of the stars—*her* stars. But *his* puzzle: the preparation for deterring a rebellion. Or defeating it.

"Hal."

'Tenderness?' he wondered. "Empress?"

"What went wrong, Hal?" Her eyes were fixed on a little star named for its planet, a place she could not completely call hers. "Why did he leave?"

The answer was not cold and calculating but spontaneous and sincere—

"Because he loved you too much."

—such a risk.

"Are you saying he left because of me?" So much for tenderness. "Because of something I did wrong to him?"

"Are you asking for honesty?"

"No."

"Then he left because he knew he could never have you."

"And if I were asking for honesty?"

He sat up, considered her image: the gentle play in her sipping the spice wine in her hand. 'Tenderness still? Fear?'

She returned his stare. No command. Request.

"He left because he felt too deeply. For you, us, everyone. And you drove him away. You listened to the Sykols instead of your conscience." He waited for the backlash. "You drove him away."

The anger came, though not as severely as he had expected:

"Those are daring words, Captain Teltrab, almost treasonous. The questioning of Sykol protocols?"

"It's what they made me for, my Lady. I'm the analyst."

"And by all indications the best that ever was."

"Thank you."

"It was not a compliment."

"No, it was honesty."

She smiled. "Your impertinence amazes me." The tone was soft, the threat real.

He did not back down: "The Chief Sykol agrees with you."

The words were playful enough, but both understood the challenge. Now she sat up.

"The Chief and I *have* spoken about you."

"My loyalty is to you, and I'm not afraid of the Chief."

"Why should you be?"

"I have heard that he's been *speaking* to you about me."

"You make me laugh."

"The Chief is afraid of me."

Her eyes went wide. She hesitated. He continued.

"He fears me because I am more powerful than he is."

"Captain!" She jumped to her feet.

He rose slowly, deliberately.

"Do you want honesty?"

Her genuine shock was tinged with delight.

"Yes. I want honesty."

"With Solomon gone—" She winced. "—with him gone there is no one else but me to take his place, no one else but the analyst, the back up for all back ups. If I were to le—if I were gone, all military confidence would be lost. Power resides in you. But the confidence...everyone will look to us, to your relationship with me. Especially during a war but even after it. That will be the benchmark of your reign."

Calmly, casually, she threw the wine in his face. She knew he was right.

"And so the Empress has an Emperor at her side, is that it?"

'Perhaps two,' he thought.

"Perhaps, my Lady, if you will pardon the connotations, more like a consort."

For a moment she melted: "Do you love me, Hal?"

"I will be loyal to you and you alone. I will do whatever is necessary to preserve your rule, protect your reign. And if I think the Sykols are wrong, and if I think your actions are wrong...I will...be honest."

She nodded, moved toward him, took up the hem of her dress and began to wipe his face—not tenderly.

"I would rather have a Captain who told me 'no' for my own sake than one who loved me too much and feared. I think ours was the better end of this deal. Solomon's joining the regular army will be helpful to the war against Inmar. And he shall be used for it."

'Solomon. Captain. Perhaps that's what Sykol Central had planned all along.' The thought of it made him shiver. 'They'll find it a miscalculation.'

He said nothing more, knowing when it was time to be quiet. Somewhere inside, a little piece of him guiltily apologized to a man he felt he was betraying.

"You're from Arché, aren't you?"

"Hello. Who are you?"

"I'm Bill. My parents made me come."

"By yourself?"

"No, they're over that way. It's the touring the Palace thing."

"Oh, I see. And you left them in the Hall of Mirrors all by themselves."

"Ah it's okay. They put this bracelet on me at the regular people entrance. They can find me anywhere with this because it's a highly secure place."

"A high security area."

"Yeah, that's it."

"And do you know that high security means you have to stay with the tour guide all the time?"

"I know. They'll come looking for me, and yell at me and make us leave. That's all I want to do anyway."

He knelt down to face the boy. "That sounds like a good plan. You're pretty smart. You should come work for me."

"You didn't answer me."

"What?"

"Aren't you from Arché?"

"What makes you say that?"

"You're all white, like the originals."

"You *are* smart. Actually I'm from here, Imperial World, where we keep a few thousand pure bred Archéans, so we can have their special talents to help us, more pure Archéans here than even on Arché."

"What special talents?"

"We see things."

"I don't get it."

"That's okay."

"Well how come I don't see any others like you?"

"Most of us live on the North Pole where the heat and sun don't hurt our skin."

"My friend Rejyk's an albino, you know what that is, he looks just like you."

"Yes, but his eyes aren't like mine are they?"

"Nah, yours are grey."

"That's right, and when the people from the lost world came to Arché a long time ago and lived with us, all the humans in the galaxy had children whose skins were different colors, hardly ever this white again, but their eyes turned lighter because of our grey, because of what we see."

"If you're from Arché then you know a lot about God, don't you? Mom says that's where all the religion people go."

They came with hurried anxiety: "Don't worry, Mrs. Morgain we'll track him right down," said the tour guide.

"Billy!" his mother shouted, and, running up to the boy, "William James Morgain Jr., you're in big trouble, young man! Wait till—"

"Oh my goodness! chimed the guide. "Captain Teltrab. Oh I'm sorry I let him go sir—oh this is such an honor—oh, I'm sorry, sir. It's these proximity alerts. They're set for a hundred meters; I keep telling Mr. Jacobi we've got to reduce these monitor warning distances, but he—"

"It's alright."

"—just ignores—"

"It's alright"—looking at the young guide's name tag—"Emily. Bill and I were just having a conversation."

"Oh, thank you sir; it's a real honor. Mrs. Morgain, this is the Captain of the—"

"Would you excuse us for just a moment." And looking back at the boy: "Bill I've never even been to Arché. We have a chapel here in the Palace. I've been there and you're going to get to see it on the tour. But I don't know very much about God." And then he whispered in the boy's ear: "Not as much as I know about his adversaries."

All she knew was that she was running for her life. Somewhere in a deep dark place down narrow labyrinthine passages.

"Please God, oh please." Panting.

She'd been asleep. Yes, that's it. She'd thought it was a nightmare. There were lights and voices. A loud blasting. And then the clawing thing tearing at her. And when she woke up, she hadn't been asleep. She was covered with blood and she was running.

"Oh!" Suddenly a wall and she fell in a heap. The floor hard and cold and above her lights flashing: darkness and then red. Dark again, and red like the blood flowing from her nose and mouth mixing with tears and sweat.

"Please." Pleading. "Please God, oh please."

The red, sticky circle at her hip oozed slowly down her white sleeping gown—the thigh, her knee, slippery between her bare foot and the cold bare floor as she clawed up the wall, crawled back to her feet, listening for the sounds of the monster coming closer.

"Did you see what it did to Ibanez?"

"Pipe down."

"Ripped his arm off—clean out of the socket."

"It can be reattached."

"I said quiet down, you two!"

If you had to be on a real action detail, Friberg was your man. That's what the non-coms said. Field Lieutenant Friberg was the best small unit commander in the Imperial Guard.

"Johnson."

"Sir."

"Tracking."

"Electronic signal may set off Sykol security protocols, Sir."

"They already know we're here."

"But they don't know who's here, sir."

"And we've got maybe ten minutes before they find out."

"Lieutenant."

"Who's that? Sambok?"

"Blair got a piece of it with his sword. I got a blood trail on infrared."

"Let's move."

Jekline Hyden, a promising young Sykol in behavioral research. Daughter of eighth generation Sykols. Superior in intelligence and form. Deep blue eyes and long auburn locks, matted now on one side and sweat wet on the other. She felt her way along the wall trying to hold back the sobs, clear the tears from her eyes—trying to see, trying to listen.

"Oh God. Oh God. Please. Pleeease." Panting and pleading.

And then she could hear. The heavy footfall, the tramping noise.

'Coming after me.' "Oh God." 'Coming.' "No!"

Screaming uncontrollably, she ran, she ran.

"Did you hear that?"

"I heard it."

"Who'd it just kill?"

"No one else is down here."

"Quiet down you two." And Friberg couldn't help but wonder: 'Who knows *what* else is down here.'

Sixty-seven levels and no Guardsman ever allowed past level ten. The Sykols weren't supposed to have more than twenty additional sublevels. Even the Captain hadn't known how deep they'd go or what they'd find.

Take this DNA tracer. Follow it. Wherever you go, I'll monitor from my Con. I'll try to cover your tracks.

But a siren was blaring, and warning lights strobing, and one of the ten man unit was hanging, still awake and lucid, over a friend's shoulder and watching their backs as he was being carried out to an extraction team, fully conscious that he'd been beaten by something which couldn't possibly have moved that fast, and fully aware of the fact that his partner carried *him* over one shoulder and his severed right arm over the other.

'We do it with eight, then,' thought Friberg as his team moved swiftly down featureless corridors.

Then the alarms turned off. Silence and darkness.

"Captain's bought us some time. Night vision." Helmet visors glowed green giving each man a cyclopean countenance.

Every breath was a whimper, a helpless little girl whimper. But she didn't quit. She groped her way through the darkness, hugged tight to the wall, held on and didn't quit. Why was it dark now? Why dark? Afraid. So afraid of the dark.

They could move more quickly now with night vision tech. Two by two in overlapping formation they moved down the hallway, checking each niche, each door—locked. Only one direction to go.

"Quickly, quickly," chanted Friberg.

Suddenly the walls were gone and the floor began to undulate. She fell screaming.

"Did you get that audio?"

"Bearing twenty meters dead ahead."

"That was not rage, but fear," noted Johnson.

"So it could have a hostage."

"No," concluded Sambok. "It's stalking prey."

"That was a woman's voice," noted Friberg.

And Johnson: "Poor girl."

There was a fresh gash in her knee. The hip injury poured fresh blood and her right wrist was shattered. The floor was cold and uneven—damp. She crawled, thinking of arms: a loving mother's embrace, a proud father's hug, and her lover's touch.

"Oh, Rico."

She wasn't meant to be in love with Rico Ibanez, a private in the Imperial Guard. She was only supposed to marry him. But he had fallen for her the moment they'd been introduced (*you two are being considered as a viable marriage co-op; get to know each other and we will assess the possibilities further*—no one ever accused Sykol Central of romanticism). She had found him kind and uncomplicated. He was a soldier serving his charge, and he loved it that Sykol Central had made it possible for him to love two women with all his heart: Janis and Jekline. She thought of his embrace. And stopped. And lay down on the cold floor and hugged herself. And she waited for it to come and kill her.

"Lieutenant."

"Go Ryker." He and Johnson were at point.

"It's stopped moving."

"Maybe it's feeding."

"Shut up, Cornell."

"It's directly ahead—maybe ten meters."

"But it's below us," added Sambok.

"You'll never believe why." Johnson stopped stalking for a moment.

And Ryker: "This is crazy."

They were at the corridor's end, but space hadn't. It had opened up and before them was a natural cavern.

Even Friberg hesitated a moment. Then: "Watch yourselves, boys. Wake up. Give me a three meter perimeter."

They fanned out the short distance, giving Friberg enough time to think:

'What's it here for? Must've come upon it trying to dig this level and abandoned...or did they make it? Who'd build a cave? The floor drops. Uneven. Have to be careful. This thing could hide anywhere in here. It could go on forever, and we can't scan.'

"Can't scan."

"Don't have to, sir."

"Johnson?"

"I've got it in my sights."

"Approach in pairs. Wait for my signal."

"Swords, sir?"

"Negative. Guns."

Eight plasma rifles powered up. Positions were established. Each man kept his visor aimed toward the target: a huddled mass of panting, bleeding flesh lay on the cavern floor. Five meters, now four. Three. Two.

"Hold."

'So meek,' thought Johnson. 'And so beautiful.' Ignoring the blood. 'How could she be so deadly?' He wanted to reach out to her, but he'd seen the consequences of that action. He stood with the others at disciplined readiness, paired in a half-circle around it.

"Kill it, sir?"

"No."

"Capture?"

"Hold position."

Then the glow in the eyes. The growl. And a super-human adrenal gland pumped its power through the body in an instant. Senses heightened and synapses fired in unbelievable numbers. Cerebral functions shut down and artificial instincts took over. The creature was upon them faster than even their engineered reflexes could allow them to pull gun triggers.

Six of them missed completely. Friberg, in the middle, nicked a shoulder and Sambok, next to him, shot her in the chest only because she attacked him first. He didn't see the plasma bullet's impact because something had wrenched his head to the side. He didn't see Friberg, beside him, get kicked ten meters distance—didn't hear the cracking of the ribs—because, by then, his head had been wrenched completely around, the last sound he *did* hear being the cracking of his own neck.

She was between them, four to the left, two right. The right flank knew to duck and dive. The left was already firing. She had simultaneously reached Cornell, but too late. The automatic fire blew off her arms, her legs. Her chest was a cavity when she hit the floor. A brain that refused the messages the body was sending it forced the lungs to one more exhale:

"Please God, oh please."

A woman who had loved her career, loved her life, loved her betrothed, woke up and ripped his arm from the socket, fled with injuries no one could survive, killed one of the finest warriors in the galaxy, injured another, and died wondering what the monster was that had shattered her peaceful sleep.

'Scrambled channel.' "Captain, Friberg here."

"Go ahead."

"It's a mess, sir, a real mess."

"You've got two minutes to get out of there."

"Negative sir. Target is dead. Sambok is dead. We need a clean up crew or stealth is bust whether they catch us down here or not."

"Hold."

Silence.

'Come on, Captain, come on.'

At the cavern entrance, the flashing red light poured in from the corridor. The siren began blaring again.

"Alright, Friberg. Sykol Central is having fits over elevator break downs, power outages, and a supposed radiation leak on level fifty-five that has shut down it and every floor below. I have a team on the way. Pull your men out."

"Yes sir. One more thing, sir."

"Go."

"There's a cave."

"What?!"

"It's huge. Somebody should check it out."

Silence.

"Confirmed. Report to my Con."

"Yes sir."

'A mess,' Friberg thought. 'A bloody mess up.'

- 33 -
Myth

Lazarus's human moment didn't last. He sank deeper into his fragmented world. He sat there staring at Quint. Staring in the dark, sitting across from him in darkness with those shining false eyes. No fire, no light, at all. They'd lost the equipment and snuffed out the jungle. It was only dark—Quint loved it so. Quint, that cold, calculator with an angry heart sitting there with his face swollen beyond recognition, heaving stomach acid in the pool where he'd left half-digested food and stimulants five pukings ago.

"You did it, you monster," he said.

"I'm not a monster," Lazarus replied.

"I know what you are. You did it. You killed me. Sitting across from me in the dark like you own the universe—perfect body, not a bite, not a scratch while my skin bleeds and flakes off and my bowels churn and rebel. Killed me."

"There was no choice."

"None in your programming."

"I'm not—"

"You are."

"Get off my back, Quint!"

"I know what you are!"

"Do you!" He moved toward him. "Do you know the pain that walks green and tormenting beside me! The hell hound who chases—damnable demon!—(he wretched) in every vision of my sleep or waking. He is there!

"Let loose the dogs? Ha! He tore me from my mother's womb ere I was conceived and put me in his incubus—" He stood and screamed to the sky: "I proclaim it! I claim it: the Imago Diablo!...my image...his image."

"Whose really?"

He didn't hear.

"Revenge!" Looking at Quint: "You wonder why I hunger?" Kneeling beside him, breath acrid. "He killed me, Quint." Crying? "Killed me before I ever killed you." Yes, crying. "I was made to be my father's death, my mother's vengeance."

"Your mother, the Queen of the galaxy."

"My goddess," he sighed.

"Your mother is a whore."

"Stop it."

"Your father, a saint."

"Stop."

"And you. I know what you are. You're a machine."

"No!"

"They took your decaying flesh and made you computer chips—made you a machine."

"Take—"

He hauled Quint up.

"Take thy—"

Hauled him into the air, holding by his neck.

"—beak from out..."

And then suddenly he looked at me. He was holding Quint, but he looked at me.

"I know you're in there. I know what you've done to Quint."

That should've been impossible.

"Why won't you leave my mind?!"

In the program I should have been invisible to him. I didn't exist.

Then Quint kicked his chest with supernatural strength, shattering his own ankle.

"You anachro-maniac!" he screamed. The anger throbbed in his temples. "You're not even a mind. You quit! They fried your brain and you let them take your art away! They scrambled you, and you would rather have lived insane than not been! Hypocrite! Compromiser! Rather have lived a mad man's fantasy than given up your gift!"

It was then that I realized those thoughts weren't Quint's, they were mine. Quint stumbled back as Lazarus released him.

"You gave up the true image, the true making, because you thought death ended it."

Quint could not have known such things, but he was saying them anyway.

"But what you got was nothing but copy."

Pause program!

He's me...I've written myself into Quint...written him into me...the anger I feel for what Janis did to Lazarus! But I can't stop...just need a breath. Can't stop...just take a breath. Do it.

Resume program.

I pleaded: "Lazarus, Lazarus."

Then pitied: "You're a catalog of clichés."

Then comforted: "It's not your fault, boy. Mother did this to you; you've paid for your pain in full. Lazarus, look at me! You don't owe her anything more!"

He heaved. He frothed. He bellowed something primal. And screaming, "No!" over and over, he came at us, at me and Quint.

It's your last chance, Quint. Make it a good one. Without thought, the safety on our rifle clicked, a laser dot set aim right between his eyes. He followed the beam into our face.

"Go ahead. But be sure."

'I can take him. I can.'

Shoving the barrel under his chin, we didn't bluff. Quint pulled the trigger.

The Kalliphi tell a story to their children of the Maker who once walked with the Kalli people. He taught them to *make* and they lived in the earth. When the man Odys followed Him home, up the skin of the great black tree, the Maker stopped walking and Odys was no more.

Fearing His anger, the Kalliphi cut down the mighty tree. And when it fell, the red serpents emerged from its roots, killing many. Then Killes made the *off way* and the people saw how the heads could be crushed under heel. But Killes was pierced in the ankle and died from the poison for he had not spoken to the people, not told them of the dream of the *off way* which had been given him by the Maker: two falling streams, each dripping in different rhythms, first together, then apart.

It was when the people saw the light of Philagapon's blade removing the serpent's head from its body that they first walked with him.

- 34 -
From 2295:
Grace!

Solomon's first tour of duty with the *regular* army was under General Scott whose division accompanied the seventh fleet destroyer *Kokkinoscardia*. They had pursued reports of raids on fringe planet ships by men from somewhere beyond the Empire's edge.

They came upon a habitable planet whose people had a centralized government brandishing an antiquated army—an easy jewel in the Imperial Crown. They swept into the capital city, reducing it to rubble with fighters in the air and following with occupation by troop landers. Solomon led his group of servo-powered soldiers straight to the city's heart where a fanatic population threw their explosives bound bodies at the invaders with a religious lust. The effort was vain. Plasma guns were emptied and servos strained as Solomon's armored troops pushed through the sea of living/dying flesh toward the capital building.

The Grand Khan of the petty planet died in the marble halls beside his people with shouts of acclamation—something the computer brains housed within the armor of each infantryman could only translate as having something to do with "death...the hand of God...coming judgment." Solomon secured a perimeter, rounding up all remaining political officials, and operatives. A search was conducted and the *hand of God* stumbled upon.

You have, perhaps, seen holo films or read stories where salvation was attained in the remaining few seconds of a countdown, the disarming of a bomb for example. You applaud the man who, through heroic effort, "saves the day" in the "nick of time." What Solomon Star experienced that day wasn't an act of heroism.

"What is it, Devsky?"

"Colonel Star. Sir, we've found an old style nuclear device in detonation mode."

They walked briskly through underground halls of the capital building.

"As far as we can tell, sir, it's old but it'll work."

"Tonnage?"

"We don't know. Enough to destroy the city, maybe."

"Time to detonation."

"Don't know that either. Private Ib'm, our tech-pro, is in there now. It's just sitting in a big room like a meeting hall—just sitting there."

Sergeant Devsky led him to the large white room where the bomb was located. Two dozen soldiers either stood about without obvious purpose or carefully surveyed the device. Their faceless helmets looked up at Solomon with faceless expressions of worry. No one noticed that the room with its rows of benches was arranged after the fashion of a chapel, the bomb being raised on an ornate pedestal.

"Who's Ib'm?"

"I am, sir."

"Report."

"The timer's over here. The numbers weren't too hard to figure out."

"And?"

"We have about four minutes."

"Devsky, sound evacuation. Use my emergency code."

"Done."

"Non-essential personnel, evacuate."

Seventeen left. Eight remained. Ib'm and three others worked with wires where they had removed a face plate from the silver box. The only features on the mechanism were a red button on top and a time counter on the side facing away from the entrance.

"Devsky, you and your men aren't needed."

"We're assigned to you, sir. We figure this is where we need to be."

'Good man.'

"Helmets."

Air hissed as they broke the pressure seals on their masks. Solomon wanted to see them: hair matted with sweat, faces dripping with it. Their heads seemed too small for the bulking blue armored bodies.

"Status."

"It's too old," said Ib'm, his head inside the machine's bowels. He talked while working: "Too primitive. I tried to locate the timer connections—it's hard to tell what anything is—tried to find them and end the count down or separate them from the detonator. Wasted my time. Tampering would've—hey what's this?—tampering would've set it off. Crawford, trace the current here. We can't find the core, can't locate the power source—that probably wouldn't do any good anyway. I have one more idea about the detonator if I can only figure out what it looks like."

"Maybe we should evacuate too," offered a boyish, blonde private.

"Four minutes weren't long enough to evacuate the city. Three won't be either," said Devsky checking the time. "Half the division is still here."

Ib'm pulled his head from the bomb's innards.

"Other side, quick. I think I've found it."

The three hauled their tools to the opposite side of the device and began to remove the access plate.

"Hurry," urged Ib'm.

"Two minutes, thirty seconds," said Devsky dryly.

Solomon moved to where he could see the timer counting down. The others who had stayed behind followed suit, crowding together, hearts pounding in rhythm. Ib'm dived into the casing again.

Solomon heard mumbling to his right. A dark skinned corporal stood chanting something with his eyes closed, lips barely moving.

"Praying, Corporal?"

Without looking: "Yes sir."

"Keep it up."

"A minute and a half."

"This is it. Trace the wires now."

Each second was a lifetime passing all too quickly, though thoughts fled and lives did not pass before their eyes. There was only the counter and the ticking.

"I'm going to make a cut."

There was a snip. The clock continued to tick. Ib'm's head emerged again.

"I think that was it. It should count down harmlessly."

"But my scanners still show armed," said Crawford.

Ib'm stood up. "That wasn't it. At least I didn't blow us up then."

"Less than a minute."

Ib'm began to pace, mumbling a liturgy of his own, hoping for a piece of knowledge yet to be recalled. The red button on top of the machine caught his eye.

"Thirty seconds."

"It couldn't be that simple."

He stepped up to the button and pressed it.

"Twenty-five. Still running."

"It isn't that simple."

He turned with a frustrated sigh toward the others, his furrowed brow still thinking.

Someone in the back spoke: "We're not going to make it, are we?"

Solomon looked at Ib'm. He shook his head, smoothed his brow.

Solomon put a hand on the shoulder of the praying corporal, then said, "You men died well."

For a moment he wondered, 'Why did I leave the Guard only to join the army? What hold does she still have?' And with ten seconds left: 'No hold any longer.'

They watched in silence; the timer ticked down to zero.

There was a blinding flash and then a wheezing sound like a hover car engine dying. Solomon looked around. Through the spots before his eyes he could see Devsky and the others doing the same.

"What happened?" asked someone in the back.

Ib'm fanned smoke away from the bomb and peered inside. He laughed.

"It malfunctioned. The old thing doesn't work anymore!"

Devsky and some others shouted whoops and hollers of joy while some joined Ib'm in his raucous laughter. Someone in the back fainted. Solomon calmly smiled his satisfaction, watching

the corporal who had been praying quietly repeat "thank you"
over and over again.

- 35 -
Wisdom

Staring at the crowd of villagers, Solomon thought, 'At least she has no hold here.' Charlie Grace, the poacher stood beside him, quietly now, lost in the joy of an awareness Solomon was yet to discover.

Their attention was suddenly drawn to a commotion at the outer edge of the village. From another great branch, a gathering moved quickly, attention given to an unseen epicenter. Shouts filled the air and Kalliphi emerged from buildings to join the throng. Solomon, the Savage, and the great sea of villagers followed suit, leaving Grace behind.

"I'll talk to you some other time, then," he called after them.

They came to the fringe of the gathering.

"What's going on?" he asked Savage.

"Bel. His tail has stopped the breathing of Gai-ju...little boy. Gaitoni killed the separate one. Too late—"

"When did it happen?"

"They say just before we came."

'Five minutes.'

To her surprise, Solomon grabbed her firmly by the arm and turned her toward him.

"You said his tail. How long does the paralysis last?"

"Why do you—"

Squeezing tighter: "In Imperial time, how long!"

"It is guessed one standard—"

He burst through the crowd with a fighter's precision. A boy, perhaps twelve or thirteen, was being carried on the shoulders of two men, his arms swinging lifelessly with their step. The boy's father, a grey bearded, medium height, stocky man followed. And unlike the image of the strong, stern Kalli native heretofore presented, he wept bitterly. Solomon grabbed the boy and pulled him to the ground against the struggle of his bearers. He paused briefly to feel for a pulse. None. He began to beat for the child, and to breathe.

Pump, pump, pump, pump, pump, breath...breath...pump, pump, pump, pump, pump, breath...breath—then arms wrapped quickly around Solomon; hands clutched his throat. The boy's father hauled the man of light away with a fierce and disparaging cry. The Kalliphi were good fighters: He had caught Solomon by surprise.

Instinctively the warrior raked his foot down the shin into the instep, pain loosening the hold; thumb grabbed, wrist spun and twisting out, he pushed the man away. He moved toward the boy, but the irate was upon him again; this time Solomon was prepared: a lightning punch: the man on his back, blood pouring from his nose. Others approached. Plasma sword drawn, Solomon whipped an elongated end at their feet, then turned off the sword as quickly as he'd brandished it.

"You trusted my father! Trust me."

Even those who did not understand his words knew the message. Those newly arrived saw his face in the frozen moment: the Philagi. They were moved to stillness.

Solomon grabbed at the chest of the father who had been slowly coming to his feet. He pulled him down over his son.

"Watch and do."

He began the heart massage again, moving in the rhythm of life. He placed the father's hands on the son's chest, one on the other, and pressed them, showing the amount of pressure to be exerted. A desperate father learns quickly. Solomon returned to filling the lungs with life. 'Too late,' he thought. The child was probably without oxygen too long. Even if not, could this artificial resuscitation keep him alive for an hour? And what if the paralysis were permanent?

Pump, pump, pump, pump, breath...breath.

They continued for endless minutes, stopping to check for a pulse periodically. The father continued to weep, though silently. Water and blood mixed and fell from the father's scruffy face onto the hands upon the heart. The people watched in silence.

Pump, pump, pump, pump, breath...breath.

The eyes stared, half opened, perhaps alive, perhaps dead, like a dreamer. The men continued, perspiring their exhaustion: pumping, breathing, checking, sweating, pumping, breathing, aching, pumping, breathing. Solomon wondered why they continued. Life now seemed hopeless. And yet...something in him said, 'Even so.' Something of hope urged him on.

Pump, pump, pump, pump, breath...breath. Until—

A sudden gasp—the body out of paralysis. Fighting, not reviving, the boy kicked himself back into existence (or had he been kicked?), heaving and pained, but alive and undamaged.

Murmurs, some shouts, came from the community all around. The father wept for joy, son held tight in his arms. The Philagi could not understand their words and was never told what they had said:

"He breathes life into the dead," said one in the crowd.

"We have a greater *off way*," said another.

A little girl stepped from the ring around Solomon and handed him two tiny flowers, one pink, the other white. He smiled and touched her arm, feeling somewhat awkward, but genuine in his attempt to respond.

"You are welcome." Savage, who had moved to the front of the gathering was pointing to the flowers: "You are welcome."

Solomon stood to thank her but was interrupted.

"Welcome," someone echoed in Solomon's own tongue.

"Welcome."

It was repeated by a few as the clan dispersed to go about their business, casually moving this way or that, as if that for which they had anxiously waited had never come, though without the accompanying disappointment. Or perhaps it had come, but was so natural, so much a part of the soul that it could scarcely be recognized, so needed that it could never have been really lived without. The people went away, taking the boy and leaving Solomon, the Savage and the father.

"Spilled my blood," he said. "Saved my son. Justice shows. And mercy."

He turned and walked away. Savage followed with Solomon. Nearing the tree's great trunk, the father veered one way, Savage another. She led Solomon along the giant's perimeter from one great branch to another, each so massive that they separated from each other hundreds of yards from the trunk. Things were not as casual as they appeared. The people were at ease, but inactive. The crowd had dispersed. Only a few remained outside in a community that must have housed thousands. Something was still not right. No. *Right* is wrong. Everything in that place was right. Choose, instead, *normal.* No one worked; perhaps it was a weekly day of rest. There did seem to be a great deal of cooking going on—so the strengthening aromas indicated. And somewhere in the branches above, he could hear music being played: pipes like flutes, and strings—bowed not plucked—vibrating a whisper song. The flutes were airy. The violin harps were gentle, mimicking voices of a chorus—whispery *oooo's* and serene *aaahh's*.

"The music is beautiful," he said to no one.

"Yes. It is," she responded.

"You're smiling at me."

They were heading away from the tree's center now, out, up a slowly ascending limb.

"I can smile," she said, looking him in the face. She took his hand and pulled him more quickly. "I looked into your heart this morning." She spoke in perfect Imperial dialect.

"What did you see?"

"You. I saw you. The Philagi."

"Said well, have," he replied.

"Come." They stepped onto a platform, a single piece of wood. At its corners were fastened finely woven ropes that reached up to the great tree's heights. In the middle a hole was cut with a single rope running from the heights through its center to some hidden fastening below. She motioned Solomon to pull on this rope. He reached high to test the strength he would need to put the counter weights in motion. He was surprised to find the platform lift with little effort. In fact he needed to pull on the rope only every so often, a gentle prod to continue their coasting upward.

'Excellent engineering.'

The air was space about them since, near the trunk, the giant branches were without tributaries or greenery. The limbs stretching above and below were huge, even from a distant perspective. The trunk was a black wall, without boundaries, without any hint that it curved into the form of a pillar. In the distance, more of these elevators could be seen in operation. In the dozen or so mighty branches above, no pulley system, no counter weights showed. Such oneness. They approached a branch. As it neared, Solomon noticed rectangles cut along its side. Young men and women leaned casually out of these windows, talking or watching birds fly.

The birds: most of them large, like the place. Some looked like gulls, but not white—grey, green, others like ducks, still others like eagles with giant wing spans, soaring in regiments or diving alone, or floating on the spring holiday breeze.

As they passed within fifty feet of the branch, Savage called out to some friends: "Charisu T'kai, Charisu Joni."

A cluster of the watchers waved. "Charisu," they called, and watched the two disappear with countenances of expressionless ease.

They climbed higher, up between two forked branches. Here an elaborate network of rigid vines had been woven. They passed through its midst where Savage pointed out its purpose.

"See there."

Children were swinging and flipping through the vines. Their movements were masterful, expert acrobatics. They smiled and laughed, but gently—not raucous or bold. Everyone clapped when one boy completed a particularly difficult performance. Then two girls—twins—swung a duet, one holding to a vine, the other to her sister, wheeling through the air.

Solomon and Savage topped the fork. The music Solomon had been enjoying was coming from this level, though he could see no performers. On one of these branches was cut a long pit—seven feet deep and as many wide. In its bottom something smouldered orange; a light smoke rose from the burning embers. Iron rods lay across the pit every few feet. To these were fastened cuts of meat, no whole animals, only masterful cuts smoking slowly. Over the fire watched three men, one elderly, one adult, one nearly a child. The aged fellow sat on a stool, apparently watching over the meaty manipulations of the others.

"I've had little meat since I came here."

"Watch carefully. Requiring a reverence is in the eating of flesh."

Behind the pit was a hole. A woman emerged, obviously walking on steps. She held a red strip in her arms, hugging it close to her breast. As she turned it over to the elderly man, she noticed the approach of two more women bearing the body of what looked like a fawn. The meat bearer motioned them to place the beast on the ground near the limb entrance. There she spoke to the animal, hugged its neck, and joined the others in lowering it into the hole. The elderly man had been singing a song over the uncooked strip. Upon its completion, he bowed and then turned the meat over to his partners. The smoky barbeque aroma filled Solomon's nostrils and made him salivate.

He turned to see more grey haired men and women sitting on stools on the branch behind him, playing games on boards of wood. Nearby, mothers sat nursing their babies, and a varied group sat, very close together, listening to a man read from a small leathery book. Upon seeing the Philagi rise, several paused to stand and watch. Some who had been below, when he first came, made the stand for a second time. Others had not seen him yet. All were deeply contemplative, however they occupied their time. There was activity. But the people were quiet as Solomon had noticed before; the community was subdued.

One more branch and they stepped out, moving again toward the mighty trunk. There were a few people walking about. Here was even greater quiet. There were more buildings on this branch than others, perhaps a dozen, never too many. Beautiful housings with convex roofs.

"What have you seen now?" Savage asked.

He thought for a moment. "The people are good."

She said nothing, wanting more with her silence.

"And quiet. There's something wrong."

"That sees."

"What?"

She stopped. Faced him. "It is not a...wrong, wrong." She grimaced, shook her head. "The word I need."

"*Incorrect* ?"

"No."

"*Bad* ?"

"That sees better—*wicked*! That sees. It's not a wicked wrong." They joined eyes. "It's a time to worship." Pause. "It's a sad wrong."

"I know that feeling," he said.

"Good. I would explain much. Sometimes my speaking is good, sometimes not so. Sometimes—"

"Sometimes there is no explaining."

She looked at him with genuine wonder: "Yes." The nod. "Yes."

They continued toward the tree's center, then turned to their right, following the trunk in that direction past numerous trunk-cut dwellings.

'My father is dying,' he thought as they walked, but he said nothing.

They stopped at last at an entrance built into the great tree. Carved out windows, doorway and a protruding roof for porch cover were the only clues that it even was a home. The natural ebony beauty had been preserved as much as possible all over the giant. A small wooden table and two chairs sat on one side of the door and a bench against the tree on the other; its back edge was perfectly contoured to the tree's grooves. A Kalli woman, middle aged, serene, stepped out from the home. She looked familiar to Solomon. She carried a wooden plate and cup which she placed on the table without looking up. When at last she noticed the newcomers, she smiled a quiet smile, saying, "Charisu Gai-ja." She held out her arms at the elbow.

Savage approached. "Charisu Maté." They embraced gently, not moving—no pats or rubs—still. And they held their hug for a minute, ensuring their presence for each other, body and soul. At last releasing, Savage's mother approached Solomon and took his hand. Her eyes searched him deeply.

"Charisu Gaiton...Philagi."

"Charisu Maté," he clumsily replied.

She smiled. "Say Gaitan."

He smiled.

"I am Sofi. Come." She motioned him to the table and moved the plate and cup toward one chair. He sat, surveying his fare: water, a brown, steaming flat-bread with an aroma of cinnamon butter, and little pink fruit—cranberries the color of bubble gum—which he had not yet seen on Kall. Without another word, the two women disappeared through the doorway. Solomon didn't hesitate to ponder the whereabouts of his father, or to ask to see the leaders of the people. He accepted. He ate.

After an hour, Savage returned to Solomon and sat with him, speechless.

"Sofi is your mother?"

"Yes."

"And what *is* your name?"

"To you I am Savage," she said, but not in the same way she had said it before. He nodded and smiled a little, satisfying smile.

They sat in silence, each pensively watching nothing in particular. Solomon had wanted to see his father, but found himself strangely patient. Nor did he voice his question. The food had revitalized him, enlivened him, and he was full—content. His mission was the farthest thing from his mind. A new perspective had come to him; he could not put it into words. But he was glad for the silence. He needed the solitude, only it had to be here among people. So he waited, and he wondered, and he watched nothing in particular until his eye caught the still white boots, his red stained boots. And he wandered.

- 36 -
From 2288:
Disgrace

"Hello, Mother."

"Solomon! You startled me."

"Come sit with me and watch the fire."

The spacious Palace suite, reserved for the Captain of the Guard and his family, was dimly lit. Solomon sat on a long multi-sectional couch. His mother, moving with serene maturity joined him in front of the fire. She noticed that his appearance was clean and proper—he wore a standard uniform; boots, buttons and buckles were polished—except that his face was unshaven, apparently for several days. She could not be sure, for he had not allowed her in his room nor gone out or come home when she had been present.

"Why did you start a fire?"

"I was cold."

"Oh."

"I still am."

Crackling silence. Solomon stared blankly at holos floating on a plexiglass mantel above the fire place. Firelight made them come alive: Solomon's father, standing tall and proud; Davidson's marriage to Alathia—liquid grace; the Pentaf at age fourteen— there was Immanuel.

"Look at me son. No matter what you do, you cannot disappoint me. I always love you."

"I know you do."

'Such confidence in him.' "What do you feel?"

"Empty."

She put her hand on his shoulder. "You wish to say no more to me." She knew it.

Solomon stifled a response and looked at his mother with slight surprise.

"The Chief sent you, didn't he?"

"Yes, he did. But I will not betray you. I did not press you."

Nevertheless, Solomon could not help feeling annoyed.

"Why?"

"That is what they want to know."

He turned away, mumbling: "Part of the job."

"I have something for you." She stood and walked to a painting that hung to the left of the fireplace. The heat from the fire was uncomfortable. 'Why did he start it in the middle of summer?' She touched the wall to the left of the painting—an unusual blurred water color of the Palace—and it became translucent. A depression appeared in the wall behind. Alathia reached through the painting and removed a small black holo disk. She turned to Solomon.

"It's from Kall—your father."

Solomon held his expression, but he could not hide his fear from his mother.

"It arrived yesterday."

"What does it say?" He held out a tentative hand.

"How should I know?" She gave it over. He clutched tightly the cool metallic square. It seemed to pulse in his hand—'Must be my heart.' Without speaking he turned to go to his room. Then, pausing:

"Will you go to be with him?"

"My place is here."

"Always duty. Duty to the Imperium. Isn't there anything else for us?"

"Not always duty, Solomon."

He nodded. 'How should I know?' "Thank you, Mother."

The holo display in Solomon's room came alight. Davidson Star's hair was beginning to grey. Solomon thought it amusing that his father had grown a beard. The young man's eyes began to glisten.

"My son." Solomon held his breath. "I trust that this message finds you well and in good spirits. Retirement here on Kall makes communication slow and rather fragmented. There have been rumors here—whispers in the trees—about internal events on Imperial World. It remains hard, even for me, to discern the truth. The Kalliphi have a saying: 'Truth is as real as the limb that holds you up.'" Shrug. "Who knows?

"I thought that I would keep in touch. Life here gives one the chance to develop...new perspectives. Nature works with certain balances, certain harmonies. Hard to see, where you are—too many walls. But here—people here learn the lesson of balance. Sometimes you must choose balance, son." He clutched his shirt at his heart. "You have to agree in here."

Pause.

He began to cry with his son.

"You have always known, son." He nodded with a smile: 'I know what's happening; I approve.'

They had both known. The disk would have been previewed. They both understood perfectly.

Some attention should be given as to why Solomon Star was not dead, having just done what no one else in history would have dared. A great deal may be attributed to no one knowing what to do. Primarily, however, permission for the resignation of a high ranking official in the service of the most powerful woman in the galaxy, head-in-tact, was arranged for by the Imperium's own Sykols.

If a Guardsman were to become embittered or discontent with his position (situations made supposedly inconceivable by Imperial conditioning), he could resign his post. This *safety valve* clause gave psychological release to the Guard. The cycle produced is fascinating: Knowing he can quit any time helps release occasional dissatisfaction or, more often, fear of failure in a Guardsman, while the thought of giving up his duty—his way of life—or the thought of failure is so repugnant to him that it shocks discontentedness out of the mind or motivates greater success oriented behavior. More importantly, the resignation opportunity insured that vital mistakes would not be made due to lack of commitment or even attempts on an Imperial life by a frustrated guard who could not escape his situation.

Imperial Sykols depended on this technique *just in case*. Given advanced methods of Sykol engineering, it was never to be used. They were only wrong once.

They gathered in the main throne room of Imperial Palace:

A mourning Empress

An edgy, loyalty torn Guard

The Chief Sykol

The twice-broken Pentaf

A little noticed collection of disappointed young women

Alathia.

The room stretched for a half-mile in width and depth. Three stories of balconies, lining the marble white walls, were filled with onlookers: Sykols, officials, Royals distantly related to House Amric, maintenance workers, and handfuls of soldiers from the half-dozen lesser Royal Guards on station at Imperial Palace. The great main Palace doors opened directly into this chamber. From the Empress's position at the other end of the room, the doors looked barely open (when actually a forty foot gap allowed pink light to stream in from outside). A red carpeted pedestal elevated the platinum Imperial throne (ironically, a plain, undistinguished chair) twenty feet above the floor: Janis sat in regal fashion. The Chief and four members of the Pentaf stood to either side and slightly behind the throne. The Guard— all five thousand, dressed in best uniform, created a corridor with lines on either side of the throne, facing each other, extending the length of the hall.

Tension: Janis breathed quick and short; rigid Guardsmen— rigid; white frocked Chief with white knuckles.

He broke through the ranks a hundred yards from the pedestal, a shadow in the distance. Janis's heart quickened.

He had received and obeyed the message:

APPEAR BEFORE THE EMPRESS
IN FULL DRESS UNIFORM
OR YOU WILL BE EXECUTED

He marched briskly up to the stage—the semblance of confidence—and assumed an at-ease position.

The Empress mustered her regal authority: "*Mr.* Star. We regretfully accept your resignation."

Release. No one had known her decision.

He didn't flinch.

Janis handed a scroll to Hal Teltrab who, taking it, stepped away from the throne. Simon Lazar, who would now be Teltrab's number two as Hal had been Solomon's, followed him down the stairs to the floor, carrying a silver bowl, eyes clouded with disbelief, shining with panic.

They stopped before him and stood in silence. He looked at Hal who avoided his gaze. Eyes averted, he held the scroll out to Solomon.

"Ca—Solomon Star. Take this discharge from my hand and you turn your back...on your loyalty, your duty...your charge."

He could see Lazar shaking his head slightly. As he took the scroll from Teltrab, Lazar mouthed the words, "This can't be."

Teltrab started to reach for his shoulder but hesitated, fist clenching. He saw the hesitation. "Do your duty!" he barked in a whisper.

Hal looked up into his eyes of compassion.

He smiled: "It's okay."

Teltrab lifted a hand to the insignia on his left shoulder. Tore quickly, turned and dropped the insignia into the bowl. Then the right shoulder—rip! Then each of the breast buttons, in turn: removed and placed into the bowl. Then the chest insignia—the crest of the Imperium—torn off along with a patch of jacket cloth. The Lieutenant moved to his side, found the tiny tear that had been made in his sash, completed it, removed the sash and stepped back around to Lazar. He placed the cloth into the bowl, removed it, dripping rich red dye onto the floor. Teltrab knelt with it and streaked the front of the white boots. They would be a sign of the Guard no more. The new Captain of the Guard stood and returned the sash to the bowl.

Reaching for the sword clipped to the belt worn beneath the sash: Solomon Star, the man of light, beat him to the draw. He activated it and tore the air in a vertical ark before him, causing Hal to step back. As quickly, he deactivated the weapon. A gasp went across the hall. No Guardsman moved.

Solomon held up the sword and directed his gaze at the Empress. "For my years of service. I keep this for myself."

Janis dropped her iron jaw, then stood and strode to the pedestal's edge to fling her righteous fury at the impudent rebel. The Chief followed quickly and placed his hand on Janis's shoulder before she could speak. The Empress turned her head a moment, but stopped before she eyed the Chief with indignation. What the Chief had intended to warn her about caught her attention by itself.

In the right column of guards, not far from the pedestal, a single Guardsman, a field lieutenant named Friberg, was looking at the Empress. 4994 men stood at perfect attention: hands to side, eyes front. Every guard but one. His eyes, his entire head—openly turned toward Janis, and with a hand he grasped the sword at his belt. He was angry! She looked around; could see it in the others: tension, the divided loyalties. She pictured the power of the galaxy slipping through her fingers and began to tremble.

Solomon had followed her gaze to Friberg. He, too, saw, and he smiled at her reaction. And he knew: At that moment he was the most powerful man in the universe—able to topple the Empire. He felt it like a surge of adrenalin—

—and it revolted him.

Janis began to sway. The Chief reached out to steady her. "Leave!" she hissed and turned to reseat her drained body.

Solomon did not wait. He clipped his sword in place and, without looking at any of his friends, turned and began the half-mile walk to freedom. He felt content, strangely so, for the first time in years. The Guard had been instructed to turn away as Solomon walked by. None did. He was a hundred yards away by the time Janis reached her throne. She watched him go in silence.

'He will pay.

He will pay.'

As he neared the main doors, the day breeze billowed and flapped his torn, opened jacket. He picked up his pace. At the door a single man—a groundskeeper—handed Solomon the sum total of his worldly possessions, all of which he had fit into one blue duffle bag. He slung the strap over his shoulder. A *one use* Imperial Shuttle pass was pinned to the strap. The sky was a bright clear pink.

The trek to Imperial City was long and leisurely. Once there he found a *lift* to the space port. While walking through the terminal, he was stopped by an elderly woman who asked him for directions and thanked him for his help. Standing in line to check-in for his ship, he watched a mother pacify her screaming child with a treat, and he was witness to an argument between a gate attendant and an obnoxious, overbearing customer over whether or not the man's prize pet tritzu could travel in the passenger compartment. The whole commonality of the experience took Solomon completely by surprise.

He watched with fascination the passers-by while he waited for his ship. He decided that he liked the new color combination of his boots. Eventually he boarded a commercial space ship and bid the home of his youth goodbye.

I have a tendency to fall back on analysis, a sometimes annoying trait picked up from long hours spent with my mentor, Captain Telbrab. Here, then, is what I see:

Three forces moved Solomon Star: a sense of duty, a high degree of confidence, and intense compassion. Confidence gave him the ability to overcome guilt, the fear of failure at his duty. Compassion empowered him to overcome his *desire* for Janis. The balance between compulsion to duty and confidence in himself might have been maintained for years, but compassion demanded more than guilty dependence. It demanded love. Because of the darkness, however, the Empress would not give it.

In response to his ensuing apathy, the man of light turned his compassion toward his Guard. When he learned of the *Crisis*, that his people had died for nothing (to be sure there had been accidental deaths among them—in training drills—but nothing like this deliberate act—such deliberate deception), nothing remained to hold him to his duty.

But is this explanation sufficient? The event remains incredible to many. Given the elaborate systems of the Sykols (their behavior control methods, attitude adjustment tables, motivation control techniques), created for the purpose of perfect power maintenance—perfect control—that one man could pull away from that control so completely seems impossible. After all, one can only say so much for free will. I've concluded that the problem is not one of credibility, but of perception: Too many in the Empire suffer from the illusion of autonomy. No. The explanation is not sufficient. But here it is in all its simplicity: Men of light cannot endure the heart of darkness.

Eventually, the shadows fade.

- 37 -
The Rose

If the following, too, makes little sense, I can only offer this truth: It is exactly how he described it to me so many years later. I asked him to explain it. He said, "I just did."

The people abandoned their homes within the giant and without and gathered in an open space on the main limb before the central entrance—a fifteen foot arch resembling the shape of a cathedral doorway. A fire was built upon a wide slab of rock. Dozens of children walked to and from it, slowly, reverently. Those approaching brought large diamond-shaped leaves which they fashioned into spheres as they neared the fire. At the flames' edge they turned the small opening in the sphere to the heat to fill with the rising air and then released the floral balloons to the sky once filled. They rose like dull stars and disappeared into the sky. Torches were lit and placed in every woman's hand. About the fire the adults formed a semi-circle.

And waited.

And watched.

And *saw*.

Something was happening. Something wonderful. Something only half conscious. The people watched, as they had done when Solomon first entered the village, with quiet intent, participating in that silent vigil with an effort beyond that of clashing warriors. There was something electric in the air. But the flow of energy was gentle and steady, humming in harmony with the living. Whatever was happening within the black giant seemed without source, yet it produced a profound effect on those outside.

Three men broke the perimeter, walking side by side toward Leviathan. Solomon thought the light almost blinding within that circle. But the tree, unlit by man, shone even more brightly, as if fired by the planet's very molten core. The entrance was a window to another world, a world of light.

He blinked.

The two nameless men escorted him through the doorway, into the heart of light.

The Philagi fell forward head long, losing himself in the passages of the dark giant. Jonah: He floated endlessly, coursing through its veins with the rich red liquid that carried him further in with every action of the pumping heart. White cells, shining purest light, approached and examined him, then, with caressing acceptance, sped him on his way. Imperceptibly, the scarlet stream darkened and so began the return trip. A blast of wind!— and he too was refreshed. At last the heart spread out before him in glorious expanse and he joined in perfect rhythm with the song of the world which beat in the souls of every Kalli human, animal and plant. He reveled in the pure living source, experiencing an ecstacy in *That* which meant little to his thinking being. The repast was brief; the journey continued, carried on by that first blood bursting through the aorta to continue the living cycle anew—on to the final goal.

Spinning—rising...

Spinning—rising...

Rising through that familiar home, at last he was expelled onto the jelly brain. Pulses of electricity shot over its surface and through its translucent core. He tried to stand and found the surface malleable, solid enough to stand on only after sinking to his knees. Walking was impossible. He found he could make his way quite easily by bouncing on his behind and pushing off with his legs and arms. He traversed in rubber-ball leaps with a child's enthusiasm. At last he came upon a ring of gold, spinning ever before him just out of grasp. Light radiated from its center, coalescing into form. He saw images there of himself, some familiar, others not, these latter being of such a kind as could not find space for description in all the volumes of the worlds. The crystallization continued and images gave way to words, for definition is often necessary. They solidified, cohered, pulsing with a brightness in pulmonary rhythm:

THE MADE

THE MADE

'Repetition,' he thought. 'The made with the made. That's why they gave up their woods.' The ring spun away from the words and girded him round to complete an age old circle.

Solomon emerged to the reality of his father's death bed. Davidson Star, the Philagapon, lay in a small, candle-lit room on a cot beneath warm animal skins. The Philagi dropped to his knees; he bent over his father's face. It was old—the beard, the hair, white and grey; the cheeks the eyes lined, but the brow smooth. The place smelled of death. Beads of sweat rose from his forehead. An aged nurse went to wipe them away with a cold rag. Solomon beat her to it, using his own hand. The skin felt like leather: tough and cold.

"Father, it's me."

Philagapon stared blankly. His shallow wheezing filled the tiny room.

"Why is he dying?"

No one knew. Here's a rub. No one knew why he was dying. No disease had claimed him, no accident injured him. To them it would remain a mystery. To us? Perhaps the best explanation is in what Savage had said to Solomon on the river. Davidson Star was being held in the throes of a new lesson, an extension of the truth: *The made must live with the Maker*. This he now learned well. And it only cost him everything.

"Father."

The eyes focused. Recognition showed in a thin smile.

"I'm here, sir. It's Solomon." He took his father's hand and clutched it to his heart. Davidson held tight.

For hours they probed each other's eyes in silence, a tear running occasionally down one cheek or the other. They saw therein the unspoken soul and knew it after the knowing of *eisos*. It said everything.

As the sun dawned over the black giant, their vigil ended. Davidson Star turned his eyes skyward, and, seeing the universal benevolence of Being, gave himself over with his final words:

"The wonder! The wonder!"

- 38 -
Chance Meeting

They were returning. She walked beside him, not in front.

"I understand now why you gave up your woods," he said.

She looked at him without responding. Their eyes met. He continued:

"Why you signed the treaty with the Imperium—my people." Silence still. *"The made must live with the made."*

"That s—...Yes, you have seen."

"Even if *the made* means the entire galaxy."

"*Eisos* cannot be for Kall alone."

"The lesson of Philagapon."

"The lesson you have learned."

"*Oneness.*"

"And I have learned," she added.

"What have you learned, Gaitan?"

She was pleased to be called *woman*. "Knew I why you were called, but not why sent. Now does it see."

"The Imperial control I thought was missing."

"More."

"More?"

"That the Kalliphi are not so free—"

"—as you thought you were."

She walked beside him, not in front. First they came upon a dimming. Nearer, then, and smoke and stench then; they came upon bodies: Beli—dead and decaying and oozing. They found Quint propped against a tree: a corpse that would not die. He had, for some reason, desperately wanted to see Solomon with his own eyes. Not like you and I can see Solomon now, in the glow of holo projection. I...I mean *Quint*...saw the man of light with eyes! Human eyes. Look...they're there now, bending over him with compassion.

"Lazarus was faster," came his croaking voice.

"What's that?"

"Faster than me."

Solomon looked at Quint's grotesque face, the broken legs and arm.

"Who are you?" he asked.

"Huh?"

"Your name?"

"Who? Oh, Quint. He's long gone. Lazarus was faster. Faster than Quint. Quint's a dead man, now.

"I don't—"

"Given it up."

"—understand."

"The body. He's dead now!"

I look at them together. Solomon and Quint, Savage standing nearby. I remind myself that I am not Quint. He is a holo projection, not a human one.

"I had to meet you," Quint continued. "Had to...see you. I kept the lungs going—breathing by will, by will pumping the heart of a dead man. Can you hear me? Can you hear me breathing? Days now. Willing this being, shooting those dragons...."

He started to drift, then pulled himself back:

"No! I had to meet you, Star. Had to see your face." He laughed. "Without wanting to shoot it off."

"I'm sorry I—"

"Choosing...choosing...never able to choose for myself. Not—...the universal voyeur. Never completely able not to watch, even...even...even in the middle of intensest action."

Solomon was as confused, as I was becoming. Stop looking at me Quint. I'm invisible. Here's the man you wanted to see, spent days killing the Beli to stay alive long enough to see.

Solomon brought us back. "Tell me—tell me what to—"

"He's out there." The voice was suddenly urgent, alert. "Waiting for you. Lazarus."

"Lazarus?"

"He'll try to kill you."

"This Lazarus."

And then his body began to spasm, his heart to fail. He had nothing left to offer, nothing left to want. And then our last thoughts, no life left to speak them...

....Hold me. Let me....feel...

...you...as...

...I...go.

I had just enough strength to leave my secret room and stumble as far away down the corridor as I could before losing consciousness. Sykol doctors diagnosed exhaustion, but I knew better. Making Quint had almost killed me.

- 39 -
Imperial World:
One Week Before Solomon's Arrival on Kall

She woke up screaming. Shot up, flailing her arms and legs about, warring with hidden demons in the sheets, her body covered in sweat, the bed soaked, her chest heaving.

"My Lady! Are you alright?" The attendant burst in from her own sleep in an antechamber. "My Lady Janis?! The lights."

"No Rachel. Leave the lights off."

Hesitation.

"The nightmares again."

'Such sympathy,' she thought. 'Just as you've been trained to do.' And with docile voice: "Yes, Rachel. My dreams...."

"Tell me." She moved toward the bed.

"I—"

A knock.

"Oh, the guards, my Lady. They will want to check—"

"I don't want to see them."

"But they'll insist—"

"Tell them to go away!" she shrieked.

The startled servant moved quickly, fearfully. Had her eyes glowed in that panic scream?

Alone for a moment, Janis measured the dark, and stared at a picture in her mind.

"God, how I want you dead." Venom in her voice.

Then she started to cry. The tear drops became streams, the sobs screams. The attendant, Rachel, returned to find her Empress as she had a dozen times before, holding her arms out to her, begging for comfort. And against all protocol, the Sykol servant woman climbed upon the bed and took the Queen of the galaxy in her arms and rocked her gently, sprinkling her own tears on Janis's head.

"Hal."

"Lady?"

"Do you sometimes feel like it's too much for us at our age?"

"I feel like it's too much for anyone, whether thirty-four or a hundred and four."

"Yes, well perhaps we'll have it down when we're a hundred and thirty-four."

"Perhaps."

"I keep having bad dreams."

"I know."

She looked at him. Then away. "Yes, of course you do."

Silence.

"Lady."

"Hal?"

"You've the weight of the galaxy on your shoulders. Make no mistake about your strength, your stability. Your passions make you a little less predictable than the Chief would like."

"Please, let's not—"

"But they make your rule aggressive. I believe you can bear the weight." He paused. "Unfortunately, I have to make that burden a little heavier right now. I have to—"

"Good morning."

The Chief stepped from the elevator at the room's center dressed as ever in white clothing, white lab coat and with his ever present note pad in hand. He bowed curtly to Janis, then moved to the window.

"Ah, how I love the view here. I'm glad you reopened this room. *Huposthesa* truly is the great tower, and a crowning achievement of Palace architecture."

"You're in a good mood this morning," Janis noted.

"I have reason to be." He moved away from the row of windows toward the small table where Hal and the Empress had taken to eating breakfast together regularly atop the great tower. *Huposthesa*. So much had happened here. Ten years before, a falling white glove had shattered the universe. Here in the great Palace tower, even as Janis motioned the Chief to sit with them, a second shattering....

"I have reasons to be less cheerful," Hal began.

And Janis: "Oh?"

He hesitated, checked the chrono piece on his wrist. Then the orchestration began:

"It is an impressive tower, Empress. Twenty stories high." He nodded his head blankly, pursed his lips. "But did you know the Palace isn't as high as it is deep?"

"Of course. What do we have, Chief, thirty sub-levels?"

Hal: "Over sixty."

"Sixty! Chief, why don't I know—"

"Really Janis I don't know what he's talking about." The annoyance barely noticeable. "Captain, I don't know where this streak of insolence is coming from—"

"Sykol conditioning, Chief. I was meant to test the Captain of the Guard, to question his choices, analyze, and offer alternatives. Then I became the Captain and I had no one else to work against. Except you."

Sternly: "There are thirty-two sub-levels in the—"

"There are sixty-seven sub-levels. I know, because I've seen them."

He laughed: "That's nonsense."

"Why, Chief, because I couldn't get down there without your knowing? Because of the homing device planted in the heads of every Guardsman at birth? All done with the best intentions, of course, my Lady, but information to which the Guard is never privy. Here's mine." He took it from his sash. "I had it surgically removed from my skull and from those of a hundred of my key men. I found it...necessary."

"Why, whatever for, Captain?"

"In a moment, Lady, but you must come see." His tone was suddenly light hearted. "It's quite amazing." He stood and offered his hand to Janis.

"Now what's this about, Captain?" Concealed annoyance was now bottled exasperation.

As Hal and Janis moved toward the room's east windows, the Captain spoke over his shoulder:

"Dr. Gaheris, by the way, Chief." The old man was standing to follow. "One of your research Sykols. He has a brother in the Guard. That's how I got to him. He performed all the operations months ago and then applied for his sabbatical. I saw him off personally. Here now." Hal bent over the wide sill and surveyed the gardens below. Then, drawing back, he said, "Look there Empress," pointing. "The Andian lake—a full mile away."

"Yes, what of it?" She too was starting to lose patience.

"Caverns, my Lady. A vast network of passages running beneath the Palace, running as far out as the lake. All natural, but tied into the Sykol network at floor number sixty-seven. You won't believe what we found down there."

The Chief had stopped twenty feet away. He raised his hands to his hips.

"The radiation leak was your doing."

"Yes it was."

"Radiation leak? What radiation leak? One of you explain."

"Isn't it obvious. The resignation *Incident* has taken its toll on the Captain over these ten years. He was never intended to—"

"*Intended*. You mean designed, engineered. I've seen your body factories now."

"I'm calling for an immediate incompetency diagnosis. Janis move away from the Captain, we're going for a team of specialists now. Come with me, I fear for your safety."

"The elevator's locked down, Chief. You can't get out till I say so. And don't bother with your sub-vocal communicator. The signal's jammed. A handy device, I must add. I had Dr. Gaheris implant one in my throat before he left."

She moved between them, a step from Hal's face, demanding his gaze with her own.

Calmly: "Alright, that is enough." And turning: "That's enough. We're facing a civil war inside six months. I won't have one here." Then fury: "I will not have one here!" She turned to Hal again.

"Of course, my Lady. Perhaps, Chief, we can strike a bargain." His eyes remained on hers.

Coldly: "What bargain?"

"You agree to allow me to speak freely regarding certain security concerns I have with Sykol Central and afterward, at the Empress's command, I'll accompany you to the evaluation facility—let your people poke around in my head." His eyes reached out to hers: 'Say yes.'

"No. This is—"

"I think the Captain's idea an excellent one. Don't you, Chief?"

"I do not!"

Ignoring him: "Let's listen to the rest of his wild ravings." She moved back to the window, leaned her back against the sill and folded her arms. She gave Hal an introduction:

"This is all part of that security break that happened last year. The one which you embarrassed us over during that cabinet meeting."

"Yes. That's right. I broke into the Sykol network. I had been trying for five years. Ever since problems with Inmar began to escalate. I began to suspect Sykol Central when the intelligence reports from the military started disagreeing with my own. It only took one file, Chief. One mishandled communique sent to Imperial Palace from across the galaxy—one report that was traceable to its true point of origin: Imperial Palace. The Sykol Bureau. Writing the protocols took substantially longer, but once I beat your systems and masked my presence, it was easy to confirm what I'd been gathering for years: that the complaints made against the Empire by the Inmar coalition are true. The economic disruptions were real, the plagues on Irakeen and Jorda not only real but caused. By us. No real pirates in the shipping lanes of those sectors, of course; no, those were special covert operatives—military raiders in disguise commanded without my knowledge to acts of terrorism without my sanction."

"That's a constitutional violation. Are you saying the Sykols were making military decisions?"

"And carrying them out. Why? Because they're making this war happen. They intend to provoke Inmar to rebellion."

"I don't believe—"

"They've done it before. The last rebellion six hundred and fifty years ago. And another seven hundred and twenty years before that. They follow cycles. Every seven hundred years or so the Sykols create a major rebellion to make the people of the galaxy renew their loyalty to the Empire, to see the need for its protection. This one wasn't meant to come this early, though, was it? The Emperor's death, my Lady Janis's early ascendance to the throne, and Captain Star's resignation at the time of Inmar's visit to Imperial world—too dangerous a combination. Serious fears about the weakening of your power demanded that Inmar be the scapegoat for House Amric *now* rather than his heir in the next generation."

"Conjecture, Captain."

"No, Lady. What was the one thing that would push us over the edge so quickly into war? Without the threat of a world ship, Inmar's rebellion could still have been avoided. There would have been time for negotiation. Six months from now we were to have incontrovertible proof that a world ship was near completion at a secret base in the fourth arm. Imperial World would have been under immediate threat, then, by a space folding ship. The Royal Houses and the Democratic Worlds would rally behind you out of fear that they might be attacked. War would've been absolute. But *there is no world ship*. Only a computer fabrication waiting for broadcast."

"Captain I—Hal...do you realize how hard it is to believe that. I don't believe *you* Chief. The Captain here is not having a nervous break down. But Hal, the old man is my father of a long line of fathers to my ancestors—more of a father to me than my real one ever was. How can I believe a conspiracy?"

"I have the proof. This computer disk has all the data on the—"

"Those can be faked!" The Chief could finally stand no more. "This is over. Now!"

"But sixty Sykol sub-levels can't be faked. Come with me now Empress. Let me take you, show you what I've seen."   His agitation stunned her. This wasn't calm, cool Hal Teltrab.

"What have you seen, Captain?"

"I've seen their monsters. The genetic manipulations in their countless laboratories. The behavior tanks where they program human minds by erasing them first—making machines in their own image. And I've seen the rejections, the failures. Down there in the caves—hundreds of preservation tanks, maybe thousands with freakish man beasts, accidents or raw genetic material. The psychotics, the mental deviants. The breeding stock. Some are kept alive down there, blind in the darkness and hard wired for pain. They keep the Imperial stock on level fifty-eight. Unused clones. Frozen fertilized eggs. They could reproduce Amric I himself if it suited them."

"I'm well aware of the cloning programs in the Sykol Bureau."

"Your father is down there."

"Well of course, the cloning—"

"No, I mean your *father* is down there. Check the Imperial Crypt. It's empty. They take the dead and use them."

"That's enough."

"Two hundred years ago they reanimated your great grand—"

"Enough! Very well, then, Chief. Take the Captain to the med facility. Captain, listen to me. I am your Empress. Obey! Unlock the lifts and go."

"You don't believe me because you can't imagine that kind of disloyalty from the Chief servant of the Empire. That's because he's not your servant."

"Hal, go."

"He's your cousin."

"Teltrab! 025A, initiate," the Chief commanded.

Hal cocked his head and winced, the right eye twitching under some strain. Then release:

"That won't work either, Chief. Both the homing beacon and the control circuitry were removed and the behavioral conditioning has been overcome. You can't usurp my will, and soon the will of no guard.

"He doesn't want you to know, Lady, why it is that every major post in the Imperium is inherited, why even Sykols and Guardsmen are born to their positions. The cover is genetic purity and control—improving the Empire by improving its leaders. The real reason is because Amric I had a brother—*the first Chief Sykol*. He renounced his claims on royalty, the throne, because therein he knew he could have real power, the power to control. I would have never found out either, Chief, but for the conflicts in the last year between Guard and Sykol leaderships— you were trying to control too much and I couldn't help but wonder why. That first Chief wrote the power principle. He knew how best to preserve it. To fall behind the scenes, to control and manipulate in unseen ways. To maintain power by pretending to serve the power of another. It wasn't five generations before the Amric heir forgot that the Chief Sykol was also Amric. And that's just as the Chief wanted. Do you know why he feels no hesitation at thieving and pickling your ancestors? Because he feels no inequality toward them. He considers himself your equal in power in the galaxy. And up to now he's been right."

"Can you prove all this, Captain."

"Yes, I can."

"Janis this—"

"I am your Empress."

"My Lady, Janis. This changes nothing."

"Perhaps it doesn't. Captain, retire to the other side of the room. I have some things to discuss with the Chief. Keep the elevators shutdown. I'll call you when I need you."

"I'm afraid I must disobey your order, Empress, for the sake of my primary duty; I believe your life is now in danger."

"From this old man? Nonsense."

"No, Lady, perhaps not directly, but you and I both know the Sykol penchant for control. Back ups and fail safes. Always plans."

"Always plans," she echoed.

Hal moved closer to Janis, his eyes fixed on the Chief manipulator.

"What would happen, Empress, if a Royal were to lose control, begin making foolish decisions that denied the code of power?"

"To preserve power." The mantra.

"Yes, Lady. What would happen?"

"They'd have a back up plan."

And Hal knew he had won. The calm demeanor indicative of his nature returned to him. The Chief's pale face, on the other hand, began to redden, his anger as obvious and uncontrolled as he'd ever revealed before:

"Captain Teltrab, the next words you speak had best be weighed with care."

"Or else what, Chief? You'll call one of your assassins? A thousand Sykols, Empress Janis, hidden in non-descript positions, functioning as good scientists should—every bit of meekness and unassuming passivity. But genetically engineered and behaviorally conditioned to be the deadliest fighters in the galaxy, even better than the Imperial Guard, better than me or Jo Isacson."

"No one's deadlier than you or Jo."

"You're wrong. Why only a few weeks ago, a lovely young Sykol woman who had never known she was a walking death machine killed one of my men and wounded several others before they could terminate her. An armed squad of Imperial Guards, my Lady, against an unarmed child. Imperial Guards! You expressed disbelief. And you should. How, for example, could the Chief possibly think he could cause Inmar to rebel before he was absolutely sure that you would go to war against him?"

"Sykol behavioral engineering, I should think."

"Surely. But as he learned from Captain Star's resignation, the Chief could not be absolutely sure of that engineering, not even with you, his own personal project."

"There had to be a back up plan."

"Now that your heir is growing in another woman's womb, the Chief can feel free to make sure the war goes on, even if it means killing you using people within the Palace that even a Guardsman couldn't defend you against. How simple: blame your death on Inmar; proclaim himself regent till your son comes of age to rule. The Empire wonderfully well re-established inside fifty years. Of course you probably would have agreed to the war anyway. Till now, that is. Till me. So you see, my Empress, I cannot leave you, not, at least for another five minutes."

Both Janis and the Chief, who were about to explode, stopped short, stared at the calm Captain of the Guard with question mark faces.

"What happens in five minutes?"

"In five minutes, Chief, I will receive a signal indicating that all one thousand of your killers, here and on the seven key worlds on which the rest are planted have been subdued and arrested, or killed where necessary."

The stone faced silence of the next minute was concluded by the stone cold voice of the Empress of the galaxy:

"Hal, kill the Chief Sykol please."

"I don't believe I ca—"

"You would not be so quick to obey that order had you every secret in the Palace, Captain. There are those that Janis and I kept which no computer could reveal to you. Shall I tell him, child, of your hungers, your vengeance. The two men heading to one's death on that planet—"

"Say another word, old man, I'll kill you myse—"

"However you may have corrupted her, Chief, I will not blame my Empress for it. My loyalty is, as you taught me, to my charge. Now she'll know what you are, and whatever she's *been* will mean nothing to me. But as I was about to say, my Lady, I don't believe I can carry out your order to kill the Chief. I've taken a serious security risk here. Not in the arrests—I knew my men could handle them by sheer numbers. What we must learn from the Chief is who we missed. He may have a dozen, a hundred more secret killing machines whose identities are hidden in the myriad of Sykol digitiles."

"No, Captain," she corrected cooly. "If your plan is succeeding, as I'm sure it is, the Chief's subordinates are right now enacting their own back up plans—sifting through files, destroying evidence, covering their tracks, inventing false records that the Chief alone knew of this program, this *heinous back up plan that threatened the very life of the Imperial Person*. That's how they'll word it. And they will terminate these remaining super soldiers on their own."

The Chief quivered with the recognition.

"In fifteen minutes the Sykol cabinet will convene to plan their salvation from execution. Of course your guards will gather them up and bring them here. They'll be screaming for the Chief's head, their loyalty to me. Do give me the Chief's head, Captain."

"Of course, Empress. An excellent analysis, worthy of a Sykol."

"Or his sister." Her words, acid.

Hal began to unbutton his jacket.

The Chief's struggle for composure was brief. He was still the master manipulator.

"You did take a risk, Captain. More than you thought."

"Yes." Not questioning.

"Oh, yes." A sure, slow nod. "Did it not occur to you that among those perfectly engineered assassins might be the Chief Sykol?"

It was Janis's time to turn pale. Hal stood between her and the Chief, his coat now unbuttoned completely, the flaps from the double breasted cut hanging down and open.

"As a matter of fact, Chief, I assumed that very thing. That you, an old man even, might be able to kill me. That even that ubiquitous note pad of yours might contain or be used as a weapon, given the skill. Which is why" —slowly pulling one side of his jacket open— "I have activated this incendiary grenade."

The oval device belted to a shoulder harness blinked a yellow and red silent count down.

"Trying to determine my bluff with one of your own, Captain?" The Chief put his note pad on the floor. "Surely you can do better." He began to remove his long white coat, his own silent crown of royal authority.

"Not quite, sir. Of course, *I'm* prepared to die. You would have expected that." Hal began to reach slowly but obviously for his side arm. "But to be willing to kill the Empress...."

"Oh yes, Captain, that's perfect," Janis smiled. Her approval perplexed the old man.

"Yes, my Empress. You see, Chief, even you have been genetically engineered and behaviorally manipulated by your own father (just as you have done with your own son) to one end: the preservation of power."

"Power expended is power lost," quoted Janis.

"The thought of losing your power, losing your control, losing your life—that's difficult enough. But" (Hal's hand halted on the gun handle), "the thought of the pure chaos that would spread across the Empire at the deaths of the Empress, her Captain and the Chief Sykol..."

Now he understood.

"...horror. Total loss of control, total expending of power, civil war, and, in all likelihood, the rise of Inmar to the rule of the galaxy. Even Magnus hasn't the strength to stand against him."

The Chief's mind raced with calculations.

"And I'm willing to take the risk, Chief, that you'd rather be dead than see the destruction of your precious Sykol machine."

Jo Isacson, his right arm in a sling, entered the tower room with a quick step, plasma sword in hand. The smoky stench of sizzling meat filled his nostrils, clouded his eyes, but did not obscure his vision. Something red and gooey smouldered in a heap on the floor near the elevator. Sitting together on the window sill close and holding hands were Hal Teltrab (a deactivated grenade in his other hand) and the Empress of the galaxy. Isacson bowed.

"Speak," she commanded.

"Success."

"All taken?" asked Hal.

"Taken or killed. They were good. You were right, Captain. Some had cybernetic implants, super strength and psychic programming. Honestly, they weren't the tough ones."

"The genetically enhanced."

"Yes sir. The one my group took went critical—turned lethal in seconds. He broke through a wall, made brilliant tactical choices in trying to escape, almost killed a guard. Had it not been for our preparations—"

"Had you not decided to take him on alone without your team, your arm wouldn't be broken."

Isacson smiled. "Sorry, Captain. I wanted to know."

"If there's someone better than you in a fight? Find out on your own time."

Janis broke in: "Commander, bring the Sykol cabinet here to me immediately."

"Yes, my Empress. Shall I have this mess—"

"No, not yet."

"Post guards outside the doors, Jo. You and Simon should come with the cabinet, and a full squad of our best. Let's be intimidating for a while. Every Guardsman remains armed and on alert."

"Sir. Majesty." He left.

Janis released Hal's hand, stood and turned to survey her world. The Captain did not turn, but rather stood at attention monitoring communications about the Palace through the transceiver in his head.

"That was dangerous, Hal."

"There was no other way."

"Of course not, and no one knows better than you. Did you see how quickly he moved?"

"Not fast enough."

"How did you know?"

"That was the biggest risk," he said. "The Chief might have been a mutate or not. I couldn't be certain and needed another edge against him. In the end, the thought of chaos in the galaxy made him hesitate."

"Along with the promise that his heir would not be executed."

"The boy shall live—elsewhere, of course—it's a promise that we'll keep." It was not a request.

"And he knew we would," Janis concluded.

"He knew you loved him despite things."

"Yes."

"And we slowed him down enough. Enough indecision for me to draw on him and fire before he could surmise that he might make the grenade in time."

"Yes."

"But I didn't know how fast he was. It *was* dangerous."

Silence.

"Captain, call a meeting of my cabinet for this evening. We'll give full disclosure."

"Certainly."

"I won't be able to trust anyone but you to take the Chief's place, but, of course, not officially."

"Nevertheless, you'll want me to turn a number of my security duties over to Lieutenant Lazar."

"Yes, to Simon."

"You're an excellent strategist, my Lady. Perfect choices."

"The Sykols trained us both well."

Her tone betrayed gentleness. So much had happened in the Palace of the power principle. But not enough.

And she said, "We'll instruct the military to proceed with Strategic Plan One immediately."

Shock. "Empress!?"

Something old in her, something deeper than Sykol caverns took over. "What, Captain, don't you see? The Chief's timetable assumes his having to manipulate me into believing war is my idea. That's no longer necessary. Delaying six months will give Inmar precious preparation time."

He continued to stare in disbelief.

"I thought that..."

"Yes, thought what?"

"That...with the truth revealed, we would inform the Overlord of the Sykol plans, that his grievances about raids and economic sabotage were true, part of the design. That we'd sue for—"

"Peace! Don't be stupid! The Chief was a traitor but hardly himself a fool. He was right. My youthful ascension to the throne must be compensated by visible strength. That was no mistake."

"So...when you say we're going to give full disclosure to the cabinet...we're really not."

"No. We'll send that communiqué *now*, proving that a world ship is under construction. In your debriefing to the cabinet—"

"*My* debrief—"

"In your debriefing you'll remove all references to Sykol responsibility for the war. You'll focus on the Chief's treason instead, the threat to the Imperial Person's life. You'll suggest collusion with Inmar."

"I see." 'So we will disclose lies.'

Silence. He stared.

"Captain."

"Yes, my Lady."

And he realized he hadn't won a thing.

"For prudence sake, issue a second order reprimand on yourself for threatening the life of your charge. That grenade trick was brilliant, but a bit desperate."

"It *was* dangerous."

"A calculated risk, yes."

"However, I will issue the reprimand as appropriate response to the Guard's rules for charge protection." 'A Sykol Manual.'

"Excellent. I suppose some commendations also."

"Condem—commendation. Alright."

"You're the finest Captain in the Guard's history."

"Thank you." Lifelessly.

"We'll restructure this Empire together."

"Yes." Deathfully.

"We'll lay siege to three dozen solar systems."

He did not answer. He thought about a white glove folded in the back of his belt. He thought about reaching for it. Then he thought,

'No, that's been done.'

- 40 -
The City

The Kalliphi emerged from the forest in hundreds, following the body borne on the backs of their fellows. They seemed more casual than when usually about the city, walking as if freed from a burden. Miners and lumberers looked up from their aimless walks, or their card games, or their drinking, or their staring at endless rows of heavy machinery lying dormant near empty holding bins, and were shocked, bewildered, elated. News spread throughout the capital and they gathered *en masse* to meet the procession. A poacher named Grace brought the first Kalli man and the first off-world miner together, joining their hands. Then from the city side another came forward, then others, until even the most cautious were running toward the Kalli people, embracing them (to their surprise) with smiles and tears, until the two bodies married into one. Somehow the months of waiting had changed the men of off-world too, and they felt a sense of community they had never experienced before.

The conclave muddled about for a moment and then took purposeful direction. The body of Philagapon, Davidson Star, was carried through the mud streets past tents and shacks, drawing the hands of all around like a magnet. All of the Kalliphi, old and new, longed one last time to feel the presence, the substance of the compassionate one. He was taken to the space port and put on a shuttle for Imperial World, to be buried with his ancestors. All but his heart. It was removed and buried at the foot of the great black tree. *Then* they had wept. Now they bid him farewell with shouts and songs sung by choirs of Kalli men and boys accompanied by whatever instruments good hearted (though not so skilled) city folk managed to scrape up. After a period of time that was not too long, nor precisely calculated, nor particularly anticipated, the elders of the Kalliphi met with Governor Pylat on no runway in particular and unceremoniously handed their sacred pledge-to-treaty to him.

That evening, the folk from the many worlds celebrated in their own ways: the old Kalliphi in quiet camps around the city (with some of their new world brothers whose company was found to be mutually satisfying), the new ones in boisterous dance and games in the streets. All save one. One lone worker whose job was done passed in contented silence along the mud roads of the city, one, who had been made inconspicuous for some reason he did not quite understand, passing as if unseen and finding satisfaction in his solitude-in-the-context-of-community and pleasure in participating vicariously in the festival about him. The smell of pine and methane permeated the air. He did not notice— he had gotten used to it.

Moving along the mud roads of the city, the ankle deep mother muck, he thought back to earlier suspicions; he wondered if what had happened here had been an elaborate, calculated plan dreamed up by people in white coats some fifty years before. If so they had best be careful. Tampering with the righteous is like trying to diffuse an ancient nuclear warhead. But he concluded they had not calculated this day into being. What had happened on Kall was something new to his experience, even after years in the more loosely run regular army. It was the experience of the Empire's limitations, of freedom from control. Still he wondered at the *thing* that had occurred but three days before, wondering if perhaps the plan that had failed were not the plan at all. For a moment he doubted the possibility of freedom, perplexed over who, in truth, had been sent there to die? Wondering how internecine was the...*thing*? Remembering...floating through the ankle deep mother muck, remembering, passing through the city, what *thing* had happened when, three days before, Solomon almost died:

They were returning to the capital city. She walked behind him, not in front. It was just the two of them, wondering and wary of Quint's warning of the day before. The mass of Kalliphi who had intended to see the Philagapon's body off to its final rest had gone on before them.

Then darkness came: Lazarus—as if he were a black hole sucking light into his very body. He was a shadow in the purity of the planet; he seemed to Solomon a dream.

The first shot should have hit: clear, unanticipated, the man/equinn toyed. Solomon heard the distorted voice:

"Kill you, you demon, kill!"

A half-second later his sword was streaking plasma protection in time to deflect the second shot. He was a green streaking blur diving for cover to one side while Savage disappeared to the other.

Cat and mouse began.

Lazarus pulled out knowledge he should not have known—not tactics with which a master assassin analyzes, but deeper knowledge: of a brilliant genetic warrior.

'Best there is...hah!'

It's all utterly clear to me: every thought in the mad man's head: He'll keep moving, Lazarus. He'll take the fight to you; wading in the dark, you'll counter his parabolic approach, moving in behind as he moves behind, the two of you running like tapestry knights wearing hundred pound armor. But how much noise you make in your expert movement. And how he makes none. Moving between trees and underneath bushes and sucking up light, you approach unseen, remembering too: 'There was a woman with him.'

But Solomon has adjusted his curve and turned straight down an accommodating line of trees, hopping one to the other, hoping to be first.

'He'll take the fight to me—never pause,' thinks Lazarus.

And Solomon: 'Now wait. Time is key—like hide-and-seek when we were all just boys. Now move—first low.'

There was a depression, not deep, in the tree roots where water had flowed. Solomon moved away from the arena, hoping his enemy would still be moving to overlap him, hoping to turn him in circles till he hopefully found his opponent first.

'Then high.' He ascended up a fallen tree's gentle gradient.

And Lazarus: 'He's good. Oh he's good,' smiling. He backtracked to find Solomon's break off point.

And then I can't help but speak to him: You think you'll be first, Lazarus?

"Get out of my brain."

First to find him?

"I killed you, Quint."

I'm not Quint.

"Killed you."

And as if that settles the matter, he ignores me, his thoughts turning to the obsession that matters to him most, even more than Solomon.

'Sweet white Mother/Queen.'

Janis is his all. Suddenly, thoughts unwilled play on his stained-glass shattered brain—of white coated men, and the Empress robed in scarlet.

Solomon was lowering himself from the fallen tree by vine and overgrowth, his plasma sword held deactivated in his hand. Crouching beneath the dead wood's roots, he watched. And Lazarus remembered:

What is your name?

'No!'

What is—

'Lazarus.'

No!

'I've risen.'

Doe!

>Gone back so far we'll never know.

The files?

"What is your name?"

'Sweet Mother: "Lazarus, my Lady."'

"An unusual name. Such an unusual man."

>*Yes!*

'She birthed me and we made love.'

>*He's tapped into everything in the database.*

More than we could ever know.

>*What've we done?*

"Come with me in the evening."

>*What've we done?*

"Ravish my body as I have ravaged your mind."

Then Lazarus screamed.

Solomon moved quickly. There was an area filled with young shoots barely a foot wide and fifty high: ashen white-barked trees spaced narrowly together. Seeing through them was like a view through strobe light. Every sight was only a glimpse, changing perspective as he moved.

'Good place to get caught,' he thought.

But there was a shadow in the saplings. Something moving, daring him to enter. He obliged.

Something was eating its way out of Lazarus's brain. He breathed through clenched teeth and grunted lightly on every other exhale. His thoughts were madness:

'Demon...demon killed my mother. Kill you, make your eyes pop. Corrupted her flesh. Wear your entrails around my neck. Made her play the...'

"...Whooore!!"

Solomon heard an animal howl and saw it in glimpses through the trees: retching, convulsing, foaming. Legs and arms moved Lazarus among the sapling maze like a puppet, hauling his rebellious torso along. They danced about the trees looking for advantage or shot.

'Must be a trick,' Solomon thought. 'He's too good to be blundering about. But there he is, sometimes stealthful—better than I've seen in years—then why sometimes lumbering? Must be a ploy.'

You need to get control Lazarus.

'Whore. Being whorish. Whoring me—'

Yes.

'—for a price.'

That's it.

'Paid in full, then.'

Yes.

'This day.'

Yes. Pick up that shard and hold it before you, that beautiful red piece of broken glass. See how it dams up your water running mind. See how you return to the task at hand—to the shadow.

Solomon could sense the change: 'We're on each other and he's ready.' The blundering had ended. 'No more mistakes.'

Their movement was a chess game. Find the advantage offered by the terrain, move and feint to draw your opponent in, pull back to bring or press forward to push:

Lazarus: 'Get him to this place where the trees run a row—clear shot.'

Solomon: 'Got to withdraw, bait him, then watch for movement. Hmm. Yes. Where does he *want* me to be?'

Solomon moved a quick reckless moment.

Lazarus recalled: 'There was a woman with him.'

Solomon's sword flashed on.

'There you are.'

Lazarus fell out of the shadow.

'Now you're mine.'

A shot blasted the tree behind Solomon (ducking) in half. He leapt between two other trees and rolled to his feet. His blade cut down and toward his target. The tree fell toward Lazarus, though not quickly enough. But Solomon was moving again and cutting—one, two, three trees and more, falling at the assassin at every turn, just in time to stop his eye from taking aim, blasting the trees to splinters (one log hit him in the shoulder, only knocking him off balance).

Lazarus countered by moving against the circle, giving up his prey for the moment. Then analyzing Solomon's trajectory, he blasted a line through the trees, bringing down dozens. Solomon wasn't there.

Smoke filled the air, and tiny fires burned here and there on fallen trees or emasculated trunks.

The dance was much less tentative now. They moved to quick confrontation, until a narrow tuft of trees held them only six feet apart. Staring at pieces of movement and silhouette, each feinted left or right, ducked or sprinted and turned, trying to out maneuver the other. Finally, Lazarus began taking chance shots, through the tuft, blasting at every movement. The first few didn't penetrate (toppling trees), and Solomon took the advantage to move around toward Lazarus. But the killer followed him perfectly and shot at the first clear glimpse. Several trees fell, then green plasma sparked off a green shield. Solomon stumbled back to cover, Lazarus followed with inhuman speed. The man of light rolled with his imbalance, used the momentum to catapult himself through a hole Lazarus had blasted in the tuft. He came quickly around. Lazarus was just spinning, late in realizing Solomon's move, who ducked under the first shot, deflected the second on one knee, then lashed at his enemy's feet. The height of Lazarus's jump startled Solomon, but his mind, working faster than time, evaluated and moved him. He carved an arc of protection, narrowly avoiding plasma fire, dove under the arc which followed him around, then swung furiously a whipping plasma strand which, as Lazarus touched down, struck the energy case on his rifle causing it to explode in fiery green fury, knocking the contestants out of each other's sights.

Solomon scrambled for his weapon. He wanted to take no chances. Sure of his opponent's death, he nevertheless approached with caution, threading through the tightly grown trees as before. Lazarus was no where to be found.

'It can't be,' Solomon thought. 'The blast threw me twenty feet. Even with the quick breakdown of plasma outside the magnetic field, I felt the heat.'

There was no trace of blood, or flesh. Only a few ragged pieces of cloth (not that Lazarus had had much clothing left to wear after battling the planet), only the faint smell of something burning—something not wooden: flesh? But something else, too.

'Not a big blast. But enough to kill. He should be dead.'

Following instinct, Solomon left the sapling field. His direction was definite without being defined. Save for crackling fire, the jungle was silent, the wildlife fled. Row after row of trees in all directions stood motionless. He continued his relatively straight line for fifty feet, then turned and began to circle back. The going was slow because every tree was a potential ambush. This gave him just enough time to worry over Savage. He fought the thinking, trusted her *eisos*, focused as he needed to. Ten minutes passed without a hint of the enemy's location. Solomon grew unsure.

'I've lost him.'

He stopped. Stood erect, still, open. He puzzled. Then he felt. Just a little feeling, passing over him like a breeze. Then he knew; he opened his mind to the feeling, tried his best to trust himself to the *oneness* as she would doubtless be doing. He reached out for the planet's rhythms, felt for the darkness of a soul not quite one. He was a moment adjusting, but a moment too long.

Lazarus's fist was only a glimpse in the corner of Solomon's eye when it smashed into his temple. Solomon reeled from the blow and fell into the hard root earth. Though stunned, he was quick to his feet. Through the spots in his blinking eyes, he saw a figure moving toward him. He stabbed straight with his sword; the figure side stepped right; Solomon did the same to buy a second for his vision. Weaponless, Lazarus continued to approach.

'He's crazy.'

The sword came down, Solomon stepping into the swing; Lazarus dodged left and kicked at the obvious forward knee (to cripple) which Solomon lifted as planned, shifting his weight back for the heel kick to the jaw. It connected. But the effect was not as expected. Lazarus stepped back off balance but, shaking his head, recovered quickly and retaliated in Solomon's moment of surprise with a forward snap kick into his ("demon's") chest, slamming him into a tree behind. The shock knocked the sword from his hand, but Solomon managed to swing away from the punch that followed. Lazarus took a chunk out of the tree. The man of light backed away in fighting stance and got his first clear look at his nemesis:

He stood naked and scorched, like a god of fire. Tall and muscular. Slender, strong legs and a wide swelling chest. Black hair. Eyes...his face...somehow unbecoming the man. Evil shone in the eyes, but their shape, and the face, were, to Solomon, of a familiar gentility, even behind the stretching cheshire smile. He stood there an oxymoron in appearance, a contradiction in terms. The gleam and black of burned flesh had its epicenter in his side—where the gun had exploded—and radiated up, down, or around his body. Blood plasma streaked down his leg from a red chunk in the very middle. His gun hand, which Solomon thought should've been blown off, was black and caked but whole. His trigger finger was bent to the side in an impossible contortion as if purposely placed there that the other fingers might still make a fist.

"Who are you?"

"Your son."

'What?' "She sent you."

"Your son, Father!"

"You're a beast of her making."

"I'll kill you!"

He lunged at Solomon with screaming primal rage, a rose colored shard stuck in his mind's eye. He would not end his screaming until he had been saved.

They danced again, in fluid motion: kicking, blocking, punching, leaping—gradually sliding into a cadence. Solomon found that he could not match the speed or strength of his assailant. But his tactics were better, his speed nearly as inhuman. Still he was on the defensive and did not know if he could take the advantage. He was surprised by the fact but not afraid.

It was time to be more creative. He dropped his guard, stepped in, limboed below a punch, grabbed the extended arm as he fell back, shoved his legs into the madman's gut (he was sure to dig a heel into the blast injury) and flipped him over as his back hit the ground. The advantage he sought was lost, however, as Lazarus got a clamp on his ankle and pulled Solomon with him as he flipped over.

Solomon mule kicked his face with the free leg, rolled, snap kicked one cheek, heel kicked the other, then stamped down on the wrist, finally forcing Lazarus to release his grip. He kicked up to his feet but Lazarus, only a trickle of blood running from his nose, was already there. He got the one good connection he needed.

Solomon felt the stomach punch in his spine. He doubled over against thought and even instinct, then fell to his knees. Gasping for air and retching at the same time, he tried to stand and move away. Lazarus, wailing, lifted him by his collar and spun him. The charred right hand began squeezing his throat and lifted him into the air. The healthy left hand reared back like a claw, aimed at Solomon's skull. Lazarus wasn't about to let his victim choke to death.

Still hanging by a clutched throat, Solomon gave Lazarus half a dozen quick punches to the eye. Next, he swung both legs up and boxed his ears. Lazarus staggered, stalled just enough for the dance to turn.

Savage came from the perfect invisible rhythm of the planet. The plasma sword sliced down near Lazarus's right shoulder. Sparks flew—silver and gold. Solomon gasped deep as he fell to the ground. Lazarus back peddled before the fire works cascading from his stump of arm. She positioned herself between them, to protect her charge; she didn't press the attack. Solomon stood beside her and stared mouth-opened at the red, green, blue, black wires, some still arcing and sparking electricity. The arm on the ground continued to clutch convulsively. Lazarus stopped screaming. His face betrayed as much surprise.

"You're a machine!"

Silence.

"A machine that bleeds."

"No." He cringed.

Solomon took the sword from Savage.

"I'm a man," he snarled.

"Not anymore."

He shook with rage. "I'm a man!" He charged without thought or care. Solomon sliced his stomach open, stepping aside as Lazarus fell past them.

They approached slowly, the blade tip leading. Lazarus lay on his back at the foot of a tree, his head propped against its bark. With his remaining hand, he held bloody guts and wires in place. He looked at the sword hanging now just above his chest, looked up at the man and woman standing over him. Something eating its way out of his brain made him wince. But he did not rave, and his anger was lost.

"Father."

And then something changed in him.

"No, it's...you, Captain."

There was a look of thanksgiving on Lazarus's face, one Solomon suddenly realized he could never forget it.

"Immanuel?!"

The sword clicked off. Solomon dropped to his knees and put his hand beneath the man's head.

"It can't be you. Why are you here? What—" He looked at the wires—"what did they do to you?"

The cyborg's breathing stopped for a moment. His head began to twitch, barely. His eyes wandered, looking here and there at unseen things. He became catatonic as a single crystal clear piece of cut glass ate its way into his memory. Solomon watched in silence the struggle he could not see. In shock, he waited, holding his dead friend's head with his hand. Savage waited with him, confused but calm, stroking his back with her hand.

Immanuel Proshemeis was remembering: things he couldn't possibly: seeing his corpse exhumed and taken to a white room with many machines and instruments. Seeing his body cut and pasted—pieces removed and better ones added. The pictures were clear and sequential, clearer than ever his thinking had been. At least, that's how I choose to imagine it. He watched, from outside himself, times he could not have known. I could not leave him broken and fragmented, could not leave him so incomplete, whose sinful resurrection could not be blamed on him. And so I helped him to see:

He watched them awaken him with the push of a button, saw the lies filling his brain through proliferous rainbow of wires, saw the glitch (it's always a glitch when no one knows why) and grinned at his self-remaking—probing the databases, the libraries of all human history and shattering his synapses with his artist's mentality and making a mad killer who had come too close to God, a killer possessed, instead, by the Devil himself. Ending with pictures of the woman of his dreams, the purpose of his youth, of what she had become and was becoming him into, he saw it all, and in seeing was made whole again. That at least is how I imagine it. And I have as evidence what the man of light told me were Immanuel Proshemeis's dying words.

His eyes came to focus on Solomon at last.

"Captain?"

"Yes, Immanuel."

"Ca—" He tried to speak, but pain tensed his whole body. He reached up with his bloodied hand and grabbed Solomon by the collar.

Then he forced his last words: "I'm not a god. I'm a man."

He smiled. A narrow and loving smile. Then he began laughing quietly, a pleasant chuckle—without remorse. Rather contented joy.

He died laughing.

Solomon had thought, while watching at his father's side, that he knew what Savage had meant that first day in the forest when she said she was taking him to die. What he had experienced then was little more than sleep. Here, holding his twice dead friend to his chest, Solomon felt something in him pass, some warmth in his heart whose absence was neither thought nor feeling, only cadaverously cold. But some deaths only begin that way. Look at Immanuel, who died laughing.

Remembering it, Solomon lightly laughed himself. The swelling on his head, the soreness at the back of his stomach, did not stay the feeling that this bizarre twist of but three days before was a distant memory in which the negatives trickle out with the passage of years, and only a melancholy goodness leaves itself to recollection. So he found himself contented as he walked through the mud among the revelers. He knew it had never been about this—about restoring production, about saving a planet for its people. It had been about his death. She had failed, and he had won, even managing to successfully complete the official mission as she had ordered it. His stride was brisk, like his contentment. If only it could have lasted.

The man who bumped into him was deliberate enough to raise Solomon's guard. He turned and faced the offworlder—a pale skinned man in the uniform of a trapper, one far too clean for anyone who worked on planet Kall. The man read Solomon's gaze quickly.

"My apologies, sir," he said, "I did not mean to alarm you."

"Then what did you—"

"Only to deliver a message."

At that moment Solomon felt the object in the hip pocket of his tattered singlesuit.

"You're from Imperial World, aren't you?"

"Those of us who live up at the pole prefer the Amric appellation, Colonel Star."

"Pure blood Archeans, like Captain Teltrab."

"Who sends his greetings, sir. And some regrets."

"What—"

"The message is marked urgent, Colonel. Good evening to you."

Solomon read the words on the mini-holo screen before they vanished and the device fused into an inert lump. The news was, to say the least, discouraging.

He walked at a markedly slower pace past the bars and the brothel, past the military complex to the municipal building, through quiet corridors to the room where he had begun his odyssey. When he stepped inside he found he was not alone.

It was Savage.

"I would take off my clothes for you," she said.

Solomon knew it was a question. He fingered the metallic lump in his pocket. The hesitation in his parting lips was enough to both blush her face and harden its expression.

Seeing her reaction he quickly recovered: "Oh...no...no, it's not...I would have you do it, too. I...I would have you forever. I would go back into the jungle with you to search for what my father found there, what I glimpsed just the smallest—what I tasted for only a moment."

"Not...staying?" her voice quivered.

"I..." He sighed, sat down on the bed, took her hand in his but did not look up at her. He pulled the dead device from his pocket and looked at it instead.

"At first I thought, 'This is it. This was it all along. The backup plan to all backups. This is how she beats me.' But now I don't think so. I refuse to say I haven't won a battle, here. I won't let her say she has." Now he looked at her. "Please," he said, as much with his eyes as his lips. And she sat down next to him.

"What is?" she asked, looking at the device.

"A message." He peered directly into her eyes. Resolution came to his. "I would not take you now, and leave you tomorrow."

She smiled sadly, understanding, at least, that he loved her.

"What message?" she asked, placing a hand on his cheek.

Against any typical reserve, Solomon reached out, and drew Savage into his arms. He looked once more at the object in his hand and then tossed it aside. He looked up at what, in that moment, felt like Divine silence, then he buried his cheek in her hair and neck.

"What message?" she whispered.

This time he did not hesitate: "There's a war coming."

When war was officially declared the next day, against the rebellion of Inmar, Solomon was called back to duty on the *Kokkinoscardia*. He was right, and because he was right, because he knew he had to leave, Janis had achieved a vengeance against Solomon she hadn't even planned. How could a man of light turn his back on the carnage to come? He knew—and the message from Hal Teltrab had been the proof of it—he knew the difference he would be able to make in the war, the lives he would save even as only a colonel, or, as he likely saw it, a division general. Captain Teltrab would be watching, ready to help. Solomon could see the numbers as quickly and as surely as any calculation Hal could ever make. A billion lives, no, billions. How could a man of compassion say no to such a calling? He had always been one to respond out of duty, but that wasn't the case this time. If the decision meant she still had a hold on him, it would not be a hold on his soul. The choice was his to make. It is true that he would later doubt himself, question his calling, believe he hadn't learned a thing on Kall. And even in those moments when he remembered the Light, the beating of the great heart, the piercing green of that Savage girl's eyes—even in those moments when he knew there'd been a change, he would say to himself, 'If only I could live that moment over.' I have reason to believe he would get the chance, and reason to believe there was change to come.

- Appendix I -
2323

"Ana-? Anakapha?"

In a quiet little cottage, in a quaint little town on an off-the-beaten-track agro-planet with no name of importance, the man of light sat reading a holo disk on a stiff backed chair made of the finest wood: the black of ocean depths and heavy, like tears of granite. Greying hair adorned his brow, a neatly kept beard, his face; white boots, brilliant and yet the slightest bit dulled by time and heavy heart shod his feet. The brown stains, just the slightest hint of crimson remaining, blended with polished floor made of the finest wood.

"Ana," he called again. "Where are you?"

"I'm here, Mr. Solomon." A gentle woman, elderly but vibrant entered the room. She wore a grey smock over a flower-print, yellow dress, her silver hair pulled into a bun. Her arms were strong, her shoulders wide, her figure husky, yet feminine: a worker.

"You were so quiet, I thought you had gone somewhere."

"I was tending to my household."

"As always."

"A person should do what she does, well. Noise is optional."

"True, and it's a welcomed trait in a Landlord."

"Landlady, young man, and it keeps my tenants loyal."

"Tenants, Miss Ana? I'm your only one."

"You pay as if for three, against my wishes (most of the time). Now be quiet, I'm in cleaning mode and this room is next."

She surveyed the den: modest furniture, earth tone in theme—a couch with well padded pillows against one wall; in the corner stood a wooden shelf, filled from floor to ceiling with holo disks: books from many planets and of diverse interests; there was a small table with two chairs where Solomon sat; two windows of a typical design—square, paned with brown trim—allowed a view of distant grain fields: flat and featureless, yet possessing a simple beauty like the woman, Ana, this native-born farmer to whose home world Solomon had come after...much; small potted plants with tiny buds—purple and gold petals—sat on the window sill and drank in the afternoon sun. The walls were grey and featureless except for one, upon which hung a painting of a great palace under a pink sky—blurred, in appearance an abstraction, enduring example of the truest aesthetic: an artist pouring more into his work than even he is aware of.

"Well I see you've taken over this room nicely."

"You say that every time."

"Of course I do, it's how I keep you under the illusion that you're not the one in charge here, *General, sir*." She smiled and began to tidy up the room.

"Shall I make lunch for us?" asked Solomon.

"No. I'll do it. But thank you. What are you reading today, then?"

"This is one of those classics that everyone says to read. It's very old, one of the oldest we have from before the Empire. No one is sure when it was written or even where. But it's widespread, so some think it's from the lost world, from Earth."

"Legends fascinate you."

"Yes. I don't know why."

"What's it called?"

"*Othello*. I forget the author."

"I've heard of that."

"It's about a man of power who is convinced by a false friend that his wife is unfaithful. He almost chokes her to death. Later he learns the truth, but his wife is too severely injured and dies."

"How depressing."

"But she forgives him."

"What?"

He looked up from his book while Ana pretended not to notice. "On her death bed, she forgives him," he said.

She glanced over. "That's good, isn't it?"

"It's good. We need forgiveness."

"And I forgive you."

"For what!?"

"For being so melancholy."

"War does that."

"Not just war. But you've earned your share. Ten years of fighting—retirement wasn't the wrong choice. You've seen enough. And our quiet town has enjoyed having you here."

"I don't understand why he married her in the first place."

"Did you hear what I just said?"

"Yes. Did he truly love her, or was she just a means to an end?"

"Your life colors your thinking."

"Perhaps. I have grown suspicious of ambition."

"I forgive you for that too. Not the ambition part, mind you," she said as she began to work her way out of the room, "but the suspicion part. Trust is a risk, General Star, tenant Solomon, sir."

"But you forgive me my distrusts nevertheless?" he said as she stepped into the hallway.

She called back: "If I didn't, you'd be making your own lunch."

That night was cloudy so no one could see the new stars moving across the sky. A fine rain coated structures and clothing and filled the air with a clammy wetness that made breathing a chore, and weighed heavily on the psyche. The massive concrete slab and lone warehouse that constituted the town's space port rested in dimly lit stillness. Japru Frock sat alone in the small tower atop the warehouse, monitoring communications, despising the night shift, wishing life would become a bit more exciting, and worrying slightly that it might. With a heavy sigh, he rolled his head about, looking at the still life picture of his work place. Then the sky caught his eye.

A circle of clouds above the landing platform was brightening. At first a dim grey, it steadily increased, becoming whiter and whiter. Then the canopy cracked with a thunderous sound, and beams of light flooded the area. Frock's mouth dropped. He didn't think to wonder why there had been no signal from the large ship landing before him. He didn't think to call into the town for the Mayor or the police or even a maintenance crew. He didn't think, even, to faint when the Imperial markings came into plain view. He just stared and gaped.

A mile away, Solomon Star looked through a window in disbelief, the dull roar of engines buzzing in his ears as with a fever, the nausea of worst-fear impossibility churning in his gut.

Don't be skeptical at the odds against an occurrence. How likely is it that a rock floating through infinite space would collide with the atmosphere of a planet rotating around a sun and burn up as it fell at just the time you happened to glance up and see it as a falling star?

Solomon thought it no coincidence and so waited in darkness in the stiff backed chair for a summons. It never came. Instead the son of a neighbor came and excitedly announced that the Empress, Janis IV, had come to their world—to that very town.

"A hundred ships are orbiting overhead!" he exclaimed with youthful exuberance. "They say she was making a tour and came here to visit us. The Mayor says since you were a general and all, maybe you should come to lead the welcome."

"Tell the Mayor it's not proper for a soldier to participate in diplomatic ceremonies in the Empire. Tell him my name should not even be mentioned."

"I've never heard of rules like that before. But I'll be sure and tell the Mayor what you said."

As per procedure, a security perimeter was established around the Empress's ship by her own personal Guard. Infantry and Mobile troops patrolled the space port while fighters monitored the sky high into the planet's atmosphere. In space, a royal armada shielded the planet. No problems were expected, of course. The visit was indeed meant to be cordial. But Captain Teltrab of the forty-fourth Guard took his responsibility seriously. He had only one: protect Janis IV.

An envoy was sent into the town, followed by troop carriers with instructions on securing the area for Her Majesty's visit and regulations for how the populace were to conduct themselves so as to avoid unnecessary disorder, miscommunication, or incidents.

Predictably, an incident occurred. A young prankster threw a smoke bomb underneath an open Guard air car. The four men in the car, clad in blue singlesuits (with light body armor), girded by red sashes, shod in whitest, white boots, were upon him in seconds, dragging him bloody nosed by the feet to a detention area. The boy's father, a pompous man who fancied himself someone important (thus explaining what influenced the boy's lack of propriety), upon seeing his son hauled down the middle of the street, flew into a rage and chased after the patrol. The boy's friends, who had been standing by, followed suit when they saw there might be a fight, as did a few level-headed adults hoping to preserve the honor of the Imperial visit and stop the red faced father before any more foolishness took place. Among them walked one clad in a grey hooded cloak.

The father planted his body between the patrol and their destination and began to bellow at the foremost Guardsman whom he took as the leader. His breath smoked in the chill of wet, evening air. The crowd enveloped the sextet, maintaining a respectable (gunpoint) distance. The guards remained calm. Years of experience steadied nerves. Backup was called for while they patiently endured the red faced railings. Seconds later, a troop carrier arrived from nowhere. Guardsmen emerged and began to disperse the crowd, directing some with a pointing hand, escorting others off the street with a forceful clench about the arm or neck. Those who had followed to bring peace urged desperately that the boy's father come away with them. Then troops pushed through them and a field lieutenant, grasping an arm, turned the man around to inform him where he could register a formal complaint and learn of the disposition of his son. But taking his gesture as an act of aggression the man hit the lieutenant's arm away.

He was immediately hoisted into the air and hauled to the side. The lieutenant and two others slammed him into the grey brick wall of a nearby building. One pressed his face into the coarse stone while the other two gave quick jabs to the ribs to stop the man's struggling. Half a dozen others kept those who had come with good and peaceful intentions at a distance. One of these people, a concerned friend, saw blood on the father's face as it was ground from side to side against the brick. He stepped forward to plead that the man be treated less harshly. A guard stepped in his way and motioned him back. As the bloodied man was being thrown to the ground to be handcuffed, the friend moved quickly around the imposing guard to magnify his plea. The guard grabbed the man by the arm, spun him around, and was about to break his nose when his own arm, cocked to strike, was stayed by a vice-like grip. Instinctively he turned himself and front kicked high into the face of an opponent who was no longer there. His surprised pause was only slight. He directed a split-second back fist at a grey blur in the corner of his eye. It was blocked and the grey hooded one punched him through the store front window behind him.

The surprise in the rest of the patrol gave over to a much longer pause. Then they mobbed the grey hooded one. They were almost as good as that one, individually. As a group they overpowered him quickly; the field lieutenant, a man named Friberg, moved in for the disabling blow. Someone pulled the hood back and the man's face was finally exposed. Even after years, that face was unmistakable. The lieutenant froze. The others took a moment more to recognize him. The struggling stopped. The lieutenant stumbled backward in shock, eyes wide with fear. Guards behind him gave support. Fear was followed by anger, followed by revulsion.

From the back of his throat and with all the disgust he could muster, he commanded, "Don't touch him!" He pulled loose from his supporters. "Let him go. Let him go!" He wrenched the arms of his companions from the man of light and pushed them away.

"Get back!" he shrieked. "Back to the transport!"

Slowly they retreated from the sight, the lieutenant last, walking backwards, never taking his eyes from the man. He stared even as the transport door was shutting.

'So that's how it is. You've taught them to hate me.'

News of his presence spread quickly. The Guard was withdrawn; all festivities were canceled. It was announced that the Imperial ship would leave in the morning.

Solomon walked the two miles to his home in the drizzly rain, a bit stiff from the jostling he had taken. There was a single hover car parked in front, a man standing at attention nearby. The darkness hid his face, but his countenance spoke everything.

"Captain Teltrab," said Solomon.

"General Star," said Hal.

The formality quickly gave way. They embraced with a power, Solomon digging his chin into the shoulder of his tall friend, slapping him on the back.

"It's good to see you," said Solomon pulling away.

"And you."

"Why are you here? If she finds out—"

"I came to apologize."

"To apologize?"

"For her. I knew what they would do. It's what I've hated most, these years. They were subtle at first. But then most of the Guard began to believe. I endured it."

"You've done well."

"I knew well before the moment you turned to walk away it was the right thing and that you'd survive. So I stayed."

"Are you apologizing for her or yourself?"

A smile. "Both I suppose. And for the Guard. It wasn't their fault."

"I know. Sykols are very good at what they do."

"And for the attempts on your life. I didn't—"

"I know." His tone was reassuring. "It's alright. Are you here alone? What about Jo and Simon?"

"They're against you too. When Jo heard you were here, he wanted to come break your neck."

'True to his training.' "That would've been a shame."

"Yes. One of us would've had to kill him."

Solomon smiled.

"No. I'm not alone," Hal continued. "She wanted to see you."

The smile vanished.

"Well...where's the patrol?" He half wanted to believe it impossible. He half wanted to verify its truth.

"There is none."

Solomon remembered his old job for a moment: "And what's to keep me from walking in there and breaking *her* neck?" He meant it not as a threat, but a criticism of the risk being taken, leaving her so unprotected.

"You haven't heard?"

"Heard what?"

"They tell me I'm the best ever. More accurate even than the Sykols."

"Analysis: The Lieutenant's primary function."

"I haven't been wrong yet."

Shaking his head in agreement: "Not about me either."

Without a farewell, Solomon left his friend and walked to his front door. He hesitated, then entered. He took off his cloak and hung it on a rack next to the door, then wiped his muddied boots on the mat below him. He heard sounds in the kitchen:

"Ana, what are you doing?"

"I'm making tea for the Empress of the galaxy."

He turned away from the kitchen entrance. Across the hallway, in the living room, it was cold. He could feel the chill emanating from the darkness there. And the silence. Something hit him on the back of the head and hung on his shoulder.

"Dry your hair."

He took the towel and did so, and then quickly matted it down with his hand. Then he entered the room.

She stood in darkness, staring out the window at the steadily increasing storm. He touched a rectangle on the wall and a dim light began to glow in the opposite corner of the room.

"Captain Star." Her voice was sweet as silver, and cold like brass in winter.

"My Lady."

"Sit down, I wish you to have tea with me."

He sat in a stiff backed chair.

"This is a wonderful view, don't you think?"

"Yes, my Lady."

Anakapha brought the tea and tiny bran cakes and then left with no sound, only a reassuring smile.

At last the Empress Janis IV turned to face him. Her face was white and youthful, beautiful as when she was twenty-five. Except for her eyes. Was it the lighting in the room or faded memory? Or were they artificial in appearance? There seemed a film over them, like cataracts, yet not unpleasant to look at. They were inhuman eyes, but possessed of an enticing beauty, an *almost* to be feared. In his mind, Solomon recalled that dark chasm he had crossed with Savage so many years ago. The depth in Janis's eyes was as deep and as dark, but it was not the same chasm into which they sank.

With graceful step, she joined him at the table.

"How are you doing with your la—ah, with the people of your new home?"

"Oh...fine my Lady. They are good people here."

"That pleases me. I am glad that you are happy."

'Must you lie even now?' "Are you happy, my Lady?"

Her smile looked the slightest bit painted: "But of course."

'No. It's not me she's lying to.'

He had in many instances, for many years, felt compassion for people. For the first time in his life, he felt pity. Power as an end had wreaked its subtle damage and molded Janis after its image: the image of humanity ever so casually bent.

She continued to chat, about her son Hector, the future Emperor, her daughter Cassandra with whom the galaxy was in love, the rising forty-fifth Guard and the galaxy's new found stability, but Solomon did not listen. A face drifted before him, a weeping face he had known years before—two faced face in the literal sense, the face in his youth which turned out not to be Janis's face at all but that of a girl who had in fact been given what she'd been promised: a "happily ever" life on an unknown "happily ever after" planet—unknown by anyone, forgotten by those who know. Eventually she died of a tragic flaw inherited from a father whom she had never really had while wailing a song of madness: "I am the Empress! I am Janis IV, heir to the throne of House Amric!" And laughing: "I own the galaxy! It's all mine." And crying: "Oh Solomon," bitterly..."I'm not a clone. I'm not—" But this is something Solomon never learned of.

The image faded from his mind, and he returned to the Empress's continuing-to-chat.

Then: "I want you to know, Captain, that, regardless of what has heretofore taken place, there is...forgiveness."

He gave a look of surprise, almost anger, but changed his mind about something; he heaved a sigh, smiled, and borrowing an old familiar nod, said, "Yes, my Lady, a man needs forgiveness."

- Appendix II -
2340

He left the agro-world. He left to wander the galaxy. For a man of seventy-seven, he kept a youthful, though wearied, body. As a genetically superior man, of course, seventy wasn't yet middle-aged. There would be many years ahead. He wandered: sometimes as a tourist, sometimes as a pilgrim or a hermit.

Then he returned to her. They did not run into each other's arms, nor embrace with the passion of the ages. But with the casual air that he had seen there that afternoon once before, she greeted his approach with a smile. She rose to meet him and looked him over with quiet pleasure. Gently, she embraced him, then pulled away: "You have aged."

"Mostly inside."

She nodded. "There is a weight on you."

Pause.

"Why did you not come sooner?" she continued.

"I think I was embarrassed to—ashamed. There were things...that wounded me. It seems the son of Philagapon does indeed have limitations, as you once wondered."

"Maybe the son of Philagapon just finally found his limitations."

They walked with little purpose.

"After a while I was afraid to come."

"Why, so?"

"I supposed there would be someone else in your life. I didn't want to—"

"There was no other."

Silence.

Eventually she led him to the uppermost, outermost limb of the great black giant. They sat down and dangled their feet off the edge of the firmament. Holding hands, they watched the sun set. It was not a particularly beautiful sunset, not particularly spectacular—but serene, like a Kalli soul.

Solomon closed his eyes and watched the images that danced before him. Not hallucinations, and not purely mental constructs. Often when you close your eyes, you can conjure up pictures of things in your mind. Sometimes you see them as if resting in the center of your brain, back behind the eyes, but sometimes the pictures take on a crystal clarity, and you can project them onto the darkness before you. Such were Solomon's visions that day, not of anything in particular, but crystal clear.

She roused him: "And why did you now come?"

"I wish I had never left."

"Will you stay this time?"

"No. No, there's something I haven't learned yet. Something my father found here, but I can't."

"I see you."

"You taught me to see half the lesson."

"The made must live with the made."

"But now—"

"Now?"

"Now I must learn, no find...."

"The made must live wi–"

"I must find—"

"Or learn—"

"The Maker."

"He sees you."

"I can't stay."

"No."

"But I would consider it a privilege if you would take that journey with me."

- Epilogue -

I have assembled the pieces of a forbidden story, here in the heart of a palatial house—the heart of the galaxy...the heart of darkness. Here in a holo room of my own making where files can be recorded and forms of unknown things shaped and molded into the closest semblance of truth that can be managed in a world such as mine. It is one story only, and Solomon Star has many. Did I tell you I met him once? But that *is* another story—also forbidden. Like this one which cannot be told again. And so I must touch a button, wave a hand, and speak a word:

End program.

Delet—no.

Bury file.

Far and away.

For the future.

CHARLIE W. STARR

teaches English, Humanities, and Film at Kentucky Christian University in Eastern Kentucky. He writes a monthly column on Christians and the Arts and Media for *Lookout* magazine and has published four books: two biblical studies, a children's fantasy, and most recently, *Light: C. S. Lewis's First and Final Short Story*, a book which has released a never before published C. S. Lewis manuscript. Charlie enjoys caving, writing, reading, watching bad television, and movies of every kind. His areas of expertise as a teacher include literature, film, and all things C. S. Lewis. Charlie and his wife Becky, have two mostly grown-up children, Bryan and Alathia, and a four pound family dog named Phydeaux.

http://www.lanternhollowpress.com

CPSIA information can be obtained
at www.ICGtesting.com
Printed in the USA
LVHW080001271218
601853LV00004B/11/P